HIDING THE TRUTH, SEEKING THE TRUTH

S J Mantle

S J Mantle

ISBN: 9798699954216

Chapter 1

1184 AD – The Holy Land

The din of the raging battle was deafening. In the chaos, men shouted and roared, the sound of bloodcurdling death cries rang out. Horses whinnied and bolted in fear, in pain, in both. Metal sword clashed with metal sword. And every so often the dry hot air was alive with the hiss of arching arrows.

The midday sun took no pity on those in the melee below. Amid the dust cloud of battle stood two Knights, back to back, resolute. Dressed from head to toe in heavy chainmail, each wore a white tabard embroidered with a red cross. Templars. They stood out for two reasons: they were curiously tall and unusually energetic. The earth beneath their feet was tacky, sticky with the blood of their enemies. Holding their swords aloft they cut their way through the onslaught.

All around, bodies and body parts littered the battlefield. The unmistakable stench of death permeated the air. Still the two Knights fought on.

"For God and King," shouted one of the two above the commotion.

"For God and King," was the breathless response of his companion.

One Knight paused momentarily to remove his helmet. Using the back of his glove he wiped the sweat from his brow and took two deep breaths, but there was no air. Sighing loudly, he replaced his helmet and lifted his sword aloft.

"William, mind out!" shouted his companion. William reeled back as a metal blade passed within a hair's breadth of his face. Before he could respond, his unfortunate assailant had been decapitated by the other Knight, his head landing with a thud at William's feet.

William turned to Robert, punching his chest with his fist in thanks. Robert bowed and once more they took up their preferred positions, ready to face the enemy in the name of God.

As the sun became low in the sky, both sides withdrew to their respective camps. The battlefield was eerily quiet, save for the intermittent cries of injured combatants. Flocks of carrion birds feasted on the spoils of war. In the distance two figures moved in and out of the shadows, walking methodically back and forth amongst the carnage. They offered comfort, gently lifting those who could be saved onto an oxen cart driven by a swarthy young man. They offered those who could not be saved prayers. Occasionally, when there was no hope, they would give a helping hand to end the agony. Amid the devastation, they stumbled across a friend, a Templar, Gregory of Brecon. As they knelt beside him, it was obvious his injuries were fatal. "Can this truly be God's will?" he whispered hoarsely. The Knights exchanged glances and paused to consider their comrade's last words.

These Knights went unchallenged, for they were well known and respected on both sides of the conflict, not just for their skill and courage on the battlefield but for their compassion. They did not differentiate between wounded Christian and wounded Muslim, but tended to all who had fought, fallen and were lying abandoned on the bloody field of battle.

Their names? William of Hertford and Robert of St Albans.

It was dusk when a magnificent grey war horse carried both Knights into the Christian camp, closely followed by the ox cart. At the hospital tents they unloaded their cargo of injured soldiers, before wending their way back to the Templar tents on the northern side of the camp. As they made their weary way back, many soldiers paused to salute them. When they reached their tent Zafir, William's manservant and the ox cart driver, jumped into action. First thirst-quenching water, before he helped to extricate them from their sweat-laden chainmail. He poured each man water to wash away the blood of battle. Once refreshed, they changed into simple cotton tunics before attending evening prayers. Supper was taken in the refectory tent before night prayers at 9pm. Afterwards, each Knight was given a glass of wine and water along with their instructions for the next day. The last job of the day was to attend to their horses but Zafir had already seen to theirs, so William and Robert took a short stroll, climbing a nearby hillock overlooking the camp. It was a clear, still night. In the distance they could see the lights of the Muslim encampment and wisps of smoke from their campfires, they could hear dogs barking and the clatter of camp life. They lay on their backs to gaze at the stars as they had done many times before.

William broke the silence between them. "Do you remember doing this as boys?"

"How could I forget?" Robert smiled. "Balmy summer evenings after a day's harvesting. We would lie looking up at the heavens, chatting and laughing until a huffing and puffing Brother John appeared to scold us and take us back for evening prayers."

For a moment, the two men were lost in their memories.

"The scrapes we got into," said William. "We were so curious and easily distracted. There was always something. An injured fledgeling, the discovery of a grass snake, a favourite horse to groom. It feels like a world away."

"It is a world away, my friend. We knew nothing of war, we were two small boys learning the ways of the Monastery. Everything was new – prayer, schooling, Latin, fishing in the ponds. Oh, and ale!" added Robert, laughing.

"You saved my life today. I'm truly grateful." William was suddenly serious.

"I did. You're becoming slow, old man." Getting to his feet, Robert began to play act. Backwards and forwards, bent over, holding his back, shaking his finger at his friend. William could not help but smile. His companion was enjoying himself so much he was shaking with laughter.

"I seem to recall that you are the older of the two of us." William jumped nimbly to his feet and clipped his friend's ear. "Robert, you're a jester, always have been."

Robert of St Albans was impossibly tall with a thick ginger beard, beady little blue eyes and short cropped red hair. At the centre of his freckled face, an enormous nose.

"You do know you are referred to as the 'Ginger Giant' in camp, don't you?"

Robert did not respond immediately as he was bent double with mirth. Eventually, he recovered enough to speak.

"I am a Knight Templar. Have some respect, William of Hertford. By the way, it's impossible for me to compete in the looks department, for my best friend happens to be known as 'Pretty Boy Templar'. Look at you, with your tall, muscular chest and arms, your short dark brown shiny hair and a full beard and, oh, I nearly forgot, those large dreamy steel-blue eyes!"

They both laughed as William lightly thumped his friend on the arm.

"You see, I'm right. Look at the muscles rippling through your overshirt, your smooth chest! It's so unfair!"

"I hold you in awe, my friend. For there is no doubt that without you I would not have survived thus far." William was suddenly serious again.

Robert approached and grabbed William's head, planting a wet kiss in the middle of his forehead. "We are in this together, for God and King. We stand together, no matter what."

"Forever together, for God and King, no matter what." In salute, William struck his chest with his fist.

The two Knights retired for the night. Awaking in the early hours, William saw that Robert was not in his bed, but he was not concerned, for in all the time he had known him, his friend had struggled to sleep more than a couple of hours a night. William had never asked what he did during his nocturnal waking hours, and Robert had never offered an explanation.

Just before 4am William was woken by Zafir. He washed, dressed and walked across the camp to morning prayers. Robert was already there and greeted him with a smile and a pat on the back. But it was not his usual open and joyful grin. No, today it was distinctly reserved. As William took his seat, he glanced over his left shoulder to see a preoccupied and pensive Robert. What was it that was troubling his friend? In that moment, William felt a deep sense of unease.

Chapter 2

Present day

Christmas had come and gone in a whirl of tinsel, carols, and turkey and, although a low-key affair, the family enjoyed the closeness that the season brought. On the thirty-first of December, a dark, dank, desolate day, they buried Harriet's beloved father, who had passed away in November.

Ever since the funeral Harriet had felt strangely detached. There was a numbness within. Determined to move forward into the new year with a sense of optimism and hope she was keen to return to work, to normality. She figured that this would lift her mood. She was jolted out of her thoughts, however, by the sound of the doorbell. As she wasn't expecting anyone, she checked the camera before opening the door to Mike Taylor.

"Mike, what a lovely surprise."

"Well, I thought I'd call in on my work colleague, see how's she's faring." He gave her a cheeky grin. They'd had their differences in the past but now Mike had become a good friend as much as a colleague.

They sat in the kitchen drinking coffee and eating left-over Christmas cake.

"Kate sends her love and also apologies for not joining me but her IT consultative work with the Constabulary has really taken off."

Harriet owed a great debt to Kate Squires who had played a major role in her rescue and subsequent recovery the previous year. "That's a good thing. I'm happy for her. She's a true friend, a real support. She texts or speaks to me almost daily."

"Come on, then, how are you doing?" asked Mike through a mouthful of cake.

"I'm okay. I just feel flat. Things have changed so much, and I know that when I return to work it's unlikely I'll be able to re-join you or the rest of the team and that makes me sad. You're like family to me. Plus, my lovely cottage, my home, is crammed with sophisticated monitoring devices and alarms. And to boot, Ben and Amelia are upset by the constraints on their lives. They are teenagers, they are frustrated at the lack of freedom and I feel guilty that the entire family is subject to twenty-four-hour protection."

"Fuck me, you are being far too hard on yourself. In the last year you have been through such an extraordinary set of circumstances that I defy anyone not to be changed, not to be affected. You just have to give yourself time. For goodness' sake, you caught your husband cheating on you, then you were reassigned to work on the very enquiry led by him, and forced to work with his girlfriend – and me! And, I will admit that to begin with I was a total shit to you and you did not deserve that. Listen, you are a strong woman, but you are not superwoman!" Mike squeezed her hand. "Then there was the case itself," he continued. "It was hugely complex, and difficult and dangerous, with well respected members of the community dying in mysterious circumstances, and corruption from within the police. At the centre of all this was Cleo Morris, paid assassin and fucking nut case. Not only did you suffer physically at her hands but psychologically as well. Damn it, Harriet, she very nearly killed you and yet still you stood up to her. That is why, my dear friend, she is pissed off. And, of course, whilst all this was going on your father was fighting his own battle with dementia."

As Mike was talking Harriet recalled senior officer Derek Wynn's unannounced visit just before Christmas. He'd arrived at the cottage in a state of extreme panic. Harriet shivered as she remembered the utter terror she'd felt on learning that Cleo Morris, who she'd thought was safely in custody, had absconded from the hospital and was on the loose. It was at that moment that she realised Cleo might not have finished with her.

"Mike, thank you. You are a good friend. I have been kidding myself, indeed it's taken all my self-control to give the appearance of normality. I knew I had to remain outwardly calm for Ben and Amelia's sake. Inside, however, I've been in turmoil. It's not knowing when or if Cleo will be apprehended, not knowing what she has planned. At times I feel helpless. All I can do is wait for her to make her move."

"Ultimately, you will be fine. You just need to be patient and expect that your strength and natural optimism will return at some point. Ben and Amelia will come round. Deep down they know the protection measures need to be in place. And, by the way, it's okay not to be okay. Cleo can't hide from us forever; at some point she will be detained once more and your life will return to normal."

As Mike had been talking Harriet noticed how much he'd changed recently – well, ever since he'd been dating her good friend Annie. He was no longer skinny – that would be Annie's expert cooking – and his limp collar-length ash-blond hair was now smartly clipped, his long sideburns a thing of the past.

A couple of days later the phone call Harriet had been expecting came. She was in the kitchen sipping a steaming cup of black filter coffee.

"Morning, Harriet, it's Cheryl, the chief's secretary. He wonders if you might be free tomorrow morning to pop in for a chat, say eleven?"

"Yes, that's fine. Do I need to prepare anything?" asked Harriet.

"No, it's just a chat. Look forward to seeing you tomorrow." Cheryl's voice was kind.

The next day, Harriet rose early, showered and spent some time choosing her outfit. She settled on a navy shift dress and smart matching jacket, to which she added a large silver pendant and a pair of long flat black boots. Flat because at five foot eleven she was conscious of her height. She ran her fingers through her short cropped blonde hair. A touch of make-up and a puff of feminine perfume and she was ready to face her fate.

Cheryl met Harriet in Reception with a friendly smile and led her to the chief's office. And, as had become the norm in her life, a protection officer followed at a discreet distance. This morning it was Chris Smyth. Dave was escorting Ben and Amelia to school, although they had left the house that morning objecting loudly to the new restrictions imposed upon their lives.

As Harriet followed Cheryl she caught sight of the chief, Mark Jones, at his desk. He was lounging in his desk chair, his long legs stretched out in front of him, his skinny arms behind his neatly cut wavy auburn hair. He seemed to be chatting animatedly to another male, but it was not until she got closer that she saw it was Derek Wynn. Kind, dependable, handsome Derek Wynn. As Harriet entered the glass office, both men jumped to their feet. She noticed a pleasing aroma of aftershave and fresh coffee. The chief was the first to greet her with a handshake and a kiss, followed by Derek. Harriet took the chair that was offered, and Cheryl handed her a cup of coffee. It was not until Cheryl had exited the office that anyone spoke.

"Harriet, it's really good to see you. You look well. How are things, honestly?" Mark Jones looked concerned.

"Thank you, sir. It's good to be here. I'm doing much better, thank you. I'm pretty much healed physically. Emotionally, I'm stronger, certainly far less fragile than I was before Christmas."

"I sense a 'but' coming," said Mark.

Harriet grimaced. "But I won't lie, I'm struggling a little with the intrusion into my life. I accept I must have protection; I know it's the right thing for my family, but I suppose I feel a little suffocated. I know she's coming for me. What I don't know is when, which means I'm constantly on edge, constantly on tenterhooks. It's utterly exhausting."

"Harriet, I'm so sorry, I can appreciate that, but neither I nor my team can currently think of a better way of doing things. There are no magic solutions here."

"I know, but I worry that the situation is not sustainable. There is such a huge cost implication to it." She paused for a moment. "Tell me, has there been any progress in tracking… tracking Cleo down?" Harriet flushed slightly. She hoped it wasn't too noticeable.

"Please don't worry about the cost. It's under control. Derek, do you want to give Harriet an update?"

"Yes, sir, if you like."

Harriet knew Derek Wynn well enough to recognise when he was uncomfortable and, as she watched him put his coffee cup on the table and shift in his chair, she suspected the news would not be good. This was confirmed when he cleared his throat, his habitual tic for awkward situations.

"Harriet, I really wish I had good news for you. But the truth is that we are struggling to find her. We have CCTV in the hospital car park that shows a grainy image of a woman matching her approximate height and size getting into a taxi about half an hour before Cleo was reported missing by Mike Taylor. Unfortunately, the woman is wearing a dark hooded coat, and there are no clear images of her. We have, however, managed to track the taxi firm down and the driver."

"And?" Harriet leaned forward in her chair and fixed Derek with her green eyes.

"And the female gave her name as Rosie McLor. No trace on the Police National Computer. She was dropped off at the train station. Apart from telling the driver where to take her, she didn't speak. She paid in cash. And, before you ask, she does not appear to have taken the train. It's as if she disappears into thin air once she leaves the drop-off point."

"Did she speak with an accent?" asked Harriet.

"Not that the driver could remember. But, to be fair, he was barely able to recall her at all."

Harriet sighed heavily. "Are there any other lines of enquiry?"

"Well, a team of experienced detectives are currently engaged in interviewing her close family members," said Derek. "These are voluntary interviews, to establish a better picture of Cleo but also to see if any of them trip themselves up. Her father and brother have been nothing but co-operative and helpful. Her mother, on the other hand, has been a completely different kettle of fish. Difficult, rude, extremely unhelpful and provocative. The feeling from the little she has said is that she has had contact with Cleo. As a result, we now believe we have sufficient grounds to obtain authority to conduct intrusive surveillance. The plan is to put a surveillance team on her to see what she does."

"That makes me very happy indeed," said Harriet, and she did feel better, more reassured. Instinctively she knew that now was not the time to ask about the minutiae. That would have to wait until she could speak to Derek alone.

"Also, we've been speaking to Kate Squires, to her father, Henry, and to a friend of theirs called Cyrus Hart. What's interesting is that Henry and Cyrus both believe Cleo's mother, Veronica, had some involvement in the death of Kate's mother years ago. We've only got initial statements at this stage and need to follow up to see if there is any tangible evidence."

"I had no idea. That's disturbing." Harriet shivered involuntarily.

"It's definitely unsettling," said Derek.

"I'm embarrassed. I've been wallowing in self-pity without realising the herculean effort that has been taking place on my behalf. Will you please pass on my thanks to everyone?"

"Of course." Mark smiled. "I don't think you realise the esteem in which your fellow officers hold you. You are one of the team and they are passionate about keeping you safe and finding Cleo."

"There is one further action we have yet to complete," said Derek. "That is the trawl of less obvious CCTV both in and around the hospital, the train station and in the neighbourhood of Cleo's parents' address."

"Good, now we need to talk about work, Harriet," said Mark Jones, looking suddenly pensive.

"Sir, if it helps, I'm guessing that you are about to tell me I won't be returning to work with the old team and, whilst I'd love to, I understand why it's not possible."

Mark Jones took a sharp intake of breath. Neither Harriet nor Derek could fail to notice the look of relief on his face. "You do?"

"Yes, you were about to tell me that the whole situation is complex, that I am both a witness and a victim in the case and that I still need to be interviewed about certain aspects."

"You are correct in your assessment of the situation. It would be completely unethical to allow you to assist in the preparation of the prosecution files and your status as both victim and witness complicates matters."

Mark Jones rose to his feet and walked across his office to a large grey metal filing cabinet, from which he removed a manila file, before returning with the folder in his hand.

"This is a particularly tragic and violent case. On the face of it a double murder, possibly a domestic that went horribly wrong. Operation Juliet. It happened last week at an address in Rose Avenue. We would really appreciate your help with this, but it is harrowing. So, I will completely understand, given all that you have gone through recently, if you wish to decline."

Harriet saw Derek exchange looks with the chief, who nodded back.

"Harriet, the senior investigating officer, the SIO, for Operation Juliet is James Short," said Derek. "He's been made acting Detective Superintendent for the duration of this case. To be honest, such is the heavy resource commitment to existing cases that we have simply run out of qualified senior officers. James Short is ... well, he can be difficult to work with."

"You mean work for," Harriet corrected.

"Well, yes, you do have a point. He tends to think of his staff as there for him to direct as he pleases. He is not the easiest man to get along with. But unfortunately, we are where we are."

"On a more positive note, though, we think we've come up with a plan," said Mark. "You will work part-time on Operation Juliet. You will job share with DS Geoff Harvey. He has some personal issues right now, which means that he can't always be at work and in turn there will be times when you will need to be absent to clear up the loose ends on your last case, which may potentially include giving evidence too. You and Geoff are exceptionally able detectives with excellent people skills and – I think – you know and like each other."

Harriet nodded her agreement and the chief continued. "We are hoping that together you will be able to mitigate James's shortcomings. We need eyes on the inside. I won't lie, both Derek and I have misgivings about this but at present there is no one else available to head up this case. I have asked Derek to keep a close watching brief in case of problems. What I want you two to do is to review the investigation to date, to speak to witnesses and scenes of crime and ensure that all that can be done is being done."

"Yes," said Harriet.

"Yes?" The chief constable looked puzzled.

"Yes, I'd be happy to work alongside Geoff Harvey on Operation Juliet."

"That's brilliant, thanks so much, Harriet." Mark Jones got to his feet and handed her the file.

"Just one more thing. Does Superintendent Short know that we've been asked to review the case?"

"Yes, but I can't say that he was very happy about it," said Derek Wynn, arching his left eyebrow as he spoke. Harriet had known Derek Wynn long enough to know that he was issuing a warning: James Short was likely to be touchy, if not openly hostile, and she should prepare herself for trouble.

Chapter 3

1184 – The Holy Land

Following morning prayers, William, Robert and the other Templar Knights attended to their horses, before being permitted to return to their beds for an hour or so. Instead of going to the 6am service, they followed their orders to tack up their horses. There were twelve Knights who set off in the early morning sunshine bound for the Templar stronghold at Latrun. There would be no fighting for them that day, unless of course they were ambushed. They were to relieve their fellow Templars and escort pilgrims into Jerusalem. They rode hard over the dusty, rocky ground, sticking to the main routes. Other road users could not fail to notice them. Indeed, they kept to the side of the road to allow the Knights to pass unimpeded. They were quite a sight, resplendent in chainmail, their white and red tabards billowing in the breeze as they sat astride glossy war horses, not heavy mounts as such but broad and strong, bred especially for war.

As they rode through a particularly narrow and rocky ravine, Robert trotted forward to catch up with William, who was the lead horse.

"My friend, slow a little, will you? I want to tell you something but, before I do, you must promise not to scold me."
William laughed and turned to look over his shoulder at his friend. But Robert wasn't smiling; he was uncharacteristically serious.

"What is it, my friend?" William asked.

"Promise me," was Robert's reply.

"I promise."

"I met Saladin last night," said Robert in a subdued voice

"Who?"

"Salah al Din."

"You did what?"

"Shush, I met Saladin," said Robert, placing his index finger to his mouth.

William's eyes widened to their full extent. He made the sign of the cross. "The Saladin?" he hissed.

"Yes."

"Robert, what were you thinking?"

"Saladin is in point of fact courteous, charismatic, pragmatic, down to earth, amusing and intellectual. He is a man of faith."

"Sorry? You met the supreme leader of the Islamic forces and had a cosy chat?"

"Basically, yes!"

"And exactly how did you two communicate when you don't speak Arabic and I'm pretty sure he doesn't speak English?" muttered William.

"We got by, using a bit of French and a bit of Latin."

William hung his head. He was struggling to process these revelations.

"Look, I may not get another opportunity, so please just listen to what I have to say." Robert searched his friend's face for a hint of compliance.

Overcome with a wave of nausea, all William could manage was a nod of his head.

"For some time now, I've been struggling to rationalise the Templar way of life. I'm not talking about you or me, or indeed many of the fellow monks we know, but those in control of the larger organisation worldwide. The Templar war machine. The focus has changed. We have become a hugely wealthy organisation, about as far removed from our humble origins as it is possible to get. Our founder, Hugh de Payns, and his followers took vows of poverty, chastity and obedience. They were known throughout the world as 'The Poor Fellow Soldiers of Christ'. They relied on donations to live. Our seal illustrates these ideals, two Knights sharing a single horse. The original Templars lived by a set of austere rules. It was a way of life that worked but in less than twenty years the original band of nine Knights grew to over twenty thousand. Put your hand on your heart and tell me that our vows and our original way of life are being adhered to."

William remained silent but did slow his mount to hear what else Robert had to say.

"You can't, can you? Because you know as well as I that only a small number of Templars follow Hugh de Payn's ideals. Instead the Templar movement has become a huge business, an advanced military organisation, with sophisticated state-of-the-art fortifications, complex subterranean tunnel systems holding monumental hordes of gold and silver and holy relics."

"Stop, stop. What are you talking about, Robert?"

"I'm talking about huge vaults holding massive stockpiles of wealth."

"And how do you know this?"

"I've seen them with my own eyes."

"But I'm struggling to understand what this has to do with Saladin,"

William was frowning.

"I was coming to that but, basically, honesty and integrity."

"I really don't understand, Robert."

"Alright, I've spent many months talking to Muslims about their faith, trying to understand the differences between us, and I've concluded that we are not that unalike. It's complex, but essentially Muslims believe in one God, like Christians, only theirs is called Allah. According to their religion, God sent several prophets to teach mankind how to live according to his law. Jesus, Moses and Abraham are three of these prophets and are held in high esteem. Laws are based on their holy book called the Quran; this guides their lives. Jihad is the name they have given to struggle or effort. They use this term to describe three different types of struggle: the struggle to live the Muslim faith as devotedly as possible, the struggle to build a good Muslim society and the struggle to defend Islam by force if necessary, holy war. God sets high goals or standards for believers to follow and followers have to fight their own desires to live up to them." Robert cleared his throat before continuing. "Anyway, I digress. I met with Saladin and we talked about all sorts of things, but essentially his faith, and I really liked him."

"You did?" William no longer cared if he could be overheard.

"I found him to be a man of principle, a man of religion who lives his life simply, with no trappings, no great wealth, no hypocrisy. He is a well read, intelligent individual and remarkably funny, a man with an acute sense of humour. I won't lie, William, these encounters have led me to question my life choices. You are my most trusted and dear friend and I needed to tell you."

There was a long pause before William replied. His head was

spinning. He felt panic. What could he say? What should he say?

"Robert, I thank you for your honesty, but I need some time to process all that you've told me."

Robert nodded, and the two Knights continued their journey in silence.

It was midday when they reached the commanding fortress at Latrun, situated just twenty miles from Jerusalem and built on the highest hill in the region. The fort had far-reaching uninterrupted views which provided an obvious tactical advantage to its Templar occupants.

For the next two months William and Robert were occupied in protecting pilgrim's intent on visiting the holy sites of Jerusalem. Their role: to accompany them, to keep them safe. To help them when required. They had several pack animals at their disposal to carry food and the odd fatigued traveller. Despite some down time, however, neither William nor Robert spoke of Saladin again. But, privately William often thought of their conversation and couldn't help but feel that Saladin might yet have a role to play in both their lives.

Chapter 4

Present day

Following her meeting with the chief constable and Derek Wynn, Harriet headed home to her desk in the corner of the dining area. Here she began to read the contents of the file given to her. As she did so, her stomach tightened and her mouth became dry. The crime scene photos were horrific. She had to force herself to look. She knew she must try to remain detached, but she also knew that she must study the images if she were to have any chance of understanding what had occurred.

When she'd finished, she grabbed her handbag from the floor and searched for her mobile, before deftly sending a text. *Are you able to meet up later this afternoon or some time tomorrow?*

Five minutes later she received a reply.

"Yep, meet you in the Lyon Café on Fish Street at 3pm."

Geoff Harvey was waiting outside for Harriet, who arrived complete with protection officer. They chose a table at the back of the café and ordered two mugs of tea and two slabs of chocolate cake.

Harriet was the first to speak. "Geoff, I can't tell you how happy I am to be working with you again. Thanks for agreeing to a job share."

"It's my absolute pleasure. Besides, it suits my situation very well, which I'm sure you know all about."

"I don't, actually, and I don't want to pry. Tell me if you want, but the last thing I want is to make life any more difficult than it clearly already is. You look like you've been through the wringer."

Geoff laughed. "Are you saying my good looks have suffered? That's mighty cheeky of you."

Harriet smiled. "You've lost weight and look tired, that's all." Geoff had once been a stocky man but not now and, although she would never tell him, he looked older than forty-three. But his kind eyes and his witticisms remained the same.

"Oh, not much then! Seriously, though, can we just be honest with each other, and support each other? I know that you are still recovering from the physical and psychological injuries you sustained before Christmas. My situation is simply that my wife is suffering from a severe form of agoraphobia. Judging by the frown on your face, you're wondering how it affects Helen?"

"I am." Geoff stroked his bald head for a moment before answering. "In Helen's case, it's an extreme fear of open spaces. She's not left the house for a year and, put simply, there are days when I just cannot come into work."

"Oh, gosh, Geoff, I'm so sorry. I had no idea."

"No, I did my best to keep it quiet. Anyway, it is what it is, and we are trying to deal with it. Now, I see you were given the same briefing folder as I was. It's a disturbing read."

"Oh my God, Geoff, that truly is an understatement. If it's okay with you, I'd like to check that you see it as I do, so that we are both in agreement for Friday's briefing?"

"Good idea, but I'm not sure that it will matter what we think to the senior investigating officer. I understand that he has already made his mind up and is set upon an investigation course."

"That's not encouraging news, but I'd say all the more reason we should talk about what we've learned so far," said Harriet.

"Indeed," said Geoff. "So, what do we know for sure? Well, we know that last Thursday evening, some time before 7pm, Mr and Mrs Wilson, the occupants of 7 Rose Avenue, were eating supper. I think it's plausible to assume their young children, a boy aged seven years and a girl of three years, were upstairs in bed. They had not long started eating, judging by the amount of food left on the plates, when an incident occurred which resulted in two deaths, Mr Wilson and the young boy, believed to be their son, Archie. A small female child was later found unharmed and asleep at the address but there was no trace of Mrs Wilson. There was, however, a monumental amount of blood concentrated in the kitchen/diner area. We know that Mrs Wilson's silver Ford Fiesta is missing from the driveway, that a neighbour heard it drive off at speed at approximately 7pm. The neighbour was sure it was her Fiesta as it has a starter motor problem and he distinctly heard the loud grinding noise of the ignition when it engaged. Police were called after a friend of Mr Wilson's turned up at 8pm to take him to skittles. When there was no reply from the front door, he made his way down the side path to the back door, which leads straight into the kitchen. He did not notice the blood on the outside of the door. He knocked but did not wait for a reply, before opening said door onto the bloody scene. It appears he did not enter, but instead ran into the garden screaming and subsequently threw up multiple times. He was discovered in a terrible state by the same neighbour who heard the car start up, and it was the neighbour who dialled 999."

"Yes, your summary of events corresponds with my understanding," said Harriet. "Initial police attendance occurred within four minutes of the 999 call. It would seem therefore that there was virtually no opportunity for the scene to have been compromised. As luck would have it, the initial officers to the location were experienced, so their route into the scene was intelligent, circumspect. They touched as little as possible and did their best to avoid the blood. They used their head cams to record their route and their movements in the house. The adult male victim was cool to the touch and they were unable to find a pulse. The child at the bottom of the stairs was also cool to the touch with no discernible pulse. CPR was unsuccessful. Upstairs, they found a young female child asleep later identified as Chloe Wilson. The officers stayed with Chloe until paramedics arrived. They also arranged for the colleagues who'd arrived shortly after them to secure the outside, and to commence a log so that everyone entering and exiting the address was recorded. I'd really like to see the head cam footage, though."

"Yes, I agree. I'd also like to speak to scenes of crime, to try to get up to speed with what they think," said Geoff.

"Absolutely."

"I'm told, however, that the SIO believes this is a domestic murder. That during a heated argument Mrs Wilson murdered her husband, and his son from his first marriage, who had likely disturbed them arguing, before fleeing the scene in her Fiesta."

"Really? Is there even a history of domestic violence between them?"

Geoff shook his head.

"So, isn't it a little early to be making such assumptions?"

"I'd say so. That's why I've arranged for us to meet with Steven Leach, the senior scenes of crime officer, tomorrow at 2pm."

Chapter 5

July 1187 – The Holy Land – Three years later

William stood motionless, head bowed, eyes resting on a shallow unmarked grave at his feet.

"For God and King, my old friend." He struck his chest in salute.

The late afternoon heat was stifling and digging the grave had sapped what remained of his strength. Feeling lightheaded, he knelt. The corpse now encased for eternity in the dry arid earth was laid out according to Muslim tradition, on its right side, facing Mecca. The location of the grave had been deliberately chosen by William for its isolation. Away from prying eyes.

Whatever it was he was feeling, it hurt like mad. It burned into his very being. William stood up. He picked his way carefully across the bleak rocky headland until he had sight of the Holy Land stretched out below. As he gazed across the rolling landscape he recalled the skinny seven-year-old with piercing eyes and mop of ginger hair who'd chased him into the fishpond before pouncing on him and punching him squarely on the nose. Not the most auspicious of starts to a friendship which had endured nearly thirty years.

He turned and reluctantly made his way back to the graveside, where he removed his gloves and bowed his head. Placing his large hands palm to palm and shaking violently, he paused to wipe his tear-stained face with a dusty hand.

"The Lord's my shepherd I'll not want; he makes me down to lie. In pastures

green; he leadeth me the quiet waters by …. Yea, though I walk in death's dark vale, yet will I fear no ill; for thou art with me, and thy rod and staff me comfort still."

Teardrops crafted a maze of zigzag tracks down his grimy cheeks. Deep heavy sobs followed; William's raw grief was unfettered. For the first time in his life his faith was sorely tested, for he felt no comfort, just the utter agony of loss.

Zafir had been watching from the shade of a nearby tree. William observed his sobbing manservant turn away and look around before darting across the rocky ground to get a better vantage point, for he knew Zafir was nervous. They were deep in occupied territory.

William stood to attention, his heavy sword hanging loosely at his side. He clasped his dented helmet in his left hand.

"Rest in peace, my old friend. You are forever in my heart."

Zafir joined William.

"I am utterly broken," said William. "Robert was the best friend a man could ever wish for and I lost him. I hoped one day to be able to tell him how much he meant to me and now I shall never get the opportunity."

Zafir let out a series of huge sobs. William placed his helmet on the dusty ground before encasing the young man in his arms. Only when Zafir became silent did William let go. He surveyed the young man before him, who must have been in his early twenties now, about five foot seven, with olive skin, huge dark eyes and the whitest of teeth. A survivor. The child had become a man.

Horses' hooves approached at speed. There was no time to flee. As William turned, five mounted soldiers appeared. Leading the group, a young man perhaps in his mid-twenties, proud and fierce looking. He skidded to an abrupt halt in front of them. William's hand immediately gripped his sword.

"Greetings, William of Hertford," said the soldier in French.

William nodded.

"I am Sayf, nephew to our supreme leader, Saladin. I have been instructed to bring you to him. We leave immediately."

William wasn't sure why he felt no fear, no alarm, but was instead curious. He understood that his fate was pretty much sealed, for word had reached him that Saladin had slain all Templar Knights to survive the recent Battle of Hattin.

A short time later, they arrived at the bustling Muslim camp. Not so different from the Christian camps. Rows of tents, campfires, dogs fighting, soldiers chatting, training, cleaning kit, seeing to horses. William was shown to an unremarkable large tent and invited to enter. Zafir was instructed to remain outside with William's horse and his sword. The tent was poorly lit, but fragrant. Roses perfumed the air, and they immediately took William back to his early years, before he'd been sent to St Albans Monastery, to happy summer days in the garden with his mother. How his life had altered.

The floor was covered in rugs and cushions. Sayf stood next to him, too close. But it was not long before a man entered from an opening at the rear of the tent, accompanied by several other males and a woman. As he approached, William could see he was tall, but not as tall as William's six foot. The man was of slim build, wiry looking, with a neatly trimmed beard. William guessed he was aged about fifty. He was smartly dressed in a long black robe, worn over loose black trousers, slipper-like pointed shoes and a black turban. He smiled as he approached and, on reaching William, bowed.

"Welcome, William of Hertford. Please take a seat." The man had a heavy accent. William did as he was bid.

"We speak now in French; my English is, what they say, broken?" William couldn't help smiling at this. However, the man's French proved to be fluent.

"I am Saladin, but I think you already know that. May I say it is a sincere honour to at last meet the man I've heard so much about. I would tell you that you have nothing to fear from me, but I see from your demeanour you are not in the least bit apprehensive."

William bowed to the man before him. "Thank you for the invitation. It is a privilege to meet the leader of the Islamic armed forces in the flesh."

"Good, well then, before we talk in earnest, please allow me to offer you some refreshment. You look fit to drop from exhaustion and grief, no?"

William looked directly into Saladin's eyes. He saw immediately there was no point in issuing a denial, for the man before him was astute. "That would be much appreciated."

Water containing rose petals was brought in individual bowls for hand washing, then a feast was laid out in the centre of the seating area. Large platters of flatbreads and yoghurt. Cheese, dried fruits and nuts, huge plates of steaming roasted lamb and beef. Colossal bowls of fruit containing plump grapes, cherries, strawberries, figs, dates, bananas and oranges. There was also a sort of honey-based alcoholic drink.

"William of Hertford, please help yourself, you are most welcome."

"I am honoured, thank you. May I take some to my manservant who has just as much need of this as I." William wondered as he said this, if this might actually be his last supper.

"Zafir has already been attended to. Do not worry, his belly is full. You are as you have been described, a selfless man who thinks of others before his own needs." Saladin spoke between mouthfuls of meat.

William bowed in thanks. "May I ask a question?" Not waiting for an answer, William continued, "I notice you are serving alcohol; I was under the impression that this is not permitted by your religion?"

"You are well informed. Fermented grapes or dates are an atrocity, an outrage. However, drinks produced by means of honey, wheat, barley, or millet are lawful, so long as they are not drunk lustfully."

When the food had been cleared away, the tent began to empty, leaving just William and the woman who had first entered with the supreme leader in the main body of the tent. Until now, she had remained at the back. As Saladin was absorbed in giving orders to his departing guests she approached. William got to his feet. She was, he thought, about five foot seven, which was unusually tall for an indigenous woman, of slim build, strong looking but graceful. She was dressed in a long-sleeved dark grey embroidered fitted jacket to the mid-calf, worn over a full length light grey dress. Her head was covered in a grey veil with only her eyes remaining visible. What extraordinary eyes they were too. Large, oval, nut brown, luminous. William realised he was staring and dropped his gaze immediately.

"William of Hertford, it is an honour to meet you at last. I have heard so much about you. I am Rabia, Robert's widow."

Startled, William looked up and into Rabia's eyes. "You speak very fine English," he stuttered.

"Thank you. I had many opportunities to practise with my

29

husband."

"You were married to Robert? I had no idea."

"It was the will of my Uncle Saladin. He was a good and kind husband."

"I'm sorry for your loss," said William, remembering his manners.

"Thank you."

An awkward silence ensued, until Saladin returned. He gestured to both Rabia and William to sit.

For a full hour they talked about William's faith, Saladin's faith, the differences and the similarities between their ways of life. William found Saladin every bit as fascinating as Robert had described. Learned, engaging, amusing and intelligent.

"William, I am a symbol of hope to my people for a united Islamic world and I will not rest until I have achieved this. And, whilst I admire you immensely, I'm afraid your faith dooms your soul to damnation."

"Sire, whilst I admire you too, I will take my chances concerning my soul." William winked at the supreme leader of the Muslim world.

Saladin roared with laughter. "Good retort, good retort." Then he frowned and got to his feet. "William of Hertford, it gives me no pleasure to touch on a subject that I fear will bring you much pain. However, I feel it is my moral obligation to do so. I understand you were absent from the recent Battle of Hattin."

"I was, but how did you know?"

"Well, for a start, William, you stand head and shoulders above any of my men. So, I always know which sector you are fighting in and often make a point of sending my fiercest soldiers to attack you!"

Both men laughed.

"Your absence was confirmed by your Grand Master, Gerard of Ridefort, upon capture," Saladin went on. "He told me he sent you on a secret mission to ensure that you did not return in time."

"In time for what?" asked William, neither confirming nor denying the existence of a mission.

"In time to save Robert. You see, he got word that many of your fellow Templar Knights had made a pact to chase down Robert of St Albans. In their minds he was a traitor. Gerard knew that if you were present you would do your level best to prevent this and many would die in the process."

The colour drained from William's face. Should he, could he believe this man?

"My uncle speaks the truth. There was a plot to seek out and murder Robert in the heat of the battle." Rabia wiped away her tears, but they just kept falling.

William dropped to his knees; head bowed. No one spoke and it took several long minutes for William get to his feet once more. "I am a man of God. I have dedicated my life to his service. I have strived to live by his word. But this is too much. I'm not sure I can turn the other cheek. Whilst I struggle daily to understand why Robert converted to Islam, I do try to respect his decision. Initially, I was furious with him, I still am if I'm truly honest. But I loved the man as a brother. Such a bond cannot be broken. To learn that many of my fellow Knights took it upon themselves to exact some sort of mad revenge is devastating. May their souls be damned." William's voice was hoarse.

"William, it may be poor comfort, but you should know that all those involved in slaying Robert have paid for it with their lives. History, however, will no doubt record another verdict and say that the great Saladin slaughtered these Templar Knights because he feared their proficiency in battle. But you and I and Rabia will know the truth."

"Tell me, where is Gerard of Ridefort now? I should like to speak with him." William's right hand had formed into a tight fist.

"He is my prisoner and has been transported to Damascus."

"May I ask, just why did this battle turn into such a disaster for us Christians?"

"Failure to plan, combined with political skulduggery, my friend. My spies reported that Gerard of Ridefort was highly confrontational during the planning stage and informed King Guy that for his honour he should advance and attack my forces. This was against the advice of Raymond of Tripoli, who Ridefort called a traitor. But this was shockingly poor strategic advice and left the king advancing straight into my trap. On the third of July," Saladin went on, "your Knights Templar joined the rear of the king's vast army as it made its way to Tiberias. But it was very hot, too hot to be marching through the desert, especially when you are reliant on replenishing your water supplies from natural springs along the way. The army stopped at the town of Turan, but its fountain was wholly inadequate to quench the thirst of twenty thousand men together with their horses and pack animals."

"So, they were essentially marching to their deaths," said a sombre William.

"War is war and I had sent outriders to fill in every well and block every spring on their route."

"But how then did you supply your own army with water?"

"Camel trains from the rear, bringing supplies of fresh water from the Sea of Galilee."

"I see."

"As soon as the Christian army left Turan I had my forces take the town, essentially cutting off their retreat route and with it any water supply. I sent out small units of troops to skirmish with them along the way, with the result that they advanced to a high, rocky, dry plateau. They were now surrounded and with no water. The following morning, they made slow progress towards a place known as The Horns of Hattin, an exposed rocky outcrop. By now, man and beast were gasping for water and shelter from the harsh sun. I then had my forces set fire to the desert brush surrounding them, before attacking. And the rest is history."

"You completely outsmarted them. And what of King Guy?"

"I spared him in this very tent. He too is on his way to prison in Damascus. It will not be many moons, Allah willing, before I take back the jewel in the crown."

Rabia stepped forward. She was sobbing. She took a minute or so to compose herself. In her hand was something wrapped in red silk. "William of Hertford, have you heard of the Greek writer Homer and his tale, *The Odyssey*?"

"I have indeed," said William gently. "It was a great favourite of both Robert's and mine. Many times, we listened to travelling poets and singers in our camps recount Odysseus's trials and tribulations."

"Such an astonishing set of tales. Robert and I often read the adventures to each other. It was very special." Rabia's eyes lit up momentarily.

Rabia removed the silk cloth to reveal a large leather-bound book. She opened the cover. William saw that it was an exquisitely illustrated, translated version of *The Odyssey*. Extremely rare, and incredibly beautiful. As she slowly turned the pages, William gasped.

"A wedding present from my uncle to us. I know that Robert wished you to have it." Rabia placed it in William's hands, the anguish on her face plain for all to see.

"I am deeply honoured and thank you for this remarkable gift, but I regret I cannot accept it. It belongs with you. You see, I am not permitted by my Order to keep personal items. Treasure it and keep it safe and think of the Robert you loved when you read it." He placed his hand on Rabia's and was completely unprepared for the emotions this aroused in him. William turned to Saladin and bowed.

"I will take my leave now. Thank you for your hospitality, thank you for your honesty and your empathy."

"God be with you, William of Hertford," said Saladin.

"God be with you, Saladin." William could see Zafir, just outside the tent, deep in conversation with a serving girl. As he exited the tent he got the feeling he was being watched.

Chapter 6

Present day

Steven Leach, the senior scenes of crime officer for Operation Juliet, had arranged to meet Geoff and Harriet outside the crime scene at 2pm. At first glance number 7 Rose Avenue was an unremarkable house. Most probably built in the 1970s, semi-detached, constructed in brick with large square windows to the front.

Harriet and Geoff arrived ten minutes early, parked and sauntered down the tarmac drive. They had gone no more than a couple of feet before a tall, gangly man in a white protective suit and noticeably large ears protruding from his mop of black unruly hair, accosted them.

"DS Harvey, DS Lacey? I'm Steven." The man stretched out his hand with a wide grin.

"Good to meet you, Steven. Please call us Geoff and Harriet," said Harriet, unable to stifle a giggle.

"Will do!" said Steven enthusiastically, exposing a large gap between his top teeth. "So, you've noticed my customised headphones then? You no doubt thought you were being confronted by an over-sized white rabbit! Long story, suffice to say, these earphones were a birthday present from my colleagues."

"Say no more," said Geoff smiling widely.

"As you know, this job can be hauntingly difficult. You have to have a sense of humour to survive. This case has already taken its toll." He was suddenly solemn.

"I can understand that. Where are you with it?" asked Geoff.

"We have literally just finished processing the scene, which as you can see was extensive. Your timing is good. If you want to suit up in the tent over there by the fir tree, I'd be happy to talk you through it, and bring you up to speed."

"That would be really great, thank you. Are you able to give us an idea of what the SIO's impression of the scene has been?" asked Harriet.

"No, I'm not, because he hasn't been out."

"Seriously?"

"Seriously. Apparently he feels there is no need, preferring instead to study the video footage and photographs."

"But…" said Harriet.

"I know, I know. I'm about to seek advice about it from my boss, DS Paul Jones."

Geoff and Harriet exchanged glances.

"Look," Steven added. "I've probably said too much already."

They kitted up in white protective suits and shoe protectors, latex gloves and face masks. They knew that this was necessary to avoid contamination in case in the course of their briefing they identified items or areas of the scene which had not been processed. As they entered the property it felt to Harriet like entering a moment frozen in time. Everything was as it had been at the moment of death, except that the bodies had been removed.

Steven Leach proved extremely articulate. He gave them a detailed account of what had been found. And, although both Geoff and Harriet were seasoned detectives, it really helped to understand how this particular scene had been processed, how it had been documented and recorded and how the scenes of crime officers had conducted their painstaking search for physical evidence. Leach explained that in order to prevent the loss of trace evidence, they had transported the bodies to the mortuary with plastic bags secured over their heads, hands and feet.

The kitchen/diner was the last room they entered. The ferocity of the attack was clear for all to see. Steven explained that processing this room had been extremely challenging due to the volume of blood present. Each of hundreds of samples had to be sealed in polythene bags, recorded, labelled, transported and then frozen to maintain biological integrity.

Harriet stood in the doorway to the kitchen trying to take in the scene of devastation before her. There were a couple of huge pools of blood within the vicinity of the table; there were also some distinct transfer stains, a partial shoe print and what looked like drag marks leading to the door to the garden. From where she was standing she could not see much evidence of blood spatter on the walls.

They went outside, back to the driveway, to finish the briefing. It was less intense and easier to talk without the face masks.

"Okay, before I say any more, do either of you have any observations?" asked Steven.

"I was struck by the contrast in scenes between the kitchen where Mr Wilson died and the bottom of the stairs where his son died," said Geoff.

"Yes, the evidence strongly suggests that little Archie Wilson was asphyxiated. We think a hand wearing a latex glove was initially placed over his mouth. Whilst it is now possible to get fingerprints from some surfaces through a thin latex glove, I'm not aware of any success in lifting them from skin. It would appear that a cushion from the sofa was ultimately used to extinguish life."

"Poor little man." Geoff shook his head.

"It's such a tragedy," said Harriet. "The ferocity of his father's death suggests to me that this was a crime of passion, of anger, maybe even rage."

"I think so too," said Leach. "But my problem is that the SIO is adamant there was no intruder. I think the evidence tells a different story. Mr Wilson stood six foot three inches tall and Mrs Wilson five foot two. From the blood pattern analysis I've conducted, I believe that Mr Wilson was standing when his throat was cut. It would have been impossible for Mrs Wilson to reach his neck unless she stood on a chair, and there is no forensic evidence to suggest that this occurred."

"Okay, let me ask you something then," said Harriet. "You said inside the house that the murder weapon, a kitchen knife, was found at the scene. It had apparently been taken from the knife block, which was on the side towards the far end of the kitchen. So where do you think the victim and perpetrator were in relation to each other?"

"The blood pattern suggests that the victim was standing near the table, that the perpetrator was standing behind him. I think this suggests the element of surprise, that the perpetrator slit his carotid artery without Mr Wilson having any idea that the attack was coming. Mr Wilson fell to the floor, and grabbed his neck, in an attempt to stem the spurting blood which continued to be pumped out by his beating heart."

"Go on, what else do you think happened?" asked a wide-eyed Geoff.

"I think Mrs Wilson fell to her knees and tried to stem the flow of blood before she was dragged across the floor to the back door. And, although she was short, I think she struggled. There is evidence of transfer blood and drag marks on the floor. There is also a partial footprint and smudges of blood on the door to the garden. I think it's a possibility Mrs Wilson was abducted."

"Oh my God, Steven! Have you told the SIO?" asked Harriet.

"I have but he is not moving. He is adamant that the evidence points to a domestic murder. No intruder. Mrs Wilson snaps, kills her husband. She is interrupted by her stepson and has to deal with him before fleeing in her Ford Fiesta."

"Seriously?" Harriet was running her hands through her hair.

"Seriously. The SIO says there is no evidence of anyone else being at the property. He says the latex gloves were worn by Mrs Wilson and, as we don't have these, we cannot confirm this. He says there is no sign of forced entry and therefore no one else was there. He is not for turning." Leach looked downcast.

"Then we must find the evidence to change his mind," said Harriet. "There is potentially an innocent woman being held out there, and every hour that passes she is more likely to come to harm, if she hasn't already. Bloody hell, it happened a week ago tomorrow, didn't it?"

"Yes!"

"Okay then, we go through the evidence again. I noticed that there was a kitchen roll on the side in the kitchen, with what looked like smudges of blood on it. Has that been analysed?"

"Off the top of my head, I don't know," said Steven. "But I can find out."

Geoff had walked some way down the drive to answer a call. Harriet went in search of him.

"It's okay, love, take deep breaths. I will get someone out to you. No, I can't come at the moment. Don't cry. Look, just breathe."

Harriet pulled her mobile from her bag and called Dave Flint. As she checked her watch, she realised he would be collecting Ben and Amelia from school.

"Dave, I need a big favour. Geoff Harvey and I are unable to leave the Juliet crime scene at the moment and Geoff's wife is having what I think is an anxiety attack. She is very poorly, and you are in the vicinity – is there any chance you can swing past Geoff's house. I'll text you the address, it's near the kids' school. See what you can do to help? And please let me know how you get on."

"No problem, Mrs Lacey, you were on loudspeaker, so Ben and Amelia are briefed!"

"Thanks, Dave, thanks, kids, I really appreciate it."

Harriet texted the address and then went back to Geoff's side, just in time to hear that Dave, Ben and Amelia had arrived.

Five minutes later, Harriet's phone rang. It was Dave Flint.

"We are with Helen; Amelia is making her a cup of tea. We'll stay with her until you arrive."

With that crisis averted, Harriet suggested to Geoff and Steven they return to the scientific support building at police headquarters to continue their review and to look at the evidence more closely. Harriet's stomach churned, for she knew full well that if Eve Wilson had indeed been abducted they needed to act fast.

Chapter 7

July 1187 – The Holy Land

As William walked across to Zafir, Sayf stepped out of the shadows and grabbed him roughly by the arm.

"Christian, I'm not so easily convinced by your charm as my uncle. You appear to have him under some sort of spell, just as Robert of St Albans did. I will not allow it to continue. Consider yourself a marked man. Do not come near my uncle or my family again. Do you understand?"

"I want no trouble. I respect your uncle, despite our differing beliefs. All I want now is to be on my way, if you don't mind. And if you do mind, then you'd better draw your sword."

"Sayf, let go of William's arm now!" shouted Saladin, from the entrance to his tent.

"May God's curse be upon you, Templar," spat Sayf as he stepped away.

"Sayf," Saladin continued, "in my experience, individuals fall broadly into two categories, those who are predominantly honest, kind and selfless and those who are predominantly dishonest, narcissistic and selfish. Very occasionally, you may come across someone who is purely selfish, or conversely selfless. William of Hertford is such an individual. He is the most honourable man you are ever likely to meet. And therefore, a word of warning. Do not under any circumstances confuse this with weakness."

Saladin and William exchanged bows.

William knew he had just made an enemy of Saladin's rash and headstrong nephew. He also knew that their paths would undoubtedly cross again. But, for now, it was time to leave. He planned to head to Jerusalem, to warn Brother Thierry, the new acting Grand Master, of Saladin's plan to conquer Jerusalem sooner rather than later.

Zafir patiently held William's grey war horse to allow his master to mount before deftly jumping up behind him. As they headed out of the vast Muslim camp, they appeared to be a source of interest.

"Zafir, what are they saying, why are they pointing and laughing?" asked William.

"Sire, they think we can afford only one horse. They do not realise that this is how the Templars ride!"

William smiled wearily.

Back at Robert's burial site, they rested until dawn, before setting off in convoy, William riding up front, Zafir driving the cart, with Robert's horse tethered behind. As they rode, William thought about Zafir's desperate search for Robert's body amongst the dead on the battlefield. He'd insisted on going alone, arguing that it was the last thing he could do for Robert and that, as a native, he could mingle amongst William's enemies. Still, it had been an incredibly courageous act by the young man.

They pushed hard, travelling in the early morning and at dusk. They avoided the main routes, sticking to dirt tracks and relying on the kindness of villagers for bread and water along the way. William estimated it would take them six days to reach Jerusalem. As they journeyed, however, their numbers began to swell.

The first addition was a tiny puppy found abandoned by the side of the road. White and grey, tiny and painfully thin with a mournful cry, it could only just have been weaned. Next, an elderly lady. One evening they had come across an undamaged well, a rarity. Having refreshed themselves, they were about to leave the battle-scarred village when Zafir thought he heard a faint noise coming from one of the abandoned houses.

"Master, Master, do you hear that?" he asked.

William stopped in his tracks and strained to listen. He could indeed hear a female voice, shouting in Arabic. She seemed to be asking for help.

"Zafir, is she okay?"

"No, Master, she is scared. She is shouting that she has been left, discarded. She is frightened."

Beneath a trap door in the floor of one of the houses, they found an elderly lady sitting in a small deep underfloor space. She was tiny and frail, clothed head to toe in black and in tears, but William detected a faint sparkle in her eyes. William and Zafir lay flat on their stomachs to reach down into the void. Without too much difficulty they were able to hold her under the arms and gently pull her out. Too weak to stand, she had to be carried to the cart. She weighed nothing. She did not speak, just stared at William. Despite Zafir's efforts to entice her, she remained silent and continued to fix her gaze on William. She did, however, accept the water they offered and a hunk of bread. She ate hungrily, before lying down on her side with her back to them. William shrugged as he placed a blanket over her.

"Perhaps she will come around when she's had time to rest. Either way, we cannot leave her here."

Later on they rested in another deserted village. As they ate bread, curd cheese and dates procured by Zafir, talk turned to Saladin's camp.

"Zafir, the other night at the Muslim camp, I saw you deep in conversation with a young serving girl. You knew her well?"

"Master, that was Lubna, Rabia's maid. We first met when I visited Master Robert at Acre. She is kind and funny."

"You would visit Robert? When?"

"In the night, Master, but only when we were stationed near to the Muslim camps."

It had never crossed William's mind that Robert and Zafir would stay in touch after Robert left in 1185. However, Robert had been a huge part of Zafir's life, so why should they have terminated all contact? Zafir had proved on numerous occasions how comfortable he was infiltrating the Muslim camps, why not then for friendship?

"I see. Well, I'm glad."

"Master Robert always asked after you and wanted to hear news of you. It troubled him deeply that you had to live apart."

William bowed his head. Despite the passage of time, the sense of betrayal he felt was so hard to bear, the pain in his chest was crushing. And whilst he was genuinely happy for Zafir, he wondered why he had not tried harder to overcome his feelings and stay in contact? Had it been pride?

"Templar!" bellowed the old lady.
Jolted back to the present, William jumped to his feet, swiftly wiping his eyes with his sleeve. Zafir was at his side by the time he reached the cart. Sitting upright, the old lady was shouting and pointing her bony finger at William.

Although William could speak basic Arabic, mostly he relied on Zafir to translate for him.

"What is she saying?"

"Master, I'm sorry to say that she detests you, she hates you, she curses you and demands to know where she is being taken," said Zafir.

"Please tell her she has nothing to fear from me. I was planning to take her to Jerusalem, to a place I know which offers refuge to those who have been displaced. She will be well looked after, and attempts made to trace her family."

"She tells you not to bother with her family, they forsook her. More importantly, she wants to know why you stay here and why you do not go home?"

"Tell her I stay out of duty to my God and my king."

The old lady appeared enraged by William's explanation.

"What in the world is she saying now, Zafir?" said an alarmed William.

"Master, she really detests you. She says you are a Templar infidel! She says your God is not her God!"

"She is wrong, my God is her God."

"You want me to tell her that? Look, Master, she is an old woman. All her life she has been taught that Christians are the enemy, they are the devil, they are vile. You will not convince her otherwise."

"Can you at least try to tell her that we worship the same God. It does not matter that her God is called Allah. He is still the same God. Can you tell her I mean her no harm?"

"I will try, Master, but she doesn't like me much either. I am a traitor and worse for serving you."

William observed the woman, who was by now standing on the cart, furiously finger pointing and waving her arms around, screeching and gesticulating at Zafir. William knew enough Arabic to realise that she was laying into Zafir, insulting him, lambasting him. Suddenly he felt himself colour.

"Enough!" he shouted in Arabic. "That young man before you is the kindest, gentlest person you could ever hope to meet. He has dedicated his life to serving me even though it has resulted in much personal condemnation for him. I have set him free more times than I can recall, but each time he refuses to leave my side. For my part, I am more grateful than I can ever show, for he is my rock and currently the only real friend I have in this desolate land!"

The woman finally shut up. William walked off but, in the distance, he could hear Zafir talking and at last the woman was silent.

Later, Zafir sought William out. "Master, I wonder if it might be sensible to change from your chainmail and tabard into plain clothing. It might help to divert attention from you."

"Zafir, as always you are most sensible. I will do so now but, before I do, pray tell me what you and our guest were talking about just now?"

"Master, I simply explained to her that you saved my life, after my family abandoned me, told her I was a small child you rescued from the gutter, that you clothed me, fed me, and nursed my injured leg, that you encouraged me, taught me English, showed me how to look after horses, and never judged, never asked me about my religious preferences, or tried to convert me to your God. I told her I owe my life to you and would follow you to the end of the earth."

"Gosh, Zafir, I don't know what to say. Thank you. What did she say?"

"She made a huffy noise but she didn't shout or swear, so I guess progress was made!" Zafir gave one of his cheeky grins.

"Young man, you amaze me. Thank you. Now get some rest. We ride again in a couple of hours."

William moved away from the others to pray. But he could feel the eyes of the old woman burning into his back. Indeed, when he rose from his knees, she was studying him closely. He bowed in her direction before sauntering off to check on Zafir.

Next day, the conditions were even hotter, making progress slow. Whilst negotiating their way through a deep ravine, they came across a man lying under some scrub. He looked deceased but, on closer inspection, they were able to establish that he was in fact unconscious. There was a large gaping wound to his chest. Clearly a Knight, his sword hung at his side.

Immediately William and Zafir sprang into action. They cut the man's chainmail from around the wound and proceeded to clean the gash thoroughly. Then William went to the cart to a large trunk, from which he removed a smaller box. It contained dressings. Zafir also went to a box secured on the cart and removed a jar. Using a wooden spoon, he heaped several spoonsful of sticky golden liquid onto the wound and massaged it in, before applying dressings. Then, carefully, they lifted the man onto the cart. The little puppy, now well fed and curious, sniffed his new companion before positioning himself in the man's armpit and falling asleep. The old lady did not say a word, she simply watched proceedings unfold before her. The man remained unconscious. Every hour or so, they stopped to allow William or Zafir to check the dressings and moisten the man's lips with water. It was not long, however, before the old woman had taken over. They continued on. All through the night William and Zafir nursed the Knight.

This did not go unnoticed by the old woman.

The following day, the man regained consciousness. They discovered he was Egbert of Powys, a Hospitaller Knight, who had fought and been injured at the Battle of Hattin, one of only a handful of combatants to escape with their lives. Although extremely weak, he was able to describe the battle. The old lady insisted Zafir translate for her.

"I've been a Knight for many years, but I have never experienced such hell. From the start it was a disaster. No water, no cover and thick acrid smoke. Thousands of us cut down where we stood. The battlefield sodden and ruddy with the blood of brave men who stood no chance. We were no match for Saladin and his vast army. We were ambushed and slaughtered. And in the searing heat it took no time at all for the reek of death to saturate the air, for the carrion birds to swoop in and tear off ribbons of flesh, gouge out eyeballs. All around were bloodied bodies and body parts, men screaming in agony and fear. I thank God I survived, but I'm no longer sure what it is I'm fighting for. How I long to return home." Egbert's voice trailed off as once more he lost consciousness.

Finally, they reached the outskirts of Jerusalem. It was evening, too late to take the old lady to her new lodgings. Egbert, on the other hand, was in dire need of medical attention. They had done their best, but he required immediate and expert care if he were to survive. Halfway down a dark back alley they stopped outside a large gated archway. Zafir jumped down from the cart and banged loudly on the wooden door. After a brief moment, a small window in the door opened. A short conversation ensued between Zafir and the man at the window, before the main gate swung open and they were given entry to an outer courtyard. There followed some activity in the shadows, before a man holding a lamp came forth to greet them. He held out his hand enthusiastically.

"William of Hertford, you are a sight for sore eyes!"

"James of Shrewsbury, good to see you again, my old friend. I have a fellow Hospitaller here, in urgent need of your expert infirmary care. We found him unconscious on a back road about two days ride from here. His name is Egbert of Powys. It appears he survived the Battle of Hattin."

"William, that was a dark day for us all. And I fear worse is to come." The Monk immediately summoned assistance and in an instant a stretcher appeared, and Egbert was taken away.

Twenty minutes later, William, Zafir and the old lady reached the eastern side of Jerusalem and the Templar headquarters. Each time William entered the site he took a sharp intake of breath. There was just something about it. It oozed history, a place revered in equal measure by Christian and Muslim. When William had first joined the Templars, he'd been told a bit of the history. The site had originally housed King Solomon's Temple, a splendid and sizeable building consisting of ornate stone pillars, cedarwood, gold, and intricate carvings. It had also apparently contained a sanctified room where it was said the ark of the covenant had been housed. Later, Solomon's temple was destroyed by the Babylonians. The temple was rebuilt on a large stone platform, which was thereafter referred to as Temple Mount, but by the time the site was given to Hugh de Payns and his followers in 1120 it had been rebuilt once more. Also on the Temple Mount compound was the Al-Aqsa mosque, a place of great importance to Muslims and often referred to in history as the most notable and beautiful Mosque in the Arab world. Under Christian rule the mosque was referred to as the

Temple of Solomon, in tribute to the history of the site. It was remodelled into a palace for the King of Jerusalem but given to Hugh de Payns and his followers to lodge in when a new palace was built. By then, however, it was a shadow of its former self, having fallen into disrepair; the lead-lined roof had been stripped and never replaced.

In the ensuing years, however, vast sums had been spent on an ambitious programme of restoration and fortification. William found this open display of wealth unsettling. For him, this was not what the Templars' focus should be.

As he glanced over his shoulder, he saw the old woman cowering on the floor of the cart.

"Do not fret," he said in Arabic. "You are safe. I give you my word you will come to no harm."

Finally, they reached the great underground vaults, thought to have once housed King Solomon's stables and now the site of the Templar stables.

William sent Zafir to fetch food and water, while he gently lifted the old woman from the cart and placed her in a warm and freshly cleaned stall. He put her in a sitting position, before covering her with a blanket. Zafir returned and handed her a large bowl of steaming lamb and lentil stew. William took his leave, giving her his now customary bow, and for the first time since they'd met, she acknowledged him by bowing her head in return.

Chapter 8

Present day

The scientific support building was state of the art, built on a former car park at the rear of police headquarters.

"Steven, back at the scene I mentioned seeing blood on the kitchen roll," said Harriet. "Can you take a look for me to see if it has been analysed?"

"Yep, doing it now," said Steven, tapping the keyboard. "It has, and the results have only just come back this afternoon. It's intriguing, initial analysis shows the DNA is identical to Mr Wilson's but I wouldn't have expected to see that blood pattern in the circumstances."

"What the hell does that mean?" asked Geoff.

"My best guess is that if it doesn't belong to him, then to a close relative, a brother perhaps?"

"Okay, indulge me, does that blood occur elsewhere?" asked Harriet.

"Hang on a minute, I'll take a look. Um, yeah, it was also found on the back door."

"Anywhere else?"

"That would be a no."

"Next question then, were the dustbins searched?"

"Hang on… blimey, no, it doesn't look like they were. Why weren't they? Oh, because the SIO told the scenes of crime officer responsible for that section not to bother. It would appear, however, that she has subsequently questioned that decision and has submitted a report currently shown as pending."

"So, it's not been actioned," said Geoff. "We really need to get those bins and their contents analysed at as a matter of urgency."

"I can't authorise that, but I know a man who can." And with that Steven Leach picked up the phone. Five minutes later, Steven re-joined Harriet and Geoff.

"Paul Jones is going to the scene now to process the bins," said a relieved-looking Leach.

It was early evening when DS Paul Jones arrived in the office.

"Harriet, how lovely to see you." His Welsh accent seemed broader than ever as he bounded across to embrace her. "Geoff, good to see you too, and Steven, thanks for the call." Harriet was immensely fond of DS Paul Jones. Middle-aged and portly with a mass of unruly auburn hair, he loved to wear brightly coloured waistcoats. Today's she thought made him look a bit like a canary. But despite his eccentric appearance he was not to be underestimated. He was extremely good at his job and universally respected.

"Paul, I'm bursting to know what you found," said an eager Harriet.

"Ah, well, it was a very illuminating search. I did find traces of blood on one of the bin lids, microscopic amounts, but inside, right at the bottom, I found two crumpled handfuls of bloodied kitchen roll."

"How long before you can get them analysed?" asked Geoff.

"I'll fast track them. It could be a few days but, given the theory regarding a possible abduction, I will try my level best for tomorrow."

"Thank you, Paul, thank you so much," said Harriet. "And thank you, Steven."

It was about half past seven when Geoff and Harriet arrived back at Geoff's house. They found everyone in the kitchen. Amelia and Dave were on the sofa at the far end engrossed in the television, Ben and Helen were seated at the kitchen table pouring over a 'GCSE Physics' book.

Harriet glanced at Geoff. He was watching his wife intently. She happened to look up and she smiled. Geoff winked back. Then a huge grin appeared on his face. Harriet wondered if she had just witnessed progress?

That evening Harriet went to bed early, not to sleep, but to ring her mother, Jane. It was a good phone call: they chatted about the day's events and the children and made plans to meet for lunch the following weekend.

"Oh, I nearly forgot, dear, I had the most charming visitor this afternoon."

"Really? How lovely."

"Yes, an old student of your father's, so pleasant and sophisticated. We chatted for ages over a cup of tea and lemon drizzle cake."

"I'm really pleased, Mum. Dad had so many students over the years. Can you remember her name?"

"I can. Rosie McLor."

"That name rings a bell, but I can't remember why. What did she look like?" asked Harriet.

"Tall, slim, with a short blonde bob. She was wearing a smart navy blue trouser suit, and I just happened to notice her handbag was Michael Kors."

"Ooh, very posh," said Harriet laughing.

Harriet turned her light out and was soon fast asleep but a few hours later she awoke with a jolt. Quaking violently and drenched in a cold sweat, she lunged for her bedside light. Breathing heavily, she checked her mobile. It was four. With hands shaking almost too much to grab a pen and pad, she confirmed her worst suspicions. She had to speak to someone, and the only person she could think of was Derek Wynn.

Derek took less than ten minutes to reach Harriet's cottage. He checked in with the protection officer outside before tapping gently on the door.

A dishevelled Harriet wearing a onesie cautiously opened the door.

"Derek, I'm so sorry to call you out, couldn't talk properly on the phone, sorry." Harriet was still trembling.

Derek walked across and enveloped her in his athletic arms. Despite her agitated state, his embrace felt different, less intimate, and yet she was surprised that she didn't mind. Things were changing between them. She had relied heavily on him during the challenges of the past year. He had been her rock and she had been drawn to him, and he to her, she knew. But, despite this, they had not taken things further and she wasn't quite sure why.

"There's absolutely no need to apologise, Harriet. It's fine, but what were you scared of?"

"Oh my God, Derek, Cleo! She's playing with me. She's fucking with my head."

"In what way? And are you sure it was Cleo?"

"Oh, yes. Yesterday, I spoke to Mum on the phone. We were just chatting when she mentioned she'd had a female visitor in the afternoon. I recognised the name but couldn't place it. But then in the night I awoke with a start when I realised the name this woman had given Mum was an anagram for Cleo Morris."

"Good God! What name did she give?"

"Rosie McLor. I thought I recognised it, and I've since checked. It's the same name given to the taxi driver at the hospital by the mysterious woman. If you rearrange the letters it spells Cleo Morris."

"Bloody hell, Harriet. Okay, here's what we are going to do." As he spoke, Harriet noticed Derek's left hand was continuously moving through his jet black hair. "I will speak to the chief constable later on this morning. We will check CCTV in the area for images of her and undertake a security review of the cottage and your personal protection."

"She disguised herself. Mum said she had a short blonde bob and was wearing a smart navy trouser suit. That's so far removed from her usual style, plus her hair has always been dark brown and very, very long, or at least it was."

"Noted. We can look anyway, see if we can identify a vehicle and we will also take steps to ensure your mother has some technical security installed, nothing to spook her, but we need to monitor her house inside and out. We can easily do this with your help, under the guise of a crime prevention survey. I have a hunch that Cleo isn't the least bit interested in your mother. She was a means to an end, to get your attention."

"Well, she bloody has it!" said Harriet.

Derek left around seven, having briefed the day shift, and Harriet was reassured by the presence of Dave and Chris. They agreed between them that they must appear normal for the sake of Ben and Amelia, who were blissfully unaware of the drama that had unfolded in the early hours. Harriet's stomach threatened to give her away, however, as she fought waves of nausea.

Geoff appeared at the cottage at eight. "Morning. Thanks again for yesterday, for rescuing Helen. It's the first time in about a year I've seen her smile. Well done, Ben, you were a star."

"Thanks, Mr Harvey. Actually, your wife really helped me with my physics, it was really useful."

"I'm pleased. Right, Mrs Lacey, we'd better get a move on, first day on the incident room and all that!"

On the drive to George Street Police Station, Harriet hardly said a word.

"You alright? You're very quiet and, if you don't think I'm being too rude, you look like shit."

"Bad night, Geoff. Repercussions from our last case. I'm not ready to talk about it yet, if that's okay?"

"Of course." He put his left hand on her arm.

Operation Juliet was shoehorned into a room that was not fit for purpose, as was so often the case in the police world. Officers were used to making do. Geoff and Harriet were greeted and shown to the desk they were to share. At precisely nine o'clock, acting Superintendent James Short and his senior team of investigators marched in and everyone stopped what they were doing. Silently chairs were moved into a horseshoe shape. Once everyone was in position, James Short moved to the front to address them.

Harriet was struck by the formality of it all. She had worked in many incident rooms and each had its own feel, but this one felt particularly formal and stiff.

Harriet scrutinised the man at the front of the room. James Short could not have been much taller than five foot seven. She only knew him by reputation, which was not particularly complimentary. Who was she kidding? Short had a reputation for being abrupt, rude, chauvinistic and economical with the truth. This morning he was dressed in a shiny blue suit with pointed slip-on leather shoes. His short dark hair had been slicked back with gel and he was sporting long sideburns. He had a sharp pointy face and a large nose. His eyes were small and piercing. And his voice had an extremely nasal tone to it. Oh, that was not going to grate at all, thought Harriet.

"So, before we start, I'd like to introduce you to Detective Sergeant Geoff Harvey and Detective Sergeant Harriet Lacey." As he spoke he gesticulated to them to stand up. They obliged. "So, welcome to Operation Juliet. I trust you are up to speed?" This was clearly a rhetorical question, as Short did not wait for a reply.

There followed a tedious hour and a half during which each of the teams explained where they were with their various tasks. Geoff and Harriet exchanged looks on several occasions. Harriet was barely able to believe how mundane it was. With the updates out of the way, she hoped that there would be an opportunity to ask questions. But that did not prove to be the case.

"So, everyone, good job. I'm satisfied that the course I've set is correct. I will update the chief constable later today; I just need you to apprehend Mrs Wilson so I can bring this room to a close."

"There is no I in team," whispered Geoff, leaning towards Harriet.

"I couldn't have put it better myself," she whispered back.

The room was dismissed. But, not one to miss an opportunity, Harriet made straight for James Short, catching him in the doorway.

"Sir, Geoff Harvey and I really need to speak to you urgently. Could we have a few minutes of your time today? "

"Yes, I'm around all day, pop into my office." And with that, he was gone.

Harriet must have popped her head into the SIO's office ten times that day and each time she found his office empty. With a creeping sense of unease, she considered what her next move should be. On the one hand, she knew she tended to be impatient, it was something she was working on, but on the other hand, she had a strong hunch that things were not right and if there had indeed been an abduction then resources were being misdirected. Instead of looking for Eve Wilson at ports and train stations, perhaps they should be pouring over local CCTV instead. So, determined to find new evidence, she persuaded Geoff to drive her back to the scene.

"What are we looking for?" asked Geoff as they arrived at number 7 Rose Avenue.

"We are going to work through a scenario to try to explain why there has been no trace of Mrs Wilson," said Harriet.

"Care to elaborate at all?"

"Indulge me, just keep an open mind and then tell me what you think."

"Okay, no problem."

"So, my theory is this. Philip and Eve Wilson are in the kitchen eating supper when someone they know lets themselves in. I think that person has a key, goes into the kitchen and to begin with all seems normal and everyone is at ease. By that I mean the individual is a regular visitor so there's nothing out of the ordinary. I noticed a third plate on the table, which may indicate that Mr Wilson was in the process of serving food to the visitor. Anyway, perhaps while he was occupied in serving up the cottage pie, this individual took a knife from the knife block on the worktop and approached him from behind, deftly slitting his throat. Mr Wilson fell to the floor, blood spurting from his neck. Mrs Wilson makes desperate attempts to stem the spurting blood from her husband's carotid artery. In the confusion and panic, Mr Wilson's son Archie wakes up and comes downstairs to see what's going on. The perpetrator panics and grabs a cushion from the sofa and uses this to keep him quiet but uses so much force the child is suffocated. The perpetrator then goes back into the kitchen and grabs Mrs Wilson, whom he drags towards the back door, but she manages to hit him in the face somehow, her elbow perhaps? causing his nose to bleed. He wipes his nose with his gloved hand, before reaching for the kitchen roll to stem the flow. He makes sure Mrs Wilson cannot cause further problems by restraining her. He exits by the back door, with Mrs Wilson in tow and hides the bloody kitchen roll in the dustbin, before putting Mrs Wilson in the boot of her car, or maybe on the back seat. He then drives off. But rather than turning right and driving up to the main road, he turns left, and takes Old Man's Lane."

"Blimey, Harriet, that's quite a theory, but I like it. What evidence do we have to back it up, though?"

"Well, good question. I learned this morning from Steven Leach that the post mortem on Archie showed signs of bruising to the left side of his neck. There are distinct finger marks, probably where he was restrained. The marks are large, too large to be Eve Wilson's fingers, so someone else was there. We also have the blood on the kitchen roll which has come back as identical to Mr Wilson's DNA, but this does not make sense. Or perhaps it does, I'll explain in a minute. We also potentially have the blood results from the dustbin, when they come back from the lab, and I'm hopeful that we might find CCTV evidence of Mrs Wilson's car, you never know. The SIO is convinced Mrs Wilson's Ford Fiesta turned right out of the drive and headed for the centre of town. I want us to consider the possibility it turned left."

"Okay, it's beginning to look promising, but it's not yet compelling."

"I'd agree with you."

"So, who do you think the perpetrator is then?"

"Mr Wilson's brother, David."

"Because?"

"Because he's his twin, identical twin," said Harriet.

"Bloody hell, really?"

"Yep. But also, because I spoke to Mrs Wilson's best friend on the phone earlier today, Amanda Cook, and she told me that Eve Wilson had complained to her recently about David Wilson. Apparently, he was always letting himself into the house, but not just that, she confided that she felt he might be stalking her. She told Amanda that in the last month, she had seen him sitting in his car outside the school where she works at least once a week, that she'd bumped into him at the supermarket several times, that he turned up at Archie's swimming lesson twice when he knew Eve would be on her own but, most creepy of all, last week she saw him standing underneath the streetlight outside their house looking up at their bedroom window."

"Please tell me the best friend has given a statement to this effect?" said Geoff.

"It would appear not."

"Harriet, this investigation is shambolic. It's full of holes and basic enquiries are outstanding. It's not good enough. It seems to me that James Short has made huge assumptions without due diligence." Geoff shook his head.

"I know but, if we say anything to Derek Wynn at the moment, we will look like we are deliberately undermining the SIO and, maybe worse, snitching."

"But what if we don't say anything and it later transpires that Eve Wilson could have been saved, how will we live with ourselves?"

"I know! It's a real dilemma." Harriet frowned as her mobile sounded. "Paul, good to hear from you." She put the call on speaker.

"Thought you should be the first to know that the blood results have come back from the kitchen roll from the dustbin and the blood on the back door. Now, they came back as identical to Philip Wilson but, being the cynical old Welsh git that I am, I asked the laboratory to undertake some other tests when I sent the samples off and this has paid off."

"Oh, Paul, don't leave me on tenterhooks," said Harriet, eyes widening.

"Okay, well, the blood also contained nasal detritus, cells and nasal mucus, which ties in with your theory that the perpetrator had a nosebleed. There is no forensic evidence whatsoever of the victim Philip Wilson suffering a nosebleed. This nasal blood appears on the paper roll in the kitchen, the back door and on the paper in the dustbin."

"That's is fantastic! So, we are now potentially able to tie David Wilson to the scene."

"Sorry? Who is David Wilson?" asked Paul Jones.

"Ah, sorry Paul. I've just learned that the victim had an identical twin called David. I'm working on the theory that he may have been involved in his brother's death. I think he might be the source of the nosebleed."

"Well, if or when you have enough evidence to arrest him, we can then apply to take samples of his blood and his nasal area. If these match the samples we have from the scene it will confirm his presence there."

"This is massive. Thank you, Paul."

Harriet and Geoff drove up to Old Man's Lane, a narrow rural road with one or two big houses situated off long drives and a couple of farms. There was no obvious CCTV. Undaunted, Harriet directed Geoff left at the end of the lane into a road which led back to the edge of the town. After a third of a mile they came across a small industrial estate. There were two buildings adjacent to the road, a dairy and an engineers. No CCTV at the engineers but, as luck would have it, a new system had recently been installed at the dairy following a spell of anti-social behaviour in the area.

It took them a couple of hours of painstaking viewing to find the silver Ford Fiesta. But find it they did. It had driven past the camera at ten past seven, or to be exact 19.10:34, in the direction of the town centre. Driving the Ford Fiesta was a white male wearing what appeared to be latex gloves.

"Bingo," said Geoff.

"Thank God," said Harriet.

"We need to see if we can track the car further."

An hour later, they found footage of the vehicle on Haresfield Road.

"Okay, now we really need to speak to the SIO. A team must be put on tracing the vehicle. Also, we need to try to identify the male driver. If it does turn out to be Mr Wilson's twin, he needs arresting." Harriet pulled out her mobile and dialled. To her surprise James Short answered and reluctantly agreed to meet. When they arrived, he was alone in his office.

"Right, what's this about? I can give you five minutes, no more."

Geoff and Harriet outlined their enquiries. The SIO remained stony faced throughout.

"Look, Mrs Lacey, I realise you consider yourself a hot shot detective after your antics last year, but I see through you and I'm not that impressed."

"Sorry?" said Harriet taking a sharp intake of breath.

"Sir, what the hell are you talking about?" Geoff reddened. "This is not about Harriet, this is not about ego, this is about solving a double murder, and locating Mrs Wilson, who, if we are right, is at risk."

"No, I'm sorry, you turn up at my investigation and try to take over. I didn't request you, far from it. In fact, Mrs Lacey, I can't help wondering if you'd be better employed looking after your teenagers instead of interfering with my enquiry, instead of trying to hijack it. This is my enquiry, and you will do as you are told, do you understand?" James Short jumped to his feet.

"Good God, really? Really?" Harriet's hands were on her hips.

"I suggest you apologise to Detective Sergeant Lacey while you still have the chance because I just recorded that diatribe on my mobile and, believe me, you don't want to face the shit storm waiting for you if you don't." Geoff looked absolutely furious. James Short said nothing for what seemed like an age.

"I may have overstepped the mark."

Before Geoff had a chance to respond, Harriet stepped in.

"Listen, this should not be about personalities. This is about the chief constable posting us to this investigation and asking us to review the evidence. To be frank, the last thing either of us wants is to interfere, but our consciences require us to ask you to look at the evidence we've uncovered and at least consider the possibility that maybe, just maybe, the sequence of events is different to your initial assessment. Hell, stop being a dick, you can tell your bosses that it was all your work, all your idea, if you like." Harriet rose to her feet and walked to the doorway.

"Exactly, it's not about you versus us, it's about finding the truth. Now, read the email with the attached file we've sent you, and call everyone in tomorrow for urgent enquiries to be got under way." Geoff followed Harriet out of the door.

Outside in the car park, the two detectives re-grouped.

"Well done, Geoff. Oh my God, what the hell was that?" asked Harriet.

"That was chauvinism and ego at its worst."

"Do you think he will call everyone together on a Saturday?"

Before Geoff could answer, their phones chimed. Harriet glanced at hers.

"A group email requesting all officers attend the incident room, Saturday morning, nine o'clock sharp. Well done, Geoff."

"Thanks, but I fear we have made ourselves an enemy."

"So be it. As long as Short changes the direction of the investigation, I can live with that."

Chapter 9

William woke early, washed, changed, prayed and then went in search of the Grand Master, but not before issuing instructions to Zafir to take the old woman to the refuge. He found Brother Thierry alone in the library.

"Brother Thierry."

"William, how wonderful to see you again. Thank the Lord you are unharmed." Thierry embraced William heartily.

"Good to see you, my old friend." William thought Thierry looked older than when they'd last met. He figured he must be at least in his late fifties now but the years had not been kind. Short, rotund and with little hair, he was an academic before a soldier of God, but he was also one of the kindest men William had ever met and he was extremely fond of him.

"Pray, tell me how is it that you managed to find your way back from Hattin? Word reached us that all were lost."

"I'm pretty sure I was given safe passage by Saladin, who, incidentally, I met. He sent for me."

"Did he? Well I never. What is he like?"

"He's a surprisingly interesting and charismatic character. Fiercely determined and energetic. Well read, intuitive and humorous."

"Well, who'd have thought." Thierry scratched his head.

"It was a surprise to me also. Listen, we don't have much time. I've come to warn you, but more of that in a moment. Firstly, I need to discuss something Saladin told me. He claims Gerard of Ridefort deliberately sent me on a mission to ensure I was out of the way and did not fight at Hattin, for the reason that he'd become aware of a plot by Templar Knights to murder Robert for his defection. Do you know anything of this?"

William searched Thierry's face, which was serious and downcast.

"Come, sit, will you?" The two men sat down on a wide stone windowsill at the far end of the room.

"William, firstly, can I say how sorry I am for your loss? Robert was your soul mate and I know the last few years have been immensely tough for you. I cannot even begin to imagine how arduous it's been."

William was unable to speak for the kindness of Thierry's words had rendered him emotional. He bent his head as if in prayer and stared at the floor.

Thierry continued. "I was aware of the plot, yes, but not at the time. When Gerard of Ridefort was captured and imprisoned by Saladin, I was informed that I must stand in as Grand Master. Ridefort's confidant here, brother Gerald of Tuscany, proved – how should I term it? – a fertile source of information. He told me in confidence that Ridefort knew if you became aware of the plot against Robert you would fight to the death to protect him and, in short, he was not prepared to lose many valuable Knights in the process. But, more importantly, he was not prepared to lose you. He apparently described you as currently the most influential Templar in the Holy Land."

"I am but a simple soldier of God."

"You are far more than that. You command vast loyalty on both sides of the conflict."

"I don't know what you mean."

"You are a humble man, my friend, but you are immensely popular. Your humanitarian work means you are highly respected. I suspect Ridefort's motive was not to prevent you from fighting to the death to save Robert but rather to prevent you from persuading the Templar Knights from their murderous intent and thus potentially posing a threat to his authority."

"Seriously?"

"Yes. Undoubtedly."

"I do not seek, nor have I ever sought, authority."

"I know that, my friend. But clearly Ridefort is either not aware or perhaps not convinced of this. Anyway, I can only guess that Ridefort's mission for you involved one of the holy relics and its relocation. Please do not confirm or deny. The less I know the better. But I implore you not to follow his instructions which will have been to take the said item to the Templar fort at Acre. Whilst there is no doubt it's a sophisticated military complex with extensive fortified tunnels, mark my words, it will fall to Saladin. Keep the relic with you at all times. Take it somewhere safe away from the Holy Land. Use your judgement to decide on a final destination for it."

"Understood."

"Now, what was it that you wanted to warn me about?"

"My friend, firstly, can I just say how much I appreciate your kindness and your empathy? I struggle daily to come to terms with not just Robert's defection but now also his loss. My faith is being tested and, if I am honest, I feel somewhat adrift, melancholy. My fellow Knights have been wary of me. I have had little contact with them. "

"William, do not be too harsh on yourself. Prayer and time will heal your spiritual wounds."

William bowed to his wise friend. "I am convinced that Saladin has his sights set on Jerusalem. He is buoyed by his recent battle success and means to strike while he has the offensive and King Guy is in custody. He said as much, and I quote, *'It will not be many moons before I take the jewel in the crown.'* With such catastrophic losses of Christian Knights at Hattin, the kingdom of Jerusalem is now enormously exposed. My best guess is that Saladin will sweep north to south along Palestine's coastal fortresses and ports before turning his attention on Jerusalem. I also predict that he will offer these communities the chance to capitulate using minimum force and offer charitable terms of surrender. I believe we may have no more than a couple of months before Jerusalem falls."

"My friend, you have convinced me. I will discreetly set about organising our departure. In the meantime, I'd like you to protect pilgrims on the road from Jaffa to Jerusalem but be ready to leave for the fort at Latrun should the need arise. It may be that I will dispatch the bulk of the Knights we have left to my home city of Tyre. It is a heavily fortified port, so passage should be possible, if required. There is no doubt that Saladin will wish to take Tyre in due course, in which case the Templars may be forced to re-group, perhaps in Cyprus. God be with you, William."

"And you, Grand Master."

William wandered back to his small room, or cell as it was often termed. He pulled a large wooden chest from under his bed. Unlocking it, he removed an iron and leather box about twelve inches square and deep using a key which hung around his neck. He marvelled at its contents and thought about how to keep it safe, how to prevent it from becoming the focus of mighty conflicts, the fate of the Holy Grail and Covenant of the Arc. He closed the lid and locked the box before placing it back in the chest, which he also locked and put back under his bed. The stables were his favourite part of the grand Templar complex and it was here that he found Zafir tending to the horses.

"How did you get on with the old woman?" he asked.

"Good. The old woman's name is Salma."

"Is it? And what does that mean in Arabic?"

"Peaceful." Both men laughed.

"And she is happily established in her new home?"

"Yes, Master, she seems most pleased and so does the puppy."

"Ah, I wondered where he'd got to."

Later, the same day, William visited the Hospitaller infirmary to see Egbert of Powys. To his astonishment he was sitting up in bed and was being fed some sort of porridge by none other than Salma. She smiled as he entered the ward.

"It's good to see you again," said William in Arabic to Salma.

She bowed.

"And you, Egbert, how are you faring?"

"I am receiving excellent care. Thank you for all you did for me. I would not have survived had it not been for your intervention."

"You are most welcome."

Just then Zafir appeared. He handed William a note before whispering something in his ear.

"Please excuse the brevity of my visit. I'm afraid I must leave you now." William bowed to both patient and nurse.

In the dusk, dark figures moved in and out of the buildings, some legitimately, others less so. Wearing a plain hooded cape, William found the door he was looking for and knocked. It was situated about halfway down a narrow alleyway in the west of the city. The door swung open. A young woman appeared and escorted him up several flights of steps which led to a flat roof at the top. Not until they reached the roof was there sufficient light from the lanterns for William to recognise his guide as Lubna, Rabia's maid.

Across part of the roof was a screen. Lubna beckoned William to approach. He saw movement behind. As he turned the corner, there she was, seated on cushions. Rabia jumped to her feet to greet him.

"I got your note," said William.

"I am glad you decided to come. I wasn't sure you would. Please be seated." Rabia handed William a drink, a sweet juice he did not recognise, but it was not unpleasant.

She must have seen his frown. "Pomegranate."

"Ah, my first time. It's refreshing. You have put yourself in great danger seeking me out."

"I wanted to warn you. My brother Sayf is determined to destroy you by any means. I'm afraid he lives by the sword, which incidentally is the Arabic meaning of his name. Unfortunately, he is impatient and petulant and lacks restraint. It is not safe for you to remain in Jerusalem."

"I am grateful. But I do not plan to stay for long. I know Saladin is coming. It's just a matter of time. Is it even safe for you to be here?"

"Oh, I'll be fine. I've been in and out of this city all my life."

"You have?"

"Yes. When I was married the first time I was only a girl of thirteen. I regularly ran home to my mother, begging her to let me remain with her."

"And?"

"And each time I was returned for the honour of my family."

"I'm so very sorry to hear that. I cannot imagine how awful that must have been for you. How did you cope?"

"I lived in a world of make believe, I read voraciously, I tried to block out reality."

"Do you mind my asking how much older your husband was?"

"Forty-seven years."

"I cannot get my head around that. It does not seem right at all," said William.

"It is our culture. We have to accept it. We have no choice."

"But it doesn't make it right."

"No, but what can a mere child do?"

"Oh, I wasn't being critical of you at all." William blushed.

"I know you weren't; I was just playing. I was luckier than some, my first husband wasn't so bad. I was rarely called to his room and more often than not by the time I got there he was asleep."

"This is a world I know nothing of." William shook his head. William watched Rabia closely as she talked about her life. He was mesmerised by her eyes. They were so expressive, he saw a wealth of emotions including joy, sadness and amusement in them. There was a calmness and intelligence to her. She provided respite from the everyday filth and horror of war. In many ways she reminded him of his mother: gentle yet strong, kind yet determined, intelligent and well informed. Neither woman was quick to judge. Seemingly they recognised life's complications and yet amid brutality they found beauty and grace, and this despite their own personal experiences. It troubled him greatly that both women had suffered at the hands of men. Perhaps that is where their inner strength had come from?

"Let's change the subject," said Rabia. "I'm eager to learn how you became a Knight."

A faint smile appeared on William's face. "It all seems such a long time ago. A lifetime even. Let me see. I was sent to a Monastery at a place called St Albans in Hertfordshire, which is in England, when I was seven years old in 1158."

"Young to be separated from your mother."

"It was, but it was necessary to prevent me from coming to harm at the hands of my father."

"Goodness, what did he do?"

"He liked to drink. He drank a lot. Indeed, once he started, he seemed unable to stop. To this day I do not know why he chose to take it out on me, other than perhaps I was a lively gregarious child, always asking questions, and I probably got on his nerves. Anyway, he would lash out at me daily. My mother had no choice but to take me to the sanctuary of the Monastery."

"William, that's awful. Did he hurt you badly?"

"I don't honestly recall, but Brother Benedict told me once that when I first arrived I had two black eyes and bruising to my legs and arms."

Rabia put her hand on William's and for the second time in his life, he experienced a strange sensation, a quiver, that coursed throughout his body.

"I digress. So, I arrived at the Monastery and it was there that I met Robert, which I'm sure he told you all about."

"He did. If I recall correctly, you got a bloody nose at your first meeting."

"I did, yes. I must have looked a sight! So, my lovely mother used to visit as often as she could. She's a beautiful, gentle woman whom I love very much."

"She's still alive?"

"Yes, I write to her regularly. She now lives in Champagne, in Eastern France. Hugh de Payns, one of the founding Templar Knights, was her uncle. It's only relatively recently that I discovered she was a patron of the Monastery at St Albans. I realise now that had it not been for her financial contributions I may not have been able to live there as a novice and Robert definitely would not have been able to. You see, Robert was destitute, abandoned by his father, a stonemason. One day, he just left the Monastery and never returned. Robert rarely talked about it, but I know it affected him deeply. My mother saw to it that he was cared for."

"I never knew that. Poor Robert. It must have hurt very much."

"Yes, indeed." William paused for a moment. "To become a Knight is not easy. Ordinarily, at a young age, around seven, a boy will be sent to be page to his father's Lord and Lady. He will be schooled and trained in the use of arms. Under the guidance of the Lady and her ladies in waiting, he will learn to honour and protect all women. He will also be taught to ride a horse. At the age of about fourteen, if he has completed his early apprenticeship, he is promoted to Squire, or shield bearer to a Knight. He then learns to handle a sword, look after and keep equipment polished and repaired. He also learns to wear and look after armour and generally serve the Knight to whom he is assigned. At the age of about twenty-one, a successful Squire is eligible to take the vows of Knighthood."

"How fascinating. But from what you've said this could not have been the path you both took?"

"You are correct. I guess you could say we were apprentices of life." William was laughing.

"Why do you laugh?"

"Because, now I come to think of it, it's a miracle we actually made it into the Knighthood at all."

Rabia laughed too.

"The Benedictine Monks at St Albans Monastery taught us to read and write," William went on, "and to speak Latin. They also instructed us in the scriptures and, on a more practical level, in return for helping out in the stables we were taught to ride. Everything was set out for us, how we would spend our time between spiritual and physical work. The rules even dictated what we should eat, and wear, when we could speak and to whom. The rules were demanding, but it taught us discipline. When we left to become Knights, we went to my mother's family in Champagne where we received intensive training in how to handle a sword, how to wear chainmail and look after it and a whole host of other Knightly duties."

"From what Robert told me it sounds as if you thoroughly enjoyed yourselves in France."

"We both did. It was hard work but a time of shared goals and focus." William fell silent for a minute or so. "I thank you for your hospitality, but reluctantly I must take my leave. It was good to meet you again. Please take care, and may God be with you."

Rabia bowed and watched as Lubna escorted the Templar from the rooftop.

That meeting was the start of regular correspondence and face-to-face conversations between the two. They shared a curiosity about life and would often pose questions and conundrums for each other to consider. Zafir and Lubna acted as go-betweens. It wasn't long before William and Rabia had become firm friends despite their different backgrounds. But this friendship came with a real risk of discovery. Both, however, found it compelling. It tested their understanding of many aspects of life, not least of which the time they first spoke about love.

"William, are you aware that Robert only had room for two great loves in his life?"

William laughed. "You mean God and you?"

"No." Rabia paused. "I actually meant you and Zafir."

"What?"

"Robert loved you more than anyone else on this earth. You were his world. He looked up to you and tried to emulate you all his life. He was racked with guilt when he changed his allegiance. But he was also 'in love' with Zafir."

William gasped and reached for the wall to steady himself, all colour gone from his face.

"I had no idea. No idea whatsoever." He was silent for a moment or two. "Was this love reciprocated?"

Rabia nodded.

William tried to think back. Had there been signs he had simply missed? Had he subconsciously blocked out what was going on? No. He'd really had no idea. And did it make any difference anyway? On a purely personal level, did this change his feelings towards either of them, did he love them any the less? No. But there was a problem in terms of his faith.

"What about you? How did you feel about this arrangement?"

"I accepted it. I loved Robert. He loved me but like a sister. That's the way it was. Better that I had him in my life than not."

"But, but... what about God?"

"What about God?"

"Relations between men are forbidden. Leviticus 20:13."

"And what does this Leviticus say exactly?"

"In a speech, God gives instructions to Moses for the people of Israel. He tells Moses the penalty for homosexual acts is death to both parties."

"But isn't your God also about the forgiveness of sins?"

"*And all the prophets have written about him, saying that everyone who believes in him will have their sins forgiven through his name.* Acts 10:43."

"There you are, you see, God is all-forgiving," said Rabia.

"I'm not sure it's as simple as that."

"If it's not, it should be. William, no one is perfect, we are all sinners."

William fell silent. Then he said, *"For all have sinned and fall short of the glory of God.* Romans 3:23."

"You see, William, I'm right!"

"I grant you make some compelling arguments. And for now, I

submit." William grinned widely and bowed to the mesmerising woman before him.

Rabia laughed. It was infectious, and William was once more reminded of his sweet mother.

Tiberias on the western shore of the Sea of Galilee was the first Christian stronghold to fall to Saladin. Then, as Thierry the Grand Master had predicted, Acre submitted. In the weeks that followed, Saladin pushed on, sweeping up the Palestine coast conquering Beirut, Sidon, Haifa and many other Christian strongholds in quick succession. While this was going on Saladin's brother raced north and seized Jaffa. By September, Saladin was seemingly unstoppable.

William had been given his orders. By the end of September he was to leave Jerusalem and lead a troop of Knights to the fort at Latrun in the Judean foothills to await further instructions. His loyalty to God went without question, but for the first time in his life he felt conflicted because he would have to leave his friend Rabia behind. This was something he felt he must tell her in person so, a meeting was arranged. It almost ended in tragedy when Zafir was discovered by Rabia's personal guard. However, quick thinking on Lubna's part saved the day, for she managed to persuade them that she had just used him for her own gratification and was in the process of kicking him off the complex. This they accepted with much amusement.

At this meeting William detected a sadness in Rabia's eyes, as if she already suspected that they were to part.

"William, I have found such joy in our discussions. I shall miss them greatly. You are truly a virtuous man who cares deeply for others, no matter their chosen faith. I have grown mightily fond of your company, Templar."

"I too feel great sadness at our parting. You have opened my eyes to the world, lit it up, shown me its wonder. You are thoughtful and compassionate, and I shall miss you considerably. May God be with you and protect you." With that, William took his leave.

Chapter 10

Present day

Next morning there was a buzz to Operation Juliet. The group email received the night before had sparked curiosity and there was a palpable air of expectation. Acting Detective Superintendent James Short did not keep his staff waiting. At nine o'clock exactly, he marched into the office with his usual senior officer team in tow.

"This is going to be very interesting," whispered Geoff.

"You can say that again," said Harriet, also in a whisper. "I bet you a pint he presents the content of our email as entirely his idea."

Geoff chuckled. "I'm going to count how many times he says the word 'I'."

Harriet stifled a giggle.

"Morning, everyone. I've called you together as I have come across new information concerning this case and, after careful thought, I've concluded that I wish to look at some new areas of enquiry in the interests of ensuring all avenues are considered. Firstly, I want DS Brooke's team to liaise with DS Paul Jones and Steven Leach regarding the familial DNA found on kitchen roll and a bin at the scene. I understand this potentially belongs to Philip Wilson's brother, David, who happens to be his twin."

"Identical twin," shouted out Steven Leach.

James Short shot him a look. "Yes indeed."

Suddenly everyone in the room started talking. Harriet looked at her colleagues. This information had clearly come as a shock, judging by their facial expressions.

"Quiet, everyone. I want DS Brooke's team to also look at David. I want a profile built. I want to know where he lives, works, who his friends are, his hobbies, what car he drives. I want to know about his love life, if he has convictions. I want to know what he looks at on his computer. Where he shops, what he eats. Do I make myself clear? Oh, and I want photographs, and family and friends interviewed, including Mrs Wilson's work colleague, Amanda Cook. Apparently, Mrs Wilson thought he might be stalking her."

Harriet thought DS Brooke's team looked somewhat shell-shocked by the size of the task they'd just been given.

"Good. Next, I want your team, Tom, to look at Archie Wilson's death again. I want you to liaise with scenes of crime regarding the bruise marks to his neck. I want to be absolutely sure these occurred during his murder and that Mrs Wilson could not have made them."

Again, the room ignited into life as for the second time that morning staff heard new information.

"Settle down, everyone. Now, I want your team, Adrian, to look at the CCTV that's been found of Mrs Wilson's silver Ford Fiesta. You will need to go to Hudson's Dairy on the industrial estate on the edge of town. There is footage of the vehicle at approximately 1910hrs on the evening of the incident, heading in the direction of the town centre. Seize it and take stills of the driver for identification purposes. There is further footage of the vehicle on a council camera in Haresfield Road. I want you to look for more and to seize any you find. Understood?"

As the SIO was talking Harriet received a text message. She glanced at her phone to see it was from Derek Wynn.

Hi, I've been meaning to speak to you about something for a while. Is there any chance I can have five mins of your time tonight, say about six thirty?

Harriet quickly sent a reply while acting Detective Superintendent Short was engaged in dealing with a barrage of questions.

Yes, that's fine, I'm off to a party with Kate Squires at seven. Why don't you come to the cottage?

Will do, thanks, D.

Harriet wondered what it was Derek wanted to speak to her about, before she was brought back to reality.

"Sir, can you tell us where the impetus for the new lines of enquiry has come from?" asked DS Brookes.

"Quite simply, I spent last night reviewing the enquiry, which included the policy document, forensic reports and witness statements and I decided to widen the enquiry to include these facets."

"I have a question for you, sir. If we are now looking at David Wilson as a possible suspect for the murders then can you clarify the status of Mrs Wilson?" piped up DS Paul Jones from the back of the room.

Harriet hadn't spotted him until now. What a wily old fox he was, he had well and truly put the SIO on the spot and she knew why: he could see through him.

"Well, I didn't actually say David Wilson was a suspect but he is definitely a person of interest. Perhaps more than that, and I would say we don't exactly know what Mrs Wilson's status is. She may be implicated, she may not."

"Well, if she is innocent, then she is a vulnerable missing person and, as such, we should be doing everything we can to find her."

"Well, I'm not sure." The SIO was visibly ruffled. "I need to think about that. That's it for today, folks. Same time tomorrow please."

And that was that.

"That man is unbelievable," spat Geoff.

"He is. And we are definitely persona non grata. But Paul Jones did a brilliant job of exposing his shortcomings. We will, however, need to tackle his reluctance to treat Mrs Wilson as a missing person. Let's see what comes out of tomorrow's briefing. I only hope she is okay. Anyway, more importantly for now, how many times did he use the word I?"

"That would be twenty-four fucking times," said Geoff. "You noticed no doubt that he didn't give us any actions?" Geoff frowned.

"I did, but it doesn't stop us offering to do some background work on David Wilson. I'm sure Peter Brookes would be more than happy to have some help."

"Nothing fazes you, Mrs Lacey."

"Oh, I wouldn't say that. But I am quite determined, and at times thick skinned." Harriet winked at Geoff.

Later, Harriet had just finished getting ready for her evening out when she heard the doorbell. Ben beat her to the front door and was just taking Derek Wynn's coat when she got downstairs. Derek smiled and walked across to kiss her on the cheek.

"You look lovely," he said.

"Thank you. Come into the kitchen. We can talk while I pour us a drink. Lager or wine?"

"Red wine if you have it."

Harriet poured two glasses of red wine and gestured to Derek to sit at the kitchen table. Derek cleared his throat several times. Harriet wondered just what it was he was about to say.

"Harriet, you know how much I admire you, and you know how much I like you. Indeed, I think you'd agree that over the last twelve months there's been a growing friendship between us." Harriet nodded enthusiastically. "But there are some individuals in life with whom one may have a connection, a warmth for, feelings for, who one never quite captivates. The timing is never quite right." Derek took Harriet's hand.

"Derek, are you trying to break up with me? Before we've even gone out properly?" she asked gently.

Derek looked alarmed.

"I was being flippant. Sorry. I'm not sure I understand completely but I think you're trying to tell me there's someone else?"

"This is such a difficult discussion to have as I have feelings for you and a strong desire to protect you. You are a true friend and you will always be that and, whilst I'm sure that if we had got together we would have been happy for a time, there is a side to you that I cannot contend with. You possess a strength of purpose, a determination, maybe even a little craziness, that I struggle with. In short, I think we are destined for different paths. I have found love with someone you know, Rebecca Wood. We have a chemistry, and are completely comfortable with each other, we fit, we are a good team and I know we will be happy. I've asked her to marry me and she's said 'yes'."

"Congratulations, Derek. Really, I'm so happy for you." Harriet leant forward and kissed him on the forehead. It made sense. Derek and Rebecca had previously dated, and remained close. Then towards the end of last year Harriet recalled how concerned Derek had been when he'd learned that she'd been suspended from duty for allegedly failing to register an informant. He had not believed a word of it and energetically set about investigating the matter which resulted in Rebecca being cleared of any wrongdoing. The whole thing had been an elaborate plot to frame her.

"Thank you. And thank you for being so decent about it. I was anxious about telling you. You are amazing."

Harriet smiled. Inside, however, she felt a strange mixture of happiness for Derek and loss for herself. But, if she were completely honest, Derek was absolutely right. Something had held her back from getting involved with him.

Five minutes later, Derek had gone and Kate Squires had arrived. Kate looked stunning, in a sequined sleeveless emerald green top and black trousers. She, like Harriet, was tall and slim, but considerably younger, in her mid-twenties. She had long glossy, straight dark brown hair and large oval green eyes. There was an extra surprise for Harriet, for sitting in the back of Kate's Golf was Mike Taylor. The journey to the party was noisy and full of laughter as the two women caught up with each other's news. Or most of it. It wasn't until they had arrived at the party, hosted by Kate's father, Henry, an orthopaedic surgeon, and had drinks in hand that Harriet told them of Derek's visit.

"Earlier this evening, I discovered that the lovely Derek Wynn is to marry," said Harriet.

"No, no fucking way," said Mike in his usual colourful way.

"I can't believe it. I take it not to you, though. I really thought you two were destined to be together," said Kate.

"No, not me. Derek is engaged to be married to Rebecca Wood." Harriet smiled at the wide-mouthed looks this announcement had produced.

"Yes, really. Before you say anything, I'm really happy for them both. Look, Derek and I will always be friends and I won't deny we were drawn to each other, but the timing was never quite right and if I'm honest something was missing for us both."

"Fair enough," said Mike. "Ooh, I nearly forgot. The week after next is February half-term, I wondered if I could drive Ben and Amelia up to stay with Annie?"

"I'm sure they would be over the moon. But I'd better ask them first. Are you sure you want to share Annie?"

"I'm sure and, yes, they are very excited. Annie thought we'd better ask them first, just in case."

Harriet laughed. "Thanks, Mike, that would be lovely." Harriet was delighted that Mike had found love with one of her best friends. When Harriet had discovered that Ben and Amelia were in danger from Cleo Morris last summer, Annie had stepped in to help without hesitation and the children had spent the summer on her small-holding just outside Sheffield. Ben learned to drive Annie's tractor, and in a matter of weeks grew in confidence, taking over the heavy manual work, and Amelia had thrown herself into animal husbandry with gusto. In short, they had loved the experience and were keen to repeat it at any opportunity.

For the first time since they'd arrived at the party, Harriet took a proper look around. They were in a stunning large open-plan flat. She took her drink and wandered across to a display wall of black and white photos at the far end of the living room. They were breathtaking. Kate joined her.

"I see you are admiring my father's artistic side."

"Oh, Kate, these are beautiful. Is that your mother?" Harriet pointed to a smiling woman possibly in her early thirties with long dark hair and large oval eyes.

"Yes."

"I hope you don't mind my saying, but you are the spitting image of her."

"Thank you, not at all, that's a huge compliment."

"And is that you?"

"Yep, the only time I ever looked cute." They both laughed.

"Harriet, I want you to meet my father, Henry, and a very good friend of the family, Cyrus Hart." Kate turned to her left.

Harriet shook hands with a striking man in his late forties, possibly early fifties, introduced as Kate's father, Henry, and with Cyrus, an elegant man perhaps in his seventies, who was leaning on a walking stick.

After the introductions were over Henry turned to Harriet. "My dear friend here needs your assistance with a quest, if you are willing."

"That sounds intriguing. What does it entail?" Harriet asked.

"How long do you have, my dear?" said Cyrus. "Perhaps I can give you a quick overview and if that whets your appetite you might do me the honour of meeting to discuss it further?"

"That *is* intriguing," said a smiling Harriet.

"I must warn you, Harriet, before he starts, that he is very convincing, some would say persuasive," said Henry.

"Some would say bossy," said Kate laughing.

"I would expect nothing less." Harriet beamed.

"Well, whilst having a clear-out last year, I came across some personal items belonging to my late great-uncle. These included a bible. Whilst examining said bible, I realised it was medieval in origin. On closer inspection, I found a parchment slotted into the leather cover, underneath the spine of the book. This turned out to be a map. There is a symbol I recognise but can't place along with a series of what look like castles dotted across the Mediterranean. Further research has led me to believe that this bible may have belonged to a distant relative called William of Hertford. William lived in the mid- to late 1100s. In early adulthood he left the Benedictine Monastery at St Albans in Hertfordshire for the Holy Land and life as a Templar Knight. I want to understand the map, try to find out what it means. Also within the pages of the bible I found a letter written in a child's hand. It seems to be from a young William to his mother. It talks about his early weeks at St Albans Monastery."

"That's fascinating," said Harriet, "and I'm tempted. I have a deep love of history. My father was professor of Ancient History at Sheffield University for many years and I was lucky enough to study Medieval History at Leeds. Whilst I could do with a diversion in my life, I'm currently engaged in a particularly complex and disturbing case. I really don't think I have the time."

"Ah, but this would give you an outlet. And hand on heart I promise I wouldn't overload you. It would be really helpful to have you on board with your expertise, and your intuition!"

"Tempting, but still no," said Harriet laughing.

"What if I were to strike a deal with you?" said Cyrus. "You help me, and I help you with something? In my younger days I was a successful investigator for a multi-national insurance company. Over many years I became adept at locating not only people, but missing funds and property, but I know very little of medieval history."

"When I told you he is most persuasive, maybe I should have said persistent," said Henry, laughing.

"He is, but..."

"Come on, Mrs Lacey, there must be something you want to find out, something that's been bugging you, something you wake up in the night fretting about?"

"Okay, okay, I succumb! If you can help me to find out what happened to Nick, my estranged husband, I will be more than happy to do what I can to help you."

"Done deal!" said Cyrus, clapping his hands together excitedly. "Let's drink to that."

The Sunday morning briefing proved most frustrating. Every team was required to run through the progress they'd made on the actions given the day before. This was long and tedious and failed to drive the investigation forward. After two hours, Harriet could contain herself no longer and got to her feet.

"Sir, it seems to me that there is sufficient evidence to justify arresting David Wilson. Don't you think it's time to move this investigation forward, to make concerted efforts to try to find Eve Wilson? Every hour that passes her chances of being unharmed become significantly less."

Acting Detective Superintendent James Short said nothing. He simply glanced at his notebook, then turned to the deputy SIO and said something in a hushed tone, before getting to his feet.

"Well, thank you, everyone, that's it for today. Carry on with your actions and we'll resume at the usual time tomorrow morning."

Those present in the room looked at each other in disbelief. Harriet watched as Peter Brookes coloured, and got to his feet – was he about to jump to her defence? – but then he sat back down and it was her friend and colleague Geoff Harvey who interjected.

"Sir, DS Lacey asked you a legitimate question. Please have the decency to answer it."

James Short shot Geoff a look of contempt, before walking out of the room.

Within minutes Geoff and Harriet were surrounded by the other detective sergeants in the room. Peter Brookes was the first to speak.

"This is simply impossible. I don't know about the rest of you, but I cannot continue to work for that chauvinistic buffoon. The whole situation is untenable. The left hand doesn't know what the right hand is doing, and there is potentially a woman's life at stake. I don't think we have any choice but to raise this with Derek Wynn and the chief constable. Also, I would like to personally apologise to you, Harriet, for not standing up for you back there. To be honest, I was gobsmacked. Never in my twenty years have I seen such disgraceful behaviour by such a senior officer."

The rest of the group echoed Peter Brookes' sentiments and it was decided that Peter would telephone Derek immediately. Three hours later, all were summoned to the conference room at Police HQ.

Sitting at the far end of the table were the chief constable and Derek

Wynn. Harriet had been concerned that there might be some awkwardness following her recent frank conversation with Derek. But she needn't have worried.

"Thank you all for coming," said the chief. "I had no idea until this afternoon quite how difficult your working circumstances have been, and I'd personally like to apologise for that. I would also like to thank you all for remaining professional and doing your utmost to solve this violent and heart-breaking case. Now, as you know, Derek here was promoted at the end of last year to Detective Superintendent. As of today, he will be in overall charge of Operation Juliet. I'm making you, Peter, Acting Inspector with day-to-day responsibility for the running of the room. I have done this on the basis that you already have experience of acting in this rank. And, after much discussion, Harriet, you are also being promoted to Acting Inspector. Geoff, you are equally well qualified, but we concluded that you have complications to contend with at the moment which would make such an arrangement testing for you."

The table ignited into a sea of relieved smiles as congratulations rang out.

"I'm glad that you all seem to approve. But now I also need to say to you that I expect the utmost discretion from you all. These decisions were not made lightly. I have put my trust in you. For the record, we were already aware of the situation on Operation Juliet and action was being planned. As of now, Acting Detective Superintendent James Short is on sick leave and will be for the immediate future. In due course you will all be asked to speak to professional standards. Now go and make us all proud and find Eve Wilson. But before you all disappear, Derek needs ten minutes of your time in his office if you would be so kind."

Once ushered into Derek's office, he closed the door and handed out detailed action plans. Harriet and Geoff Harvey were the last to leave. As Harriet made for the door, she turned to look over her right shoulder.

"Sir, are you able to say what happened to bring us to this point?"

Derek beckoned them back into the room. "Geoff, close the door will you?"

"Yesterday afternoon, an experienced officer came to see me with grave concerns about the way the incident room was being run. He brought with him a recording of one of the recent briefings which made for difficult listening. It was clear that an urgent intervention was required. The SIO was asked to come and see me this morning and no doubt you will hear rumours circulating over the next couple of days of a loud argument that ensued. All I can say is that during this altercation I had no choice but to call for assistance, such was the level of irrational behaviour displayed by the individual concerned."

"Oh, my goodness," said Geoff.

"I'm sorry you were put in that position," said Harriet.

"It was certainly challenging."

Harriet and Geoff took their leave and walked back across the car park to their car.

"Congratulations, Harriet. Does that mean I have to call you Ma'am from now on?" Geoff was smiling widely.

"Thank you. And don't you dare! I mean it! Are you sure you are okay with it being me?"

"I'm happy to have been considered, but also much relieved that I wasn't put in the position of having to turn it down. At last Helen is showing signs of improvement. I want, I need, to be there to encourage her, to look after her. In the future, who knows. I'm sincerely delighted for you."

"You are such a kind man. Helen is so lucky. I want to thank you for being there for me too. I'm incredibly grateful that you don't push me to talk about things I'm not ready to talk about. And yet you are always there supporting me, standing up for me."

Geoff placed his hand on Harriet's arm. "Who do you think the officer recording was?" he asked.

"I'd put money on it being Paul Jones from scenes of crime. He has no time for charlatans, no time for individual glory. It's all about the team for him."

"I think you may be right."

The Monday morning briefing bore no resemblance to previous ones. It was noisy, it was animated and there was an excitement in the air. As Harriet sat and listened to Peter Brookes, thick set, his shirt sleeves rolled up, his mop of light brown hair flopping over his eyes, she realised he was an excellent choice to lead the day-to-day business of the room. He was knowledgeable, enthusiastic, empowering and energetic.

"I just want to say to all of you we have a tough job to do here but, if we work together as a team, I'm confident that we will be successful. And never, ever be afraid to ask questions, never hold back. If you have an observation or if you think you have spotted something, say so. It is important. More often than not it's the little details, the snippets of information, that lead to the successful unravelling of complex cases like this. So, please speak up. And, finally, I'd just like to say once more, Harriet, how much I regret not standing up for you yesterday. I'm only glad Geoff stepped in and did the right thing. Thank you, everyone. Happy hunting."

After a couple of days of hard work, the arrest team, the interview team and the search team were ready to move. At 5.30 am on a cold and sleety Thursday in February a team of officers arrived at David Wilson's flat.

Chapter 11

September-December 1187 – The Holy Land

"Master, Master," shouted Zafir as he shook William from his slumber.

"Whatever is it?" asked William sleepily.

"Master, thousands of pilgrims and refugees are flooding into Jerusalem. Saladin is on his way. The city is overrun. Can I offer shelter in Temple Mount?"

"Yes, do it, and find Brother Thierry for me, will you?" said William as he hastily put on some clothes.

Thierry was in the refectory.

"Brother, where is everyone?" asked William, looking around.

"I've sent them to Tyre. It's just the two of us now, we are the only Templar Knights left in Jerusalem. And it's time for you to go to the fort at Latrun."

"I'd like to stay a little longer, if I may."

"So be it, but don't leave it too late, William."

William bowed to the elder Knight and went off in search of Zafir.

For all the hordes of people pouring into Jerusalem, it was clear there were very few men to be found. Indeed, women and children outnumbered them by fifty to one.

Later the same day, William was summoned to see Thierry in the Great Hall. Here he found a group of city officials and a Christian Knight called Balian of Ibelin who William knew by reputation as a brave man.

"My lord Balian, this is the Knight I spoke of, William of Hertford," said Thierry. "He knows Jerusalem like the back of his hand. He can assist in the collection of food from across the city."

"William of Hertford, it is good to meet you at last, although I wish it were not under such circumstances." Balian strode across and shook William firmly by the hand.

"William, Balian has agreed to lead the defence of the city," said Thierry. "You are to help his men collect food in readiness for the siege that is surely coming. All able-bodied men have been armed and I have given permission for the silver from the roof of the Church of the Holy Sepulchre to be removed to swell the war coffers."

Again, William bowed, for he had no words. Whilst he applauded the efforts being made to defend the city, he was realistic enough to recognise that they did not stand a chance. And he was uncomfortable at the order to remove the silver roof from the Church of the Holy Sepulchre. This was one of Jerusalem's most holy sites. The church had been built on the location of Jesus's crucifixion and subsequent burial. Was it morally right that it should be defaced to pay for the defence of a city whose fate was already sealed?

William did as he was instructed. It took several days. Then, on the twentieth of September, word reached him that Saladin had arrived with a vast army and was camped outside the city. William knew that Saladin's first move would be to liberate the Al-Aqsa mosque on Temple Mount simply because of its colossal religious significance. He also recognised that once Saladin saw its dilapidated condition he would be enraged. It could only be a matter of days before the city fell. He must leave, before it was too late.

William was occupied in securing the metal and leather box to his horse when Zafir arrived in the stable block with Salma, the old woman, and the puppy in tow.

"Sire, she insisted. She says she feels safer with you than she would with Saladin."

It had been a long time since William had laughed, but the irony of this was not lost on him and he could not help himself. Even Salma saw the funny side of it. Eventually, William recovered himself.

"Zafir, in all seriousness, you need to tell Salma that the journey is dangerous. There is no guarantee that we will actually make it. And ask her if she can ride a horse, will you? Because where we are going it's the only possible mode of transport."

As Salma answered, it was Zafir who began to laugh.

"What? What did she say?" asked William.

"Sire, she said don't worry about her. She's old, if she dies, she dies, it's only a matter of time anyway. She also said she was brought up in the saddle and has ridden considerably more horses than men in her life but for the record she was extremely good at both!"

"Much too much information, Salma!" laughed William.

Salma threw her head back and cackled, proudly displaying her missing front teeth.

At dusk on the twenty-ninth of September, three riders entered a narrow tunnel on the north-western corner of the old city. At the very same time Saladin's forces breached a wall on the northern battlement. Salma proved herself to be an excellent horsewoman: she was lean, wiry and, despite her age, had good form in the saddle. She was also fast. At times Zafir and William struggled to keep pace with her.

They reached the Templar fortress of Latrun at midday on the thirtieth of September, only to learn that Balian and city of Jerusalem officials had approached Saladin in an attempt to negotiate a diplomatic surrender. The messenger also told them that Saladin had been initially uncompromising, hell bent on spilling Christian blood. But Balian reportedly told him straight that, unless there were decent terms, the Christian defenders of Jerusalem would simply destroy the city, burn themselves and its buildings to the ground. It seemed this was enough for Saladin to change his mind and to agree that all twenty thousand Christians holed up in in the city would be permitted to leave if they paid to do so. The poorest were to be paid for from public funds. In addition, it was agreed that the Templars would give up the fort at Latrun in return for the release of their Grand Master, Gerard of Ridefort. On hearing this, William turned to Zafir.

"We need to leave immediately. Water the horses and grab what supplies you can. I have no wish to come face to face with Ridefort. We will ride for Tyre. I'm sure this is where Saladin is headed next."

"Understood, Sire. What distance are we talking?" asked Zafir.

"I estimate it's just over a hundred miles. Salma is more than capable of riding that distance, so long as she has food, water and the opportunity to rest."

"Yes, Sire, I agree."

On the second of October 1187, whilst watering their horses at an isolated well between the coastal ports of Jaffa and Arsuf, William learned from a fellow Knight also on his way to Tyre that the Muslims had reoccupied Jerusalem. William's thoughts turned to Rabia, as they often did, and to a conversation they'd had a few weeks earlier. Rabia had told him

Saladin's forces including his allies were close to exhaustion. Why? Because non-stop campaigning had drained them both physically and financially and the federation Saladin had formed under the banner of this holy war was strained. Mistrust and scepticism amongst its leaders had resurfaced.

Five days later they reached Tyre. The city bulged at the seams with thousands of Christian refugees. William made immediately for the Templar fortress which offered a degree of peace from the frenzied activity of the main city. Once the horses had been seen to and Zafir and Salma had somewhere warm and dry to sleep, William went in search of Thierry.

William was warmly welcomed not just by Thierry but by a host of Templar Knights gathered in the refectory. It seemed that the horror of Hattin and the subsequent chaos had softened the attitude of many of the battle-hardened Knights. In the hard light of day, it did not seem right to blame William for the defection of Robert of St Albans.

Brother Thierry gave a rousing speech reminding those assembled that they were soldiers of God. He also informed them Europe was mobilising for a third crusade. This was met with much cheering. William, however, remained unmoved. He was a practical man; he knew how expensive such action would be both politically and financially and he also recognised that help was unlikely to reach them for several years. As he stood amongst his enthusiastic colleagues he felt wholly alone. He had not felt like that since being left by his mother at the Monastery almost thirty years before. Over the previous few months his sense of focus had diminished. Even God, his long-time comforter, spoke less to him. He was tired. Tired of war, tired of the struggle, tired of doing the right thing.

During the following month, the Templar Knights worked night and day to improve the city's fortifications. Situated on a peninsula, the city was heavily fortified. A man-made causeway allowed access to the city but by the end of October double battlements had been constructed to protect it.

Saladin arrived on the outskirts of Tyre at the beginning of November, and a six-week siege began. Huge wooden catapults were directed at the fortifications by his forces. Day and night the settlement was shelled with barrage after barrage of large stones. As winter set in, Saladin's army endured thick mud and icy cold tents. Hunger to conquer Tyre began to wane.

William busied himself with his duties, which included fighting as well as his work with the poor, sick and needy. Salma proved a most helpful addition to his humanitarian work. It turned out that, although she looked quite fierce, she was extremely good with children. Sometimes, William caught her looking at him, almost as if she were studying him. On such occasions he would bow to her and she in turn would bow back, before each went back to the task in hand.

One evening in late December, William was in the chapel at prayer with his fellow Templars when he caught a movement out of the corner of his eye. Zafir was in the doorway urgently but silently gesticulating to him. William discreetly excused himself.

"Master, I am so, so sorry to disturb you, but Salma did not return this evening. It is most unlike her."

"Yes, indeed. Where was she last seen?" asked William.

"As far as I can ascertain, near to the quayside on the east side of the port. She was attempting to coax a young boy from his hiding place to offer him bread."

"Then we will go down to the dockside to start our search. See if you can get some of the other grooms and manservants to join us and bring lanterns."

"Yes, Sire."

William went ahead. Before long Zafir arrived with a large group of men including some of William's fellow Templars, and the search began. Half an hour passed before a shout went up from behind a boat in dry dock. William and Zafir ran across. There on the floor lay Salma's dog. The grey and white puppy was lifeless, covered in blood.

"No, no." William picked up the tiny stiff innocent body. Things did not look good for Salma. The search continued late into the night before they agreed to resume at daybreak.

At dawn, William was awoken by Zafir, who was excitedly waving a note in his hand.

"Master, Master!"

"What is it, Zafir?"

"I know who has Salma!" he exclaimed.

"You do?"

"Yes, but it's not good. She's alive, but she has been roughed up."

"Tell me, who has her?"

"Sayf, Saladin's nephew."

"How do you know this, Zafir?"

Zafir pointed to a parchment in his hand. "Lubna smuggled it to me. It's from Rabia. It appears Rabia has intervened and for the time being Salma is with her, but she says her influence is not as great as it was with her brother and she fears for Salma's life. She pleads, however, that you do not try to mount a rescue, as this is what Sayf is counting on. He plans to kill you and take your head to Saladin."

"Does he indeed?" William was trying to think of an appropriate resolution. "Does the note say where Salma and Rabia are?"

"It says they are camped where the river runs purple," said Zafir.

William ran his hand through his beard. What did that mean? Where the river runs purple? What was Rabia trying to tell him?

And then it came to him.

"They are camped downstream from the textile quarter. The purple pigment used to colour the cloth is washed off in the river, and consequently the water is coloured. So, they are away from the main camp."

"Is it even possible to reach them there?" asked Zafir.

"It will be difficult, but it's possible, if we can create a diversion. Zafir, who can pass unchallenged in any camp?"

Zafir remained silent for a moment or two until his face lit up. "Travelling musicians, minstrels, bards and poets, Sire."

"Exactly! Sayf expects me to charge in like a fool. Salma was a means to get my attention. He knew that Rabia would intervene. I think Rabia is actually the inducement. He knows about our friendship, I'm sure of it. So, we will have to outsmart him. We will send in a troop of minstrels and poets as a diversion."

"Sire, are you actually suggesting that we mingle amongst them?"

"Whilst I don't have a bad voice, no. They provide a distraction."

"They will have to be good, Sire, and we do not have the funds to pay for such a plan," said Zafir firmly.

"We don't, but I know a man who might help us. Meet me in the stables in an hour."

Unbeknown to Zafir, William went straight to Thierry and managed to persuade him to finance the rescue attempt on the basis that Salma had proved most hard-working and helpful to his charitable work and did not deserve to be used as a pawn. He also persuaded him to send a message to Saladin via diplomatic channels alerting him to the threat posed by Sayf to his sister, Saladin's niece.

And so it was, that a colourful troupe of musicians and poets entered the Muslim camp on a dark wintry night in late December. At the same time a couple of figures clothed in dark peasant garb slunk to the North Quay, careful not to draw attention to themselves. Here a small boat was waiting, captained by a merchant who traded with both Muslims and Christians, but sided with the Christians. The little rowing boat slipped out of the harbour unnoticed and made its way to the textile quarter situated on the eastern edge of the Muslim camp. William and Zafir disembarked and quietly scrambled towards the tree line. They could hear the musicians in the distance and as they reached the outskirts of the camp it was clear the entertainment was proving quite a draw, for there was loud cheering, clapping and laughter. Luckily, the captain of the boat had recently delivered supplies to Rabia's tent and was able to give them a pretty decent idea of its location. They would know it, he said, by the golden flag topping the tent; it was the largest of the structures; they would see six smaller ones encircling it.

The light was poor, but eventually they found it. William knew that Sayf would be guarding it, waiting for him to make a move. But he also rightly guessed the guards were stationed at the entrance to the tent and, due to the freezing conditions, they would be huddling around a central fire to keep warm.

William took a small hunting knife from his tunic and set about cutting a way through the back of the tent. He was careful to cut along a seam, which would be less obvious. Cautiously, they sneaked inside. The light was poor, but it was just possible to see cushions and blankets arranged around a central fire. On the cushions there appeared to be two figures. A quick scan of the tent suggested that for the moment, there was no one else present.

"Rabia, is that you?" whispered William in English.

Two figures immediately sat bolt upright.

"Yes, William, I'm with Salma."

"Oh, thank God. Is it safe for me to come across to you both?" asked William.

"Yes, but you will need to be quick. The guards are due back shortly."

William approached, but before he had a chance to sit down, Salma jumped on him, arms around his neck, legs clamped around his waist as she proceeded to shower him with kisses.

"You came for me. Thank you, Templar," she whispered in broken English.

"You speak English!" William kissed her back. "Of course, we came for you. You are family now." And William hugged her tighter. "We need to be quick. Can you walk?"

Salma nodded.

"Wrap yourself in this blanket and go to the back of the tent. Zafir is waiting for you there."

Salma did as instructed. William approached Rabia. He took hold of her hands.

"Why don't you come with us?" he asked.

"I'm more use here. I can create a diversion, give you a chance to get safely away."

"But Sayf will be furious. I'm not happy you will be safe. Please, Rabia, please come with us."

"As much as I want to, William, I cannot. Look after Salma, she is a good woman, a real character. Our paths will cross again. I know it." Just then, a guard announced his intention to enter the tent.

"Go, William, please!" entreated Rabia. William pulled her close; he could feel her heart beating against his chest, her sweet breath on his face. At the last moment he tore himself away, but there was a pain in his heart.

As they scrabbled away, there was no immediate alarm raised. William guessed Rabia had made it look as if Salma was asleep under the covers. William and Zafir took it in turns to carry Salma on their backs. Progress was slow, the ground was uneven and slippery with mud, and it was pitch black. Eventually, they were able to make out the glow of a lamp on the boat. As they reached halfway across the harbour, it began to snow, large flakes like goose down floating silently through the still night air. By the time they reached the harbour the ground was covered. Their raid would now be all but invisible. God had been kind to them.

Chapter 12

Present day

Operation Juliet was a hive of activity despite the early hour, each member of staff busily employed. To the untrained eye it might have looked like chaos. But it was far from that. There was an air of anticipation. And when word came that David Wilson had been arrested, a cheer went up. Harriet was in charge of the Section 18 search at his address. Specifically, her team were looking for evidence relating to the murders of Philip and Archie Wilson, but also anything to connect David to the disappearance of Eve Wilson.

Later the same morning, a briefing took place during which the interview team reported back. David Wilson had presented as supremely confident, totally denying any involvement in the terrible events. Interestingly, he'd displayed distress at the deaths of his brother and nephew and concern for Eve's disappearance. But lead interviewing officer Geoff Harvey was not convinced by his performance.

"I will grant you he is a good actor, but there is something insincere, even sinister about him. As an aside, he does not have a corroborated alibi for the time of the incident. I have a gut feeling he is our man. It's early days, but it will be interesting to hear his explanation when I tell him his blood has been found at the scene."

Peter Brookes turned to Harriet. "How did your team get on at the address?"

"There is nothing obvious to link him to the murders or the

disappearance of Eve. The flat is spotless. It actually has an almost sterile feel to it. But I did find photos and correspondence relating to an address in Ragman's Lane. Rock Farm. Judging by the photos it's been in a derelict state for years. It seems as if it originally belonged to David and Philip's grandparents and was a working farm in the 1940s. I'd urgently like to take a look at it. To that end I've sent a Section 8 PACE warrant application across to the magistrates' court."

"I definitely approve of that course of action. Once you have the warrant, make sure scenes of crime as well as specialist search officers are with you. We have twelve hours left on the clock, but I'm happy to apply for an extension. Just keep me updated."

Harriet nodded.

"And bloody good work everyone," said Peter Brookes.

By the time the teams reached the farm, the light had begun to fade, not ideal conditions in which to conduct a search. But with the help of some large floodlights it went ahead. First, they tackled the house but this was hampered by its neglected state, crumbling damp walls, rotten floorboards and stairs. They found nothing in the house, nothing in the first of the corrugated iron clad barns. Spirits were beginning to flag, when one of the officers stumbled across a pair of car registration plates. Not immediately recognising their significance he ran them through the Police National Computer. The result that came back, however, elicited an excited shout, loud enough to send Harriet scurrying across the yard.

"Boss, I think I've found the index plates for Eve Wilson's silver Ford Fiesta."

"Really? Where?"

"At the bottom of that pile of wood over there at the rear of the barn."

"That's fantastic work. Okay, I think we know we are in the right place now. Gather round, everyone, I want you to concentrate on locating the car itself. We also need to tackle the other barns. I suggest you split into two teams. I'll update Inspector Brookes."

Harriet accompanied officers to the final barn to be searched. It was quite some way from the house. It was an old stone building located on the corner of a concrete yard and had once been a milking parlour, judging by the abandoned equipment contained within. At the far end, they found a solid wooden door. Curiously, it was secured with a shiny heavy duty padlock. The search team used bolt cutters to remove it and slid back the lock. The door creaked open. It was pitch black inside. It smelt musty. In the torchlight, it was just possible to make out a huddled figure at the back of the room. As the officers approached, they could see it was a woman. She was sitting on the floor with her back against the wall, her torso secured with a series of chains, her mouth taped. Harriet could see the whites of the woman's eyes in her torchlight. She knelt beside her.

"It's okay, it's okay, we're police officers. We've come to get you out of here. Don't be frightened." Harriet gently clasped the woman's ice-cold hands in hers. "It's okay, Eve, you're safe now."

The woman shook her head.

"You don't feel safe?"

The woman nodded, and then it dawned on Harriet. "But you're not Eve Wilson?"

Again, the woman nodded her head.

It had gone midnight and staff were waiting for Harriet to return from the hospital.

At about ten past midnight, she arrived to take her seat in the incident room. "So sorry everyone, it took longer than anticipated."

Inspector Brookes was the first to speak. "So, it would seem that there is far more to this case than any of us first thought. I think I speak for all of us when I say I was absolutely flabbergasted to learn that the woman you found was not Eve Wilson."

There was much nodding of heads in the room.

"I know, I know. To be honest, it did come as a huge shock," said Harriet. "So, here's what we know so far. The woman we found is called Eleanor Bridgeman. She is thirty years of age, and was reported missing from Slough by her boyfriend approximately a month ago. In summary, her car broke down on the edge of town and a male fitting the description of David Wilson, who called himself Danny, pulled up alongside and offered her a lift into town. It was raining, it was cold and dark, and he seemed 'nice', so she assented. She now accepts that this was a completely foolish and out of character thing to do. Anyway, it seems Danny made an excuse to call by Rock Farm, where he overpowered her, dragged her to the barn and raped her."

"Poor Eleanor," said Peter Brookes.

"Indeed," said Harriet. "She has been through a horrendous ordeal, but she is strong and wants to talk. She's been admitted for observation and tests as she's showing early signs of pneumonia. I think we should see how she is later on this morning and try to obtain a statement then. SOCO has taken full forensics, including nail scrapings, and I have a record of Eleanor's first account."

"This is brilliant work, well done everyone." Peter Brookes looked exhausted. "I've already sent some of the teams home to sleep. Those of you remaining are needed to prepare interview packs and arrest details for the additional offences. I've got a Superintendent's extension for an additional twelve hours, as David Wilson is now in his rest period. If we meet back here for a briefing at nine, we will have about eight hours left on the clock before we have to apply to the court for an extension. Thank you again for all your sterling work. We must keep going, as there is still much to do, not least of which is finding Eve Wilson."

Shattered, Harriet finally climbed into bed at 3am. It seemed only minutes before her alarm was filling the room with chaotic noise. She found herself unceremoniously jerked out of slumber. She reached for her phone to turn the alarm off. She felt groggy, achy, her head was sore, her mouth dry. But as she lay there feeling sorry for herself, she reflected on Eleanor Bridgeman and Eve Wilson. With renewed resolve, she threw off the covers and forced herself into the shower. Half an hour later, she was showered, dressed and eating a slice of toast as Dave Flint opened the car door for her. She mused that she could get used to being driven around – but then perhaps not. The circumstances which had led to this being a daily occurrence were not something she cared to repeat. She did not want to think about Cleo Morris and forced herself instead to consider how her lovely Ben and Amelia were enjoying their half-term holiday with Annie and Mike on the outskirts of Sheffield.

The briefing that morning was short and business-like. Harriet returned to Flint Farm to resume the search of the site. In the morning light, it looked even more ramshackle and overgrown than it had the day before. The early morning mist was hanging around, making the location look almost supernatural. Underfoot, the remains of a heavy dew, a distinct aroma of leaf mould in the air. As Harriet approached the barn in which Eleanor Bridgeman had been found, she saw a figure at the far perimeter fence. She squinted, but it was too far to get more than an outline. Surely not, she thought. No, it couldn't be. Cleo wouldn't be that reckless, would she? Harriet shook her head, before forcing herself to look again, but the figure had gone. She shivered and hurried around the corner to the search teams who were waiting for her.

It was about midday when a shout went up. One of the teams had found a silver Ford Fiesta at the bottom of a deep pond. It was missing its index plates, so the working assumption was that this was Eve Wilson's car. The fire service were dispatched to assist with raising the vehicle. It was only when it was recovered from the water that the grim discovery of a female's body was made.

Harriet immediately rang Peter Brookes. "Pete, this job is growing. We've just found a female's body in the boot of what we think is Eve Wilson's Ford Fiesta, which was submerged in one of the ponds at the farm."

"Fuck. I did not see that coming. Is it Eve?"

"We don't know at this stage. Steven Leach from scenes of crime is here. He's made a cursory examination of the body and says it's not possible to tell without further tests. The victim's hands and feet are tied and there is a maceration of the exposed skin."

"Sorry, maceration?"

"Yes, it's when the exposed skin has started to break down as a result of its exposure to the water. There is some detachment of skin which Leach says tends to suggest that the body has been there for about two weeks. So, it would fit with the disappearance of Eve. It may be wishful thinking on my part, but I'm not convinced it is Eve. She's been variously described as a slight woman, petite, tiny, with small hands. The woman in the boot is taller, perhaps five foot six."

"Okay, thanks, Harriet. I'd better inform Derek Wynn and the chief. See you for the six o'clock briefing."

Later that afternoon, Harriet got a call.

"Boss, I'm DC Cutter. I'm in the process of taking a statement from Elly Bridgeman. I thought you should know that she has described hearing a male and a female arguing on several occasions whilst held captive in the barn. She described the quarrel as coming up through the floor from below her."

"Thank you, that's really helpful. If she says anything else that you think might help, please don't hesitate to call."

"Will do, Boss."

Harriet went to look for the sergeant in charge of the search teams. In less than ten minutes, they were back in the barn where Eleanor Bridgeman had been discovered. At first there did not seem to be anything out of the ordinary but, just as Harriet was about to return to the incident room, one of the officers found a trap door in the floor. It had been masked by old sacks and a discarded metal pig feeder. Like the barn door, a shiny padlock secured it. This was cut off, and the door creaked open. It was pitch black. Torchlight revealed a series of rickety wooden steps which led to another locked and secure door. Harriet carefully followed the search officers down the stairs and into a cold shadowy cellar. It appeared to be empty. Professional as always, the team began a detailed search of the space. As they reached the far end, they came across a wall. On closer inspection it appeared to be made of wood. Perhaps it wasn't a wall after all, but a partition? Further scrutiny revealed a door hidden behind an old wardrobe pushed up against the panel. This door too was secured by a padlock. The lock was removed, and the door opened. What lay behind the partition was a tiny space, perhaps two metres square, and in it they found an unconscious female.

Chapter 13

1188-1190 – The Holy Land

The following morning, New Year's Day to be exact, William went in search of Salma. A bitter winter wind forced him to pull his cape around him for warmth. The icy blast stung his cheeks. He found Zafir and Salma in one of the inner fortress courtyards burying the grey and white puppy. William joined them, kneeling next to Salma, who turned abruptly to see who the intruder was. Her eyes were wet with tears. William used the edge of his cloak to wipe them away. He was startled by the bruising to the old woman's face.

"Oh, Salma, what did they do to you?" he exclaimed in poor Arabic.

"I'm fine, William," she replied in English.

"You are not. Who did this to you?"

"That pig Sayf." She spat on the snowy ground.

"I'm so sorry."

"Don't be, I was saved from worse by Rabia. She is a brave and noble lady. Sayf is a bully and a cad who loathes you. You would do well to be wary of him."

"I know, and I'm deeply sorry that he hurt you to try to get at me."

"Ha, I'm made of tough stuff, Templar."

"You are indeed. It's good to have you back."

"It's good to be back. Now tell me, William, what are you hiding in your clothing?"

William smiled as he carefully opened his shirt. There nestling in the warmth of his chest was a tiny black puppy. Gently he handed it to the old woman, whose face immediately lit up.

She bowed to him in thanks, before stuffing it inside her dress.

"What will you call this little fellow?" William asked.

"Dog," came the reply.

"But the last one was called Dog," said Zafir, laughing.

"And this one is called Dog too," said a beaming Salma.

Salma's face turned suddenly serious.

"Templar, Rabia speaks highly of you. She talked at length about your compassion towards your fellow man as well as your ..." Salma turned to Zafir to request a translation "...humility." As she spoke Salma studied William's face closely. "Why look so sad? You have given so much of yourself, you are the most honest, how you say? principled, beautiful soul I have ever had the fortune to meet. Not bad for a Christian, eh?" A smile briefly passed across her face before tears once more formed in the old lady's eyes; William stooped down and took her hand which he kissed gently. For a moment they fixed gazes and there was nowhere to hide for either of them.

"Salma, your English has improved beyond measure. I thank you for your generous words." William led her back to the infirmary, back to tend to the sick and injured.

Later the same day Saladin launched an offensive on the causeway of the city of Tyre, a brutal assault and one in which William found himself immersed. The weather conditions had not improved, indeed alongside the bitter wind there was now driving sleet.

The following day again William was involved in defending the boardwalk when he noticed a figure hurling himself towards him, nostrils flaring, waving his fist, pure loathing on his contorted face. William immediately recognised the man. As the soldier approached, he shouted, "Today, Templar, you will die a horrible death. I will take you apart, limb by limb."

"Ah, Sayf, God willing, today is not my day to die."

Sayf lunged at William who caught the blade of his sword as it approached his head. Metal on metal, the two men were locked together, blow after blow. But William's experience soon showed and he pushed Sayf back until he lost his footing and fell into a quagmire of blood and mud and had to be rescued by his men who dragged him away, kicking and screaming.

"You pig, you bastard, you dog, you will die, you will die!"

"He doesn't seem to like you much," laughed a fellow Templar as he passed by.

"Do you think?" William replied with a smile but, in that moment, he wondered why Sayf had such a fierce loathing for him.

Wiping the sweat from his brow, he took a deep breath and threw himself once more into battle. The fighting was every bit as chaotic, noisy, bloody and brutal as the battles he'd fought with Robert at his side.

Eventually, William and his fellow Knights succeeded in pushing Saladin's troops back along the causeway until they had no choice but to turn and retreat. Word subsequently reached them that Saladin and many of his elite troops had left Tyre to spend the remainder of the winter months in Acre.

In the spring of 1188, a small band of Christian Knights brought news that Saladin was on the march again, this time through Syria and Palestine, seeking out exposed or weak Christian fortresses and settlements to subjugate.

William remained in Tyre helping those in need and working with Brother Thierry and his fellow Knights to secure the city. But the news that Saladin was actively targeting Christian settlements was hard to bear. When Jerusalem fell, the Templar headquarters had been moved to a tent on Mount Toron in the Lebanese mountains. William was keen to head there and offer his services to help to rebuild the Order. He couldn't help thinking how Robert would have approved of the Order's change in fortune, a return to its impoverished and humble roots. He was beginning to comprehend what had motivated Robert to leave the Templars. He now understood his longing for a simpler, more honest, way of life. For Robert this had been manifested in conversion to Islam. William too longed for a modest more straightforward existence.

That summer, Christian spies reported that Saladin had released King Guy from his imprisonment. But it appeared that rather than sticking to his promises to renounce his claim to the throne and leave the Holy Land, he began to rally forces and personally reach out to Templar and Hospitaller Knights to stand behind him, to help him take back Acre.

Nothing much changed until in the heat of midsummer 1189 King Guy arrived in Tyre. William and Thierry were amongst the Templar Knights present when he made an impassioned call to arms for his cause. Amongst Guy's courtiers was Gerard of Ridefort, who rumour had it had also been released by Saladin but not without Saladin exacting a hefty price from King Guy.

"Thierry," whispered William in some distress. "Ridefort is here. I'd heard he'd been released but cannot believe the king has brought him back into the fold."

"I would advise discretion, William; he is not a man to cross. Keep your head down. Now is not the time to settle old scores. He is deliberately giving you a wide berth. I think he may be nervous of you, and rightly so. Privately he has made it clear he wants the relic he entrusted to you returned to him."

"I'm sure he does, but it is safer with me than it would ever be in his hands."

King Guy of Lusignan spoke eloquently and powerfully to promote his assault on Acre. He promised support from Europe, which he said was on its way. He spoke as if victory was a mere formality. By the end of the day many of those who had gathered had pledged to join him, swelling his troop numbers significantly.

"We have been waiting for help from Europe for two years and still it hasn't arrived," mumbled William bleakly under his breath.

"It will, it will, my friend, have faith," replied Thierry.

After the rally, the king took refreshments in the Templar refectory. William chose to excuse himself, but Thierry was in attendance. Later that evening Thierry sought William out in the stables, where he found him playing draughts with Zafir and Salma.

"Sorry to interrupt, Brother William, but may I have a word?" asked Thierry.

William jumped to his feet. "Of course."

As the two men sauntered down the stable block, Zafir and Salma followed at a discreet distance, but close enough to be able to listen to the conversation taking place.

"My friend, I know you well. I know you to be an honourable man of God. But we find ourselves in uncertain and shadowy times and I worry for your safety. There are complex political games afoot, involving self-important individuals engaged in power plays and personal squabbles. It's a far cry from the godly behaviour we expect. And I need to tell you that both Grand Master Ridefort and the king have personally requested that you ride with them to Acre."

William looked at the ground. "Do I have a choice?"

"You do not. I do not. But we will keep our wits about us, and we will strive to maintain those principles we hold dear."

"When do we leave?"

"Tomorrow, my friend."

"Then I should tell Zafir and Salma. They should at least have the choice as to whether they accompany me or not," said William grimly.

"Can you refuse?" asked Salma.

William jumped, for he had not been aware of their proximity.

"Apparently not. I'm a Knight Templar, and must do as the king directs," said William through gritted teeth.

"Then we go where you go," said Salma firmly, arms folded across her body. Zafir nodded vigorously in agreement.

On the twenty-ninth of August 1189 William recorded the Christian army's arrival at Acre in his diary. Its numbers had been swollen by the arrival of several boatloads of Italian troops and fifty ships containing thousands of Danish and Dutch soldiers. Then, in late September, Italian nobleman Conrad of Montferrat reached Acre with a thousand Knights and twenty thousand infantry. William was well aware of the disdain with which Conrad held King Guy. The political manoeuvrings and squabbling grew daily amongst the Christians. He was conscious that there were now sufficient forces capable of blockading Acre from the sea as well as managing a partial hold by land. It was only a matter of time before King Guy made a move. He wondered how Saladin would respond. Whatever happened, he was sure they were on the verge of a prolonged and bloody siege.

On the fourth of October 1189, William watched from the Templar headquarters on Mount Toron as the Christian force consisting of thousands of soldiers was given the order to advance at walking pace across the plain of Acre towards Saladin's camp. The Templars had been divided into two groups, one led by Gerard of Ridefort, the other by Marshall Geoffrey Morin from Tyre. The king had ordered William to keep the Templar headquarters out of enemy hands. He was therefore required to watch from his vantage point as the action unfurled. As the battle progressed, he noticed Gerard of Ridefort charge with his troop into Saladin's base camp, closely followed by Geoffrey Morin. But instead of pressing on, they became side-tracked by the booty they found in the camp. This recklessness allowed some of Saladin's troops to re-group and attack. Flabbergasted, William could do nothing to prevent the outcome. Ridefort and his Templars were cut off from the rest of the Christian army and overrun, their precious flag lost. Later that day news reached him that Ridefort had been executed on the battlefield and Geoffrey of Morin had also been slain.

From where he stood William watched as panic ran through the rest of the Christian army, soldiers lost their nerve and fled, horses neighed and bolted. It was only William's quick thinking, along with the king's brother,

Geoffrey of Lusignan, that prevented the capture of Mount Toron. Although a fierce battle ensued, they held on and were able to defend it from Muslim hands.

In the aftermath of the battle, many seriously injured soldiers staggered back to camp, some so disfigured by their injuries they were unrecognisable. Zafir and Salma worked tirelessly through the night with William and Thierry and many other volunteers to save as many as they could. It was horrifying work even for battle-hardened soldiers. William felt ashamed at the way some of his fellow Knights had behaved. The Templar name for him was now tarnished.

In the early hours of the morning William went to grab a few hours' sleep, only to be woken less than an hour later by Zafir.

"Master, Master, wake up please. Your help is needed."

"Whatever is the matter, Zafir?"

"Master, Saladin's men have gathered up our dead from the battlefield and thrown them into the river that runs through the camp. The stench is already overwhelming. We need to bury the dead away from the river now."

"I'm on my way. You go ahead," said William.

The odour was so appalling that William was forced to cover his face. Every so often he retched violently. In his life as a soldier he had seen many horrors, but the sight of the bloated, bloodied bodies of fellow soldiers was heart-breaking. As he worked with the others to bury his comrades as deep and as quickly as possible, he was reminded of the dying words of Gregory of Brecon some years before: *'Can this truly be God's will?'* And in that moment William had to wonder.

A few days, later, William was with Thierry when a messenger arrived. They learned that, although they had come out worse from the battle, with greater losses, Saladin had also lost troops, many of whom had fled during the fighting and had not returned.

"I tell you this, I watched as Saladin moved what was left of his exhausted, battle-weary troops back, away from the filthy and soiled battlefield. My contacts tell me he awaits a promised influx of fresh troops," said the messenger.

December 1189 brought particularly wet and miserable conditions for both sides which resulted in a lull in the fighting, as they endured lashing rain and mud-filled trenches. There was only one thing to do: hunker down and wait for the weather to improve. With more time on his hands, William's thoughts increasingly turned to Rabia, so much so that one morning he could bear it no longer and sent for Zafir.

"Zafir, I am reluctant to ask this, but is there any way that I might be able to enter Acre undetected?"

Zafir grinned widely, showing off his beautiful white teeth.

"What?" said William. "She is my friend."

"Master, you know full well what. And, yes, it's possible but it will involve some skulduggery and a little money."

"But I don't have any money. And it can be nothing illegal, do you understand?"

"Yes, Master. Although you don't have money, I do. But firstly, I will need to contact Lubna to see if her mistress wishes to see you." Zafir winked at William.

"Ha, ha, very funny, young man."

A couple of days later Zafir approached William on his way back from morning prayers. "Master, can I have a word?"

"Yes, of course,"

"It's a yes, and a no."

William frowned.

"It means, she wants to see you, but she forbids it on the grounds that it is too dangerous."

"Oh, does she?" William was unable to hide a smile. "So, my friend what is the plan?"

William had to hand it to Zafir, he was an excellent coordinator. Although slightly out of his comfort zone, a few days later William found himself hidden in the back of a cart containing a contingent of young, beautiful and noisy prostitutes. They had arrived in one of the last European ships to make it to into Acre harbour. Three hundred to be exact, eager to offer themselves to the besieged soldiers. And, although forbidden fruit for Muslims, there were apparently many who made enthusiastic use of their services.

As the cart trundled its way over the cobbled streets, William could hear the hustle and bustle of everyday life all around. Merchants selling their wares, customers, friends greeting each other, disagreements. The crushing stench of overcrowding hung in the air. Eventually, the cart came to a standstill, and the ladies disembarked. No one noticed William slip out and join the throng. He quickly identified a small shop front, a bakery. He entered and immediately went down the steps into the cellar. At the rear of the cellar was a wooden door, just as Zafir had described. William opened it, entered and closed it behind him. He carefully lit the lantern that had been left for him and made his way cautiously along the tunnel, bending as he went, for the roof was low. After three quarters of a mile, the tunnel split. He took the left fork and after five hundred yards he came to another door. He knocked three times. The door opened and Lubna was waiting. She smiled and beckoned him to follow her up a steep flight of stairs.

At the top of the stairs was a small door, which led into a tiny upstairs room. Inside was Rabia seated by a roaring fire. She jumped to her feet to greet William with a hug. For a brief moment they were forehead to forehead, but all too soon Rabia broke contact.

"William, it's so good to see you, but this is foolhardy, too dangerous!"

"You are a good friend, but you have also become my counsel. I just had to see you."

"Well, then, please sit down and tell me what it is that's on your mind that's worth this danger."

"Firstly, I want to hear from you. How are you doing?" William scanned her face.

"I'm just fine, William. Sayf has kept his distance since Tyre and our uncle's intervention. He has not been near me for weeks. Now, I want to hear from you."

"Rabia, I'm lost. It's as if I'm on a path, a path that I know well, a familiar route. I have walked it for many years, but it continually leads to the same outcome, year in and year out, and I'm tired. I'm tired of the death, destruction and horror, of the greed. I cannot believe that this is God's will."

"I see, and have you lost faith in your God?"

"No, not in God, but the men manipulating God's word for their own ends."

"William, are you proud to be a Templar Knight?"

"If you had asked me that a couple of years ago, I would have given you an emphatic 'yes' but today I hesitate. I am proud of my service to the Templar Order. I hold dear its founding principles: simple living, modesty, humility, discipline, protection of the weak and sick, the promotion of justice and fairness, and humanitarian values. But too many Templars have become ruined by self-indulgence and materialism."

"And is it not right that you should push back against this and fight for what is right, and what you believe?"

"Perhaps, but I suspect that I am one of very few left now who think like this. And, whilst I do not shy from battle, this would be a monumental fight with little chance of success. So, do I lead by example, and to some extent put up and shut up? Or do I protest?"

"What does your heart tell you? Not your head, but your heart?"

William was silent for a minute or so. "My heart tells me that I should continue at least for the time being to try to effect change from within."

"Then, my dear Templar, you have your answer."

"It seems that I do. Thank you, Rabia."

"You are most welcome. Perhaps, William, you should look to Homer's *Odyssey* and take comfort from the fact that it took the great Odysseus ten years to make it home after the Trojan war. Perhaps what you are currently experiencing is your very own Trojan war. And there will come a time when it will be right and proper for you to make your own journey home."

William's face lit up and he took Rabia's hands in his. "I'm deeply indebted to you."

There was a knock at the door. It was Lubna.

"Sorry, Mistress, but William needs to leave now, if he's to make the boat. William, you will need to hurry. Take the right tunnel at the bottom of the stairs, follow it until it forks again, take the right fork until you reach a small door. This leads to the outside to a rocky outcrop where Zafir will be waiting to row you back. Take this lantern. Good luck, Templar."

Chapter 14

Present day

The paramedics had just lifted the unconscious female into an ambulance when Harriet's mobile lit up.

"Boss, it's DC Cutter again. Thought you should know that Elly Bridgeman claims that during her imprisonment she heard what she thinks was digging. It seemed to be coming from the rear of the barn. She describes hearing intermittent clanking noises. Her best guess, that it was metal on stone. It apparently went on for some time. I thought you should know."

"Thanks, that's much appreciated." Would this job never end? Seriously, could there be more bodies to come? Harriet went to find SOCO and the search teams.

Despite the fatigue felt by everyone, there was a strong sense of purpose and once Steven Leach had taken a cursory look at the ground behind the barn, the teams began to dig in two areas which showed signs of disturbance. The ground was claggy and stony, not ideal.

Harriet was by the old farmhouse deep in a phone conversation with Peter Brookes when Steven Leach came running towards her waving his thin arms in the air. She cut short her call.

"Boss, Boss, another body," he gasped, clearly out of breath.

"I'm on my way."

Harriet ran back with Leach.

At the bottom of a shallow trench skeletal remains were clearly visible wearing what looked at first glance like a pair of black trousers and the remnants of a purple jumper. To one side of the skeleton, a dilapidated black handbag.

As Harriet and Steven Leach were peering into the trench, DS Paul Jones rolled up.

"Paul, am I happy to see you," said Harriet.

"Steven called, said I might be needed." He pulled on his green wellington boots.

"Believe me, you are. I think we may have a serial killer on our hands."

"I think you could be right," said Paul, peering into the hole.

"Boss, they've found another one," shouted Steven Leach.

Harriet and Paul exchanged looks before walking across. Sure enough, there was another grave, but the occupant had not been lying there long.

The search continued for several days, but no further burials were found. The body count for the site stood at three.

Operation Juliet was frenetic, as everyone worked flat out to process the farm, to bag and tag evidence, to trace the deceased, liaise with other forces and deal with the multitude of forensic samples. Derek Wynn and the chief constable, Mark Jones, were forced to dig deep to cover the spiralling overtime budget as well as identify and post additional staff, such was the unprecedented workload.

It was a couple of days after the discovery of the unconscious female that Harriet received a request to go to the hospital. Although still groggy, Eve Wilson had asked to see her.

Harriet hesitated slightly at the door to Eve's room, why she wasn't sure. She knocked and waited for a moment before entering. On the opposite side of the room her eyes rested on a hospital bed containing a petite woman, aged perhaps thirty-five, with ash blonde hair. She had her eyes closed. Harriet approached. First one deep brown eye opened, then the other. The woman in the bed smiled weakly.

"Harriet Lacey?" she asked.

"I am, Eve." Harriet watched as the woman pulled herself into a sitting position. Harriet helped with her pillows.

"Dear Harriet, I have been lying here trying to find the right words, but nothing I can say is adequate to describe my gratitude to you. Without your intelligence and tenacity, there's no doubt I would not be here now." Eve's eyes filled with tears.

Harriet handed her a tissue from the packet she was holding and reached for her hand.

"Eve, I'm just so pleased we got to you in time. It was a team effort. I cannot begin to comprehend what you've been through; you have endured a terrible ordeal. I know you've given a first account and you are yet to give a statement, but do you feel up to answering just a few questions for me?" Harriet noticed just the hint of a frown cross the patient's brow, but nevertheless Eve nodded.

"Okay, thank you. I know this is so difficult for you, we can stop at any point. Firstly, can I just ask you if you know how David's blood got onto the kitchen roll we found?"

"Yes. I was trying to help Phil. Blood was gushing from his neck, but David grabbed me and dragged me towards the back door. I knew I was no match for him, but I refused to give up without making it as difficult for him as possible, and I managed to elbow him in the nose. At first, he didn't realise he was bleeding and when he did he reached for the kitchen roll. He was swearing at me for delaying him. He taped up my mouth and bound my hands and feet with gaffer tape, but I saw him trying to bury the kitchen roll in an outside bin."

"Thank you, I guessed something like that had occurred, but I wasn't sure," said Harriet. "Were you kept in that tiny little room for the entire time?"

Eve seemed to hesitate before answering. Harriet wondered why it had been such a difficult question.

"Er, yes. To begin with it wasn't too bad. There was a light and a heater but, as time went on and I refused to bend to his will, he took them away. The only control I felt I had left was to refuse to eat. This drove him mad. He's mentally ill, you know, no doubt about it. He has a strong sense of injustice, is completely selfish. He can't see other people's points of view. He is cruel and calculating. He makes my skin crawl."

"That's a helpful insight, thank you," said Harriet.

"You know, in some ways I do feel I was fortunate. David was rough, but he did not really assault me physically or sexually, like the other poor girl. He just kept repeating that he was in love with me, wanted to build a future with me." Eve shivered. "Years ago, when I was a teenager I went out with David for a couple of weeks, before deciding that I liked Philip better. Philip and I split after about a year, only to find each other again years later, but I don't think David ever forgave me or his brother." Eve started to weep. Harriet squeezed her hand.

"Poor Phil, poor little Archie. Oh God, how am I going to live without them?" Eve was sobbing now, and Harriet wrapped her in her arms.

"Eve, there is nothing I can say to ease your pain. But I promise you that we will do everything in our power to make sure we find the truth and that, if David Wilson is guilty, he will be punished. Given time, you will rebuild your life. You have a beautiful little daughter to cherish and care for."

Eve smiled weakly at her. She looked exhausted, so Harriet excused herself, promising to return in the next day or so. As Harriet left the hospital, she had the overwhelming feeling that something didn't quite add up. She just couldn't put her finger on it. Was Eve telling the truth? Something did not feel right. She pulled out her mobile and rang Geoff Harvey.

"Geoff, it's Harriet. Would you be in a position to do me a favour?"

"Of course, how can I help?"

"I've been thinking about the mobile phone that was found with Eve. I can't help thinking that it was a really strange thing to find. If she had a phone, she could have called for help and she obviously didn't, so what was the phone for? When initially asked about it, I'm told she was evasive. Later, she said she knew nothing about it, that David must have dropped it. So, could you possibly ask Paul Jones in SOCO to give it to Kate Squires when SOCO have finished with it? And could you ask Kate to see what it tells us?"

"Yes, of course."

"It may be nothing but, as I said, I've got this hunch that all is not quite as it seems. Thanks, Geoff."

It had been an exhausting and harrowing few weeks. As Dave Flint drove her back to work from the hospital, Harriet didn't feel ready to return to the incident room. She needed some headspace, so she asked him to make a detour. Some time later she found herself standing outside the West End of St Albans Cathedral looking up at its enormous front entrance. Her thoughts turned to Cyrus's quest and more specifically to William of Hertford.

Harriet pushed open one of the heavy carved wooden doors at the front of the cathedral and entered its enormous nave. She immediately recognised the rounded Norman arches to her left, with traces of medieval artwork on their plastered walls, and wondered at the vast wooden ceiling overhead. It was an immense space. Taking a sharp intake of breath, she took a seat at the back, and opened her laptop to research her surroundings. At that moment, she was the only person in that part of the Abbey. There was not a sound and, although she wasn't particularly religious, she sensed something – an aura, an atmosphere? Harriet sought to put herself in the mindset of a small boy arriving there for the first time. How had William felt about it? Was he frightened, excited, a mixture of both? What had the monks been like? Kind or austere? Perhaps a mixture of both? She wandered slowly up to the crossing. As she meandered through the space, she felt her interest in William grow. On reaching the shrine of St Alban, she paused for a moment before walking on again. But it was when she stumbled across a copy of a painting of the medieval Monastery by Joan Freeman that her imagination was fully captured. It was an illustration of how the Monastery may have looked prior to 1539 and she wondered if William would have recognised it: the great gateway, the long stables which had apparently housed up to two hundred horses, the cloisters, refectory, kitchens, storerooms, dormitories and even a dovecote and vineyard.

"It's impressive, don't you think?" said a smartly dressed woman standing next to her.

"It most certainly is. But not so easy to picture how it fits with what's left standing today," said Harriet.

"Yes, indeed. Did you know that the Norman church was rebuilt using Roman bricks and flints from the ruined Roman city of Verulamium?

"No, I didn't. Fascinating."

"Yes. I wonder, do you have a minute to spare?" asked the woman.

Harriet turned to face her. She was perhaps in her mid-fifties, wearing a smart bottle-green skirt and jacket. Still beautiful, with ebony hair coiffured into a classy soft bun. She had large oval green eyes, not dissimilar to Harriet's own. She looked vaguely familiar.

"Look, the last thing I want to do is to alarm you. But I really do need to speak to you, Harriet."

"How do you know my name?" Harriet took a step back. Dave was waiting for her in the car. Should she text the pre-agreed distress word? She hesitated.

"It's a long story. And I need to be quick. We don't have much time before your protection officer starts to worry and comes in search of you. Also, my surveillance team are going to work out that I'm not attending a doctor's appointment in Loughton. Look, can we sit over there?" The woman pointed to a row of seats to her left. As they sat down next to each other, the woman turned to look at Harriet.

"I've not made myself very popular with your colleagues. Indeed, I suspect they have variously described me as difficult, rude, obstructive and other less polite terms. As a mother yourself, you will no doubt agree that we have an inbuilt impulse to protect our children even if they have done wrong. But my daughter has crossed the line many times and, for a variety of complicated reasons, I wanted to warn you that Cleo is intent on killing you."

Harriet jumped to her feet, mouth wide open. How had she got into a position where she was talking to Cleo Morris's mother, Veronica? Veronica got to her feet too and placed her hand firmly on Harriet's arm.

"Please sit down. I know you have no grounds to trust me. But please let me have my say."

Harriet sat back down but this time on the edge of her chair.

"There is something that you need to know about Cleo. It is fundamental to the way she operates. Every move she makes is calculated, painstakingly thought through, premeditated, designed. When she is forced to improvise, she makes mistakes, and becomes vulnerable. The key to staying safe is to be unpredictable. She cannot cope with impulsiveness. She's currently in a bad way, out of control, drinking heavily and at times quite mad."

"Just explain to me why I should believe you?" hissed Harriet. "How do I know you are not trying to manipulate me, fool me and, more importantly, why would you want to warn me?"

"That's fair. I anticipated this so I'm going to tell you something that I have never divulged to another living soul. I used to have two best friends. One was Ella Squires, the other Ann Rayfield, your grandmother. By rights, we should not have been friends. All our lives it had been drummed into us that we should not associate. Ella and Ann had been told I was to be avoided, that I was unworthy of their attention. I had been told they were not to be trusted that, like it or not, I was an outsider. So, you see our friendship flew in the face of everything we'd been told and, as such, had to be kept secret."

"Hang on a fucking minute. Are you seriously expecting me to believe that my grandmother and Kate Squires' mother Ella were your friends? When I've been told that you were likely responsible for Ella's death."

"I suppose in a way I was, but not in the way you might think." Veronica looked down at the floor and when she looked back at Harriet there were tears in her eyes. "I didn't see Ella's death coming. I was so engrossed in the work we were doing."

"Which was what?" interrupted Harriet, her eyebrows raised.

"We were working together to build orphanages across India and the Middle East. We aimed to provide shelter, food and education for the many displaced children of those regions. It took much of our time and, in retrospect, I may not have given Cleo as much attention as she deserved, let alone craved, so she decided to make me sit up and listen and to break up my friendship group permanently. You see, one morning Ann and I found Ella stabbed to death in my kitchen."

"Really? Really? And how do you know it was Cleo? She can only have been ten or eleven."

"She was thirteen, and she left a message in Ella's blood. It said, *'Maybe now you'll notice me Mum'*."

Harriet shuddered for a second time and searched Veronica's face. Either she was an extremely good actress, or her distress was genuine.

"What happened?" Harriet softened her tone.

"It was a Saturday morning; the boys were at football. Ann and I were upstairs assembling packs of essentials to send out to one of the orphanages and Ella was downstairs in the kitchen organising their distribution.

"After about an hour we went to the kitchen in search of the coffee Ella had promised and that's when we found her on the floor, in a pool of blood."

Harriet watched as Veronica struggled to remain in control. She could not or would not look Harriet in the eye. Her shoulders were stooped, she was biting her lip and struggling to regulate her breathing.

"We rushed across to her, but there was no pulse. When we turned her over, we saw to our horror that she'd been stabbed multiple times. We never did find the knife. It would appear that she was approached from the rear and whacked over the head. She had a visible injury to the back of her head. Once on the floor she was stabbed repeatedly. Being upstairs, we did not hear a thing."

"What did you do?"

"The only thing I could think of in that mixed-up crazy moment of horror. Ann and I cleared up the blood in the kitchen and then placed Ella's body in a green and gold tablecloth – every detail is engraved in my mind – before lifting her into the boot of my car and driving to a derelict building in a deserted industrial estate on the edge of town. I was totally panicked. I could not think straight, I could not conceive turning in my daughter. I didn't know what to do, what to think. I remember having to stop the car to throw up. Ann was my rock. She remained calm but that's not to say she wasn't upset, she was, extremely. Afterwards I never spoke of it to Cleo, and nor did she once mention it to me. Then, I did the only thing I could think of. On the Monday morning, I arranged for her to go away to boarding school. I couldn't bear to be near her. I was distraught. To make matters worse, I couldn't share my loss with anyone, because five days later your grandmother died of a stroke."

"Are you seriously trying to tell me that you covered this up and no one, not even your husbands, knew of it, of your friendship? Let alone the tragic circumstances of Ella's death?"

"No one knew. If our friendship had been discovered, there would have been recriminations. I had no appetite or energy to deal with that."

Just then, Harriet caught sight of Dave approaching. She put her hand on Veronica's knee and mouthed that she had to go.

"Sorry, Dave, I got rather engrossed."

"No problem. Thought I'd better check on you. Who was that woman you were talking to?"

"I'm not entirely sure, we got chatting about loss." Harriet briefly turned back to see Veronica kneeling, head bowed.

"Oh, okay," said Dave as they walked back down the nave together.

On the car journey back, Harriet decided not to mention her encounter with Veronica to anyone, not until she could properly process it. Not until she could check out some of the details. She would need to decide if she were telling the truth. There were also Henry and Kate Squires to consider. After all, Veronica had revealed the person responsible for Ella Squires' murder. She also decided it served no purpose to cause trouble for Veronica with her surveillance team at this time. Indeed, she had put herself out to speak to Harriet and, if she were to be believed, she'd potentially provided her with vital information on how to deal with Cleo.

Peter Brookes had decided to rest some of the teams for the weekend. Ben and Amelia were off to London to see a show with Harriet's mother, Jane, so when Harriet learned she would not be required, she decided to drive to West Wales, to Aberporth, for some sea air and thinking time. Cyrus had been in touch. His sleuthing had uncovered more letters written by William to his mother, Arianne. He was in the process of having them typed up. So, on the spur of the moment, Harriet invited him to join her at to her uncle's cottage. She was eager to see the transcripts. William of Hertford was beginning to prove an intriguing and interesting diversion.

Having spent the morning preparing the cottage for Cyrus's visit, Harriet decided to take a late afternoon walk on the beach. The weather looked threatening, but she needed some sea air and some space to think. Deep in thought, Harriet stood motionless on the grey wet sand. Transfixed by the black sky, she didn't notice the wind pick up. It began to swirl around her with such force it threatened to upturn her. Seagulls raced back and forth fighting to escape the current of angry air. The wet ebony cliffs towered menacingly on either side of the inlet; the rain lashed down. With lightning speed, the tide turned, and charged into the cove like a mighty army intent on destroying everything in its path.

Harriet turned and started to run back up the beach, suddenly aware of the peril she was in, but the mountainous waves were bearing down on her. The strength of the wind made progress difficult. Harriet struggled on. And just as she seemed to make headway, she tripped and fell. A giant wave crashed over her. She struggled to the surface and gasped for air. As the wave retreated, it dragged her with it with such force that she was powerless. It was in that moment that she realised she would drown unless she could get herself to the rocks to her left. She looked over her shoulder to see the boiling sea once more advancing. With every ounce of energy she could muster, she threw herself onto the wet rocks. On hands and knees she clawed her way up the slippery rock towards the old slate cart track. She lunged forward in one last desperate attempt to pull herself onto the track but fell short. Exhausted and defeated, she waited for the inevitable, but then a hand grabbed her arm. With one immense tug, Harriet was hauled from the path of the waves and dumped face-first on the slate track.

"Are you hurt?" asked her rescuer.

"No, thanks to you. I'm fine, honestly. Just give me a minute to catch my breath."

Harriet rolled onto her back and then up onto her knees, and finally to her feet. Her saviour had his back to her. He was watching someone at the very top of the beach running towards them. Harriet also saw the figure, who stopped dead in their tracks, before turning back.

"Cyrus, I can't thank you enough. When I invited you down, I didn't dream it would be to save my life." Harriet greeted him with a kiss.

"That was close, too close. Are you really okay?" Cyrus hugged Harriet.

"I'm fine. Maybe a bit bruised, but I don't mind telling you I really scared myself back there."

"You scared me too. And Cleo." Cyrus pointed to the departing figure on the beach.

"Really? Oh God, no."

"It's okay, you are safe. She won't dare come near you now she knows I'm here. We go way back, Cleo and I."

"You do? Let's go back and get warm and dry and then we can talk."

Chapter 15

1190-1191 – The Holy Land

The siege of Acre continued and conditions in the trenches steadily worsened, a stinking mixture of liquid mud, human effluence, rotting food, rats, feral dogs, decomposing bodies and body parts. Fighting when it occurred was half hearted, but still the stalemate went on and it was not long before there was a certain familiarity amongst the soldiers on both sides, who began to greet each other, share stories, and occasionally sing together. Often the Christians could hear the Muslims' call to prayer, the Muslims the Christian bells summoning them to church. And both sides could see each other's campfires.

In the spring of 1190 the weather improved and fifty Christian ships made it to Acre from Tyre. A council of war was called during which William and Thierry argued that Saladin could not afford to allow the Christians to re-open trade with the Mediterranean coastline, which meant only one thing: he would attack. Despite initial reluctance, senior leaders of the Christian force made ready and were able to defeat Saladin's ships, with the result that they once more controlled the sea around Acre, though still not the inner harbour. For the next six months the inhabitants of Acre were close to starvation, as supplies could not get through. They were forced to eat all their surviving animals. Fighting continued with varying degrees of success for both sides but, in October, word reached the Templars that Saladin had moved his army back to overwinter at Saffaram, a camp about ten miles from Acre.

Conditions for the Christians did not improve; indeed, they became much, much worse. William spent a good deal of his time tending to the needy with Zafir and Salma at his side. It was back-breaking work and draining. William's days were spent moving from patient to patient. He would gently lift a soldier's head to allow him to take a few sips of water, before moving on to the next bed to remove a filthy dressing. As always, Salma was beside him ready to hand him a bowl of ointment, or bandages. Sometimes William's patients were small children, often wide-eyed and rigid with fear. Salma's job was to speak to them, to softly reassure them that the tall Templar Knight was not to be feared, quite the opposite, for he had been sent by Allah himself to help them. More often than not they were convinced and did not flinch as William cleaned their infected wounds. William was all too aware that he could not carry out this gruelling humanitarian work without the help of faithful Zafir and Salma. Not once did they complain about the atrocious conditions, not once did they whine about being hungry and exhausted. No, they just got on with the job to tend to the sick and the dying.

When food supplies ran out and the Templars began to eat their precious horses, William once more was active in trying to find a solution. Cases of scurvy and trench mouth were common, and the mortality rates were on a scale not seen for countless years. With the help of Hubert Walter, Bishop of Salisbury, he managed to re-organise and mobilise the crusader camp to ensure that any existing food was fairly distributed to everyone, not just the rich. Things slowly began to improve when a grain ship got through with its precious cargo.

It was a June day in 1191 when William was interrupted in the infirmary by an excited Zafir who ran in to find him.

"Sire, sire, pray come and see."

"See what, my friend?"

"King Richard I of England is arriving."

William followed Zafir and was just in time to see the king's fleet, numbering nearly two hundred vessels, moor up in the outer harbour. As they stood and watched, rumours ran through the crowd that the king had brought with him a huge personal army, considerable gold and his most reliable military advisors.

No sooner had Richard arrived than he set about making sure it was his trusted advisors who led the Templars and Hospitallers. Robert de Sable, one of King Richard's vassals, was appointed Templar Grand Master.

Richard set up camp, and then began a brutal bombardment of Acre day and night. It was not long before William was summoned to an assembly in the king's tent.

As William entered the vast and expensive marquee, incongruous amidst the filth of the rest of the camp, he saw it was filled with Knights, perhaps more than three hundred. In the middle was a platform containing an ornate throne, on which the king was seated. William stood at the back. From this vantage point he could see the king clearly. He was dressed in the finest chainmail, wearing a bejewelled crown of gold. His tabard of the finest silk contained a golden lion at its centre. William estimated the king must be in his mid-thirties. He was slim and athletic looking. His red hair was just visible beneath his crown. As for his eye colour, that would have to wait until he was closer. It was not difficult to separate the newly arrived Knights from the rest. William and his battle-weary colleagues looked a sorry sight.

Most were painfully thin, with sallow complexions, open sores and sunken eyes, their armour mud encrusted and battered.

The king got to his feet to rapturous cheering. "My loyal subjects, Europe has rallied, and the third crusade has commenced!" There was more cheering from the king's newly arrived Knights. "We stand here in solidarity with our brothers who have fought bravely in terrible conditions to defend the Christian faith." Yet more cheers from the shiny new Knights. "We will be victorious, and we will have retribution for the horrors of the Battle of Hattin. We will re-take Acre, we will re-take Jerusalem and we will drive the infidels back, far away from the Holy Land." Further enthusiastic applause for the king.

Try as he might, William was not energised by the king's words. Indeed, he was wearier than he had ever been. And, if he were completely honest, he was no longer sure what he was still doing in the Holy Land. As a young man it had all seemed so straightforward, so clear. Now, perhaps with the experience of age, he recognised that life, indeed faith, was never uncomplicated, for man had a nasty habit of manipulating it for his own ends.

Following the king's speech, his royal highness wandered amidst the throng with his officials. As he passed within a few feet of William, he happened to turn to his new Grand Master, Robert de Sable, and, so as not to be overheard, asked in Old French where William of Hertford was among the crowd. Robert pointed to William. The king turned and stared at the man before him who stood head and shoulders above the rest.

"You're seriously telling me that ragged-looking excuse for a Knight is the great William of Hertford I've heard so much about?" asked the king in disbelief. But before Robert had a chance to reply, a voice boomed out, also in Old French.

"Perhaps, Sire, it might be wiser to judge a man not by his appearance but by his deeds."

"How dare you speak to the king in that tone," shouted Robert de Sable.

The tent fell silent.

The king put his hand on Robert's arm and moved closer to William. "You speak the old tongue well, my friend. How and where did you learn it?"

William bowed to his king before replying. "Sire, my mother is Arianne of Troyes, her uncle was Hugh de Payns. It was she who taught me to speak this dialect as a young boy."

"You have true Templar lineage, my friend. Your mother did an admirable job of instructing you. I have a dear sister, Marie, who lives near Troyes, so I know it well. I sincerely apologise for my insensitivity; I can see that you have been through the mire. You were right to pull me up. A man's deeds are far more significant than his appearance."

The king put his hand up and there was silence. "Men, look at this Knight, study him carefully for he represents the very best of us all. He has fought loyally, steadfastly, bravely for the last twenty years. Sadly, there are now a mere handful of such Knights still alive. We salute you, William of Hertford. It is an honour to join you in this fight."

"William of Hertford. For God and King," came the shout.

William bowed once more. But inside he felt empty and cold, unable to summon any battle fervour.

The next afternoon, William caught up with Thierry in the refectory.

"My friend, it's good to see you," said Thierry.

"And you. Pray, what can you tell me of the king's battle strategy? Reliable information is hard to come by."

"Put simply, we are to dig in and bombard the city, endlessly it seems. The king is ruthlessly determined that Acre will fall."

A few weeks later, Thierry sought William out in the infirmary. "My friend, I bring further news. Is there somewhere we can talk?"

William beckoned Thierry to a dark corner. They spoke in whispered tones.

"I have it on good authority that the townspeople of Acre have capitulated and sued for peace. I'm told Saladin was against this but did eventually agree to terms. The city gates are once again open, and our Christian flags raised above the roofs."

"Already? And what of the king?"

"King Richard is moving into the Citadel as we speak and King Philip of France to the Templar house by the docks, but I don't think he will stay long. Rumour has it that he's fallen out with Richard."

"Why is that? Do you know? asked William.

"I understand they do not get on. Philip views Richard as over-ambitious."

A week or so later, William was summoned once more before the king. The monarch was in a jovial mood and welcomed him warmly.

"William, it's good to see you again. I'm just going to come straight to the point. I need to ensure that I have the very best advisors and the very best soldiers around me. King Philip has left the Holy Land so I'm re-organising and I'd like you to be the Royal Standard Bearer."

William was so completely taken aback that initially he did not respond.

"Well, what do you say?" asked the king, anticipation written all over his face, a glint in his steely grey eyes.

"Sire, it would be an honour. I am truly humbled by your offer."

"Good, good! Now go and see my armourer, will you? For you desperately need to look the part."

When William returned to the new Templar lodgings, Zafir emitted an enormous wolf whistle and got a playful flick of the ear for his trouble. Salma was equally vocal with a series of loud high-pitched squeals.

"Well, thank you both," said William, giving them a long low bow.

"Salma, our master is now too grand for us," teased Zafir.

"Indeed, very handsome he is too!" Salma laughed.

William rummaged under his cloak and removed two packages, handing one to each of them. As they investigated, their faces lit up.

"Clothes free of lice at last!" said a beaming Salma. She made her customary bow to William.

"Master, things are looking up," said Zafir.

"Perhaps," was William's guarded reply.

One afternoon several weeks later, Zafir took William on one side.

"Sire, my contacts tell me that once we have finished re-fortifying and repairing Acre, the king is keen to move on, to Jaffa. But apparently he is frustrated by the fact that Saladin appears in no rush to satisfy the terms of the surrender, which include considerable monetary compensation for the Muslim prisoners and the return of the 'one true cross' taken from the

Christians at the Battle of Hattin."

"Interesting, very interesting. Let's hope that the king doesn't do anything rash, for he does not strike me as a patient man," said William.

In August, Richard called a council meeting to which William was not invited as he did not have sufficient rank. His friend, Thierry, however, was present and immediately it was over sought out William, whom he found at prayer in the Temple House by the docks.

"William, my friend, I apologise for interrupting you at prayer, but I simply must speak with you."

William got to his feet and greeted his old friend warmly. "Thierry, you look troubled. What ails you?"

"My dear friend, I have just come from the king's council at which he announced his intention to behead all two thousand seven hundred Muslim prisoners taken at Acre."

"Wait, stop a minute, what are you talking about? Terms were agreed. Saladin is to compensate the king for these prisoners."

"Yes, but he has dragged his feet for too long and the king has run out of patience. He will not be moved."

"But such action would be a cold-blooded massacre, whichever way one looks at it. The king must be made to reconsider."

"Believe me, many of us tried. He will not budge. He says he must capitalise on the victory of Acre. The longer he waits for the surrender terms to be fulfilled, the less impetus and influence he has. He is an impatient man."

"He is a dangerous man. Quite apart from the fact that such an act would be morally indefensible before God, this action will be a death sentence for every Christian prisoner from now on."

"You do not have to persuade me, William. I totally agree. But I cannot see what can be done to prevent this."

William stroked his beard as he strode up and down the chapel. "Can you get me a meeting with Templar Grand Master Robert de Sable?" he asked.

"William, I might be able to, but Sable does not care for you. He believes that you are too influential amongst the Templars, and therefore a potential source of trouble to him."

"Wasn't that also Gerard of Ridefort's view of me?"

"Yes."

"But do you think he will dare to show his distrust or dislike of me if we fill the meeting room with like-minded Knights?"

"I'm not sure, that might work, but it is still a huge risk, William. You could find yourself detained for disobedience, or worse some trumped-up charge. You are in danger of playing right into his hands."

"That may be so, but I cannot in good conscience stand by. I have to try, Thierry."

"May God be with us, my friend."

For the remainder of that day and the next, William and Thierry busied themselves. Thierry managed to secure a meeting in the Great Hall with the Templar Grand Master, neglecting to tell him that it would be attended by a host of fellow Templar Knights. William rallied his colleagues, presenting them with his arguments against the planned action by the king and, to his surprise but also delight, every Knight he approached pledged their support to him.

Robert de Sable could not disguise his surprise on entering the Great Hall to find it filled to capacity. He walked to the front and took his ceremonial seat before turning to Thierry.

"So, Thierry of Tyre, what is so important that we must meet with such haste?"

"My lord, it is I who has need to speak with you," said William, stepping forward.

"I see," said a frosty-looking Sable. "I can't for one moment think why you would wish to speak to me in such a public manner."

"My Lord, I wish to raise the matter of the recent council meeting convened by King Richard in which a decision was made to behead the Muslim prisoners from Acre."

"William of Hertford, this is not for you to be concerned about. The king has made his decision and the Templars will carry out their duty as ordained by the king and that's an end to it."

"Grand Master, I have no wish to challenge the king over this. However, I cannot in good conscience remain silent."

Robert de Sable jumped to his feet. "Enough! I will hear no more of this nonsense." He walked towards the door but found his way blocked.

"Grand Master, I am James of Warwick. May I suggest that you hear William out?" And with that the entire assembly of Knights stamped on the floor as one.

The Grand Master immediately re-took his seat. William noted the colour had drained from his cheeks as he reached for his pocket handkerchief to mop his brow.

William bowed to James in thanks. "Grand Master, the Templars are devoted to God and loyal to their king. But I am not aware of a single Templar Knight who would be prepared to murder prisoners in cold blood. I cannot see how the king can truly believe this action is justified. I cannot fathom what he cites as its legitimacy. This proposed action flies in the face of everything we believe. We are monks, men of God. We believe in the sanctity of life. We fight for God, for Christianity. In my mind there must always be scope for compassion in war. So, I for one will not be party to this sinful deed."

Before Robert de Sable could reply, every Templar Knight in the room struck their chest in unison. No one said another word but, spotting a gap in the assembled Knights, the Grand Master scurried out of the meeting.

William later learned that Sable went straight to the king, but not to report the events of the meeting, as one might have expected. No, being the accomplished politician that he was, he persuaded the monarch that word was spreading of his plan and it was not being well received. He suggested, therefore, that if the king were intent on such action, he should use his own private army to dispatch the prisoners or face a significant rebellion from within his own army. He made no mention of William's intervention. A day later, on the twentieth of August 1191, the Muslim prisoners were marched out onto the plain of Acre in front of Saladin's camp where all two thousand seven hundred men were beheaded in sight of their fellow countrymen. None of the Templars was aware of this until after the event.

Two days later, on Thursday the twenty-second of August 1191, King Richard left Acre and led his army along the coast. Conditions were extreme: crushing heat and relentless attacks from mounted Muslims, who killed significant numbers of crusader horses and men with their incessant barrage of arrows. William rode just in front of the king with his colours held aloft. He knew full well that by becoming the king's standard bearer he had made himself a target, not that he could easily have refused. He anticipated that Saladin had eyes on him by now and it would only be a matter of time before he was brought down, for William believed he would be seen as aligned to King Richard, 'the butcherer'.

As he rode, hot dry air filled his nostrils. It was faintly perfumed, wild herbs maybe? William closed his eyes for a moment and tried to focus, but the slight breeze kissing his face reminded him of happier times with Rabia, of their late night conversations. Enough! he told himself. He was a monk, married to the Church, he should not be daydreaming about a woman. He would not allow himself to consider a different life, it was just too agonising. For most of his adult life his faith and devotion to Christ had been enough but, sadly, that was not now the case.

William did not fear death. Indeed, in some ways he longed for it, for he was exhausted. As they marched on his thoughts turned to his poor mood. He seemed unable to shake the feeling of hopelessness that had been with him for weeks. For the first time in his life he was unable to see a future. Rabia once more entered his thoughts. He guessed she was not far away, for Saladin was in close pursuit and the Sultan's entourage were always close to hand. William thought back to their last face-to-face meeting in Acre in December 1189 when he had sought her counsel. He recalled that this had been the last time he'd felt such despair and that it had been Rabia who had advocated that he search his heart for answers. At that time, he had determined to stay and try to effect change from within the Templars. Now, as he rode through the heat of the day, he looked into his heart once more.

Chapter 16

Present day

Whilst Harriet showered her battered and bruised body, Cyrus busied himself in the kitchen putting together a tray of cheese on toast and hot tea. When Harriet appeared, she ate hungrily, savouring the melted cheese and zingy tomato chutney that accompanied it. On finishing their toast, Cyrus poured a couple of large whiskies.

"Now, that's much better," said Harriet, appreciating the smoky sweet liquid.

"I agree, there's nothing like a bit of cheese on toast to restore the soul." Cyrus winked.

"Cyrus," said Harriet. "I know we don't know each other well, but Kate says you are one of only two men she would trust with her life. And I have a dilemma I need to run past someone. Would you mind?"

"My dear, it would be my pleasure."

"You might not say that once you know what it's about. What I'm about to tell you cannot be repeated to anyone, at least not until I've spoken to Superintendent Derek Wynn. You understand?

"Yes, of course."

"A few days ago, I found myself at St Albans Abbey. I wanted to get a feel for the place where William lived as a child. I was totally absorbed in the magnificent building; the sense of history was palpable. As I was studying a copy of a painting of the original Monastery I was approached by a well-heeled woman, as it turns out Veronica Morris."

"Bloody hell! Harriet, did she threaten you, harm you in any way? She is dangerous. I believe she was responsible for Ella Squires' death."

"No, that's just it, she went to considerable lengths to warn me about Cleo, who she said had crossed the line. She told me that to stay safe I must behave unpredictably, for Cleo does not cope well when she has to improvise."

"Hmm, she is right about that."

"She also told me a story about her charitable work with her two best friends building orphanages in India and the Middle East. The thing is, she claims these friends were none other than Ella Squires and my grandmother, Ann Rayfield."

"No, that cannot be possible!" Cyrus was on his feet.

"Please, Cyrus, sit down and hear me out. I too was disbelieving, but there is more. She told me that Cleo was responsible for Ella Squires' death. She was jealous of her friendship with her mother. Veronica blames herself for not spotting the signs. Either she is an accomplished actress or her distress was real."

Cyrus stayed silent, but Harriet noticed his face was now pale. She poured him another whisky before continuing. "She told me that after the discovery of Ella's body, she found a message written in her blood."

"Sorry? What?"

"A message written on the kitchen floor. *'Maybe now you'll notice me Mum.'* Veronica told me that from that moment on, she could not bear to be near Cleo, so she sent her away to boarding school. Anyway, I was convinced that I had been fed a pack of lies, but I went to my mother's house yesterday evening and there I found this photo in my grandmother's diary." Harriet handed Cyrus a faded polaroid photo of three women, arms around each other's shoulders, beaming at the camera. "Veronica Morris, Ella Squires and Ann Rayfield," she said.

"Oh my God, Harriet!" exclaimed Cyrus. "Have I been wrong all these years?"

"Well, there is more. I also found evidence of these orphanages in my grandmother's papers. They did exist, and they were set up under a charity which was run by my grandmother. I found evidence to show that Veronica and Ella were trustees. I think she was telling the truth. It's what I do now that is bothering me."

"This is most upsetting. Poor Henry appeared on my doorstep in a terrible state the day Ella went missing. I can never forget the look on his face. He knew she was gone. After much frantic searching by the police, friends, neighbours and the general public, a week later we learned that her bloodstained body had been recovered from a derelict building on an old industrial estate in Loughton. I think, if I remember correctly, Ella's body had been wrapped in a tablecloth and she'd been stabbed multiple times? A crime of passion, the police said. I remember Veronica was questioned at the time as her car was seen in the area by a witness, but there was nothing obvious to link her to it. I tried to speak to Veronica about a month later, but she was her usual acidic, unhelpful self which I foolishly interpreted as guilt."

"Don't be too harsh on yourself, Cyrus. Veronica herself is aware of how unpleasant she can be. I'm guessing it was her way of keeping people at arm's length. A great deal of what you've said ties in with her account. She says Cleo killed Ella in their kitchen. Ann and Veronica found her, cleaned up, wrapped the body in the tablecloth and placed it in the boot of Veronica's car, before leaving it in a derelict building in Loughton. As I'm sure you can understand, there are all sorts of issues here which I need to run past Derek Wynn. I'm sure Veronica knows that I have no choice but to report this. But I think, on balance, I would rather trust my gut instinct, which is that she is genuinely trying to help us, and perhaps me specifically, and that in some way she wishes to rid herself of some of the guilt she feels. To an extent, I can relate to her dilemma all those years ago. For God's sake, her daughter was only thirteen."

"I hear what you are saying, my dear, and, from what I've been told, you are an excellent judge of character and a brilliant police officer, but do you really think the bitter Veronica we all know has a softer, kinder side?"

"I really do. I got the distinct impression that for all her bravado she has a tender side and is actually fearful of her daughter. I might be wrong, but in any case we really need to find Cleo and stop her. From a purely selfish point of view if we don't I will never be free of fear. I'm living in a constant state of anxiety. She's never far away. For fuck's sake, she's even here! And whilst I am reassured by your presence, you can't always be by my side. I think we need Veronica Morris to have any chance of apprehending Cleo, who needs to stand trial for the murders she's committed."

"Then I will do everything in my power to support you."

"Thank you, Cyrus. I really appreciate that. So, I plan to ask Derek Wynn to speak to the Crown Prosecution Service with regard to some sort of deal for her. There are several offences she's guilty of, not least of which is assisting an offender and perverting the course of justice, but there is mitigation and with a guilty plea she may get a lesser sentence, maybe even a suspended sentence. The trick will be to gain CPS permission or approval to use her to help detain Cleo. She will effectively be a participating informant."

"Good plan. But what about Henry and Kate Squires?"

"I've been giving that a lot of thought. First, I need to speak to Derek Wynn. If he goes for it, once everything has been put in place they must be told, and sensitively. I was hoping you would consent to be present to provide support?"

"Of course, although, if it's possible, I think they should hear it directly from Veronica."

"I will certainly ask. But wouldn't that be the least sensitive way to go about it?"

"No, I think they deserve the truth and the truth from the only person who really knows what actually happened to Ella."

Harriet nodded before getting to her feet to stoke the log burner. Then she went into the kitchen, returning a short time later with a tray of fruit cake and coffee.

"Cyrus, do you mind if I ask you a question?" Harriet didn't wait for Cyrus to reply. "When you rescued me earlier you said that Cleo wouldn't dare come near me now she knows you're here, that you go way back. What did you mean by this exactly?"

"Ah, well, it's a long story but in essence Cleo and I came to blows a few years ago. Cleo was involved with a fellow called Leon Drake. A nasty piece of work. Charming and charismatic, but also dark and violent. He worked as a barman at a popular cocktail bar in the financial district in London. His MO was to identify young vulnerable females, whom he would seduce whilst Cleo stole from them. Money, credit cards, jewellery. A good friend asked me to look into the circumstances of a high-value theft from his daughter and, to cut a long story short, I set Leon up, which led me to Cleo. As tough as she is, she did not want to go to prison and, being caught on the back foot, had no plan to fall back on. Realising the game was up she offered evidence against Leon, then disappeared. I told the police all this and, with the evidence I'd gathered along with Cleo's, Leon went to prison. I handed over everything I had on her to the police and I told her so in a subsequent telephone conversation. She is still wanted for these thefts. So, believe me, she will keep her distance, because she knows full well that I will not hesitate to report her."

"Blimey, she really is something."

"She is."

"Okay, enough of Cleo," said Harriet. "Can we please have a conversation about the enigmatic William of Hertford?"

"Of course, but first I have a confession to make." Cyrus looked serious. "When we met recently at Henry's party, it was not the first time."

"Really?"

"No, I knew your father and you and I actually sat next to each other during a lecture of his."

"I'm sorry, I don't remember that."

"Nor should you, it was a long time ago, but I was impressed with your enquiring mind and thirst for knowledge, to the extent that when I stumbled across William's bible last year, I knew immediately that I wanted you involved. I tried to approach you on several occasions, but my timing was always lousy and I didn't manage to pluck up the courage to speak to you."

"You weren't by any chance the male I saw with binoculars in the car park here in Aberporth? And on the chalk escarpment near my cottage?"

"I was. Can you forgive me?"

"To be honest, Cyrus, it's a relief to know I wasn't losing my mind."

Cyrus put his hand on Harriet's before reaching for a file on the floor by his chair. "To the matter of William of Hertford. You go first, though. What did you find?"

"Well, you recall that you mentioned a symbol on the map? You said you recognised it, but couldn't place it."

Cyrus nodded.

"Well, I think I know what it is."

"You do?" He clapped his hands together.

"Yes, I think it may very well be a seal which according to several sources is thought to show Hugh de Payns, the first Grand Master of the Templars, and Godfrey de Saint-Omer riding one horse to represent the Order's early poverty. Originally, the Order was known as The Poor Fellow Soldiers of Christ and the Temple of Solomon. When the Order was first established, its Knights took vows of poverty, chastity and obedience, dressed in donated clothes and were reliant on contributions and bequests to live. The seal is a nod to this early hardship. What's more, and you may already know this, I think William's mother, Arianne of Troyes, was the niece of Hugh de Payns."

"Oh, my goodness me. This is fascinating. I did not know there was a connection between Arianne and the first Grand Master. This probably explains how it was that William was able to leave the Benedictine Monastery at St Albans to become Templar Knights. William was of high birth, from Templar royalty."

"Cyrus, this is so exciting. Now it's your turn. What did you turn up in the letters?"

"Well, the first thing to say is that William was clearly a prolific writer throughout his life. Unfortunately, however, I only have a small sample of the many letters he sent, and I know he sent lots as he refers to many past letters. But the ones I do have tell us volumes about the boy and later the man. The first few letters I discovered in my late great-uncle's things – and these relate to William's early years at the Monastery in St Albans – are childlike and innocent and addressed to his beloved mother. He talks about life in the Monastery, of his deep friendship with Robert, of their daily adventures which included swimming and fishing in the Monastery fish ponds, climbing the orchard trees, catching slow worms amongst the gravestones, spying on various monks, giggling uncontrollably in mass, learning Latin, using sign language when they were not permitted to speak and so on. What is so delightful about them is William's *joie de vivre*. Such love of life, such spirit and optimism. And he shows much affection towards his mother. Each letter must have been so special to her, as well as tinged with sadness, as he was no longer able to live with her. What is really frustrating is that none of the letters gives a hint as to why he ended up at the Monastery, just that it was a necessary situation which he accepted."

"For some reason, hearing about William generates a whole host of emotions that I can't explain. The more I learn about him, the more I'm drawn to him. Please continue."

"I know what you mean, he is getting to me as well, and it's almost impossible to articulate. Maybe it has something to do with his philosophy on life? Anyway, the second batch of letters I stumbled across quite by chance when clearing out the loft. I found them in a small wooden box. These cover the period when William and Robert left the Monastery and travelled to France, to the family estate in Troyes where they were trained to become Knights. There are also several early letters detailing their arrival in the Holy Land. Again, there is such an eagerness to make a difference, such an energy. And even when they arrive in the Holy Land their fervour remains intact. Robert and William seem dedicated to God and their king. But their humanity also shines through too as they refer to caring for not just the pilgrims they were charged with keeping safe but also soldiers on both sides of the conflict. Please read the translations yourself. I would really relish your opinion."

"Thank you, I can't wait. Did you say they tended to injured Muslims as well as their own?"

"That's what William tells his mother, yes. He argues that these men fought bravely in battle and in his view should not be abandoned to die agonising deaths on the battlefield but afforded respect and compassion."

"Oh, my goodness. I could easily fall in love with William."

"Yes, he comes across as a kind, generous, gentle, brave and principled man. But he was also a monk, so not available, if you know what I mean!"

Harriet laughed. "Do you think there might be letters still in existence in France? Do you know if the family estate is still there? Or, if not, if the family archives have survived?"

"Do you know, as crazy as it sounds I'd not thought of that. That's brilliant. I don't know the answer to either of those questions, but I can sure as hell find out. You see, I knew I was right to get your help with this quest. I'll get straight onto it on Monday. The way I look at it, the more we can learn about the man, the better chance we have of understanding the map."

"Thank you, Cyrus, for bringing me on board. I apologise for my initial reluctance. This is turning out to be such fun."

"Now, let's talk about Nick."

"Do we have to?" Harriet pulled a face.

"Knowing a bit about him would help in my search for him."

"Okay, what do you want to know?"

"Let's start with what he was like as a person, before things went awry."

"Well, let me see. He's always been a man that likes to be noticed. Aware of his good looks, but not vain, if that makes sense?" Cyrus nodded. "Nick is intelligent, and for many years was considered a fine police officer, well respected, fair and decent. He had a reputation for having a good feel for cases. Nick was a good father, and until a couple of years ago was involved with the kids, although not hugely hands-on, but he would go to sports days and school plays if he possibly could. And he often took the kids to the park, to football and netball practice. In terms of us as a couple, the mad passionate can't-be-without-each-other phase lasted I'd say until Ben was born. After Amelia was born we had two children to cope with and, well, it wasn't the same. Not bad, just different. Nick could be impulsive and funny. But also moody and monosyllabic. I always thought we were a normal happy family. However, what do they say, hindsight is a wonderful thing?"

"What do you mean?"

"Looking back I now see things I didn't notice at the time. Nick's drinking just seemed to creep up on us. Almost overnight he changed from being laid back and cheerful to short-tempered and secretive. It took me far too long to work out that he was self-medicating. He would carry a water bottle around with him everywhere and I'm pretty sure it contained vodka. What makes me really mad is the fact that for at least the last two years he seems to have been pretty much constantly inebriated, during which time he was driving to and from work, driving at work. Driving our children around. His judgement started to go too. But do you know, I still don't know what initiated the drinking. Was it one event, was it a predisposition? An illness? Or something much more sinister? I'd really like to know. There was no warning that he was about to jump ship. He simply disappeared, leaving his job, his family and as it now turns out his country. He ran away. In my book you just don't do that."

"Oh, Harriet, I'm so sorry. I can see how painful this is for you. It was not my intention to upset you, it's just I wanted to get a feel for the man."

"No, it's fine, Cyrus, really. I'm struggling with the fact that I really didn't know the man who I lived with for twenty years. I'm angry, with him, yes, but also with myself. I took my eye off the ball and the reality is that his behaviour had a profound impact on many good people who maybe I could have protected, had I been on top of my game. I'm not feeling self-pity for the fact that my husband was a serial adulterer and gambler, I'm feeling rage at how his actions adversely affected others and, rather than face up to the consequences of those actions, he fled. I want to find him; I want to confront him. I have hard questions for him."

"If you don't mind me asking, does that mean you want him back? Do you want a reconciliation?"

"Oh, good God, no! I'm done with Nick Lacey, but that doesn't mean I don't care what happens to him. It's just I no longer wish to be part of his life. He will always be the children's father."

"Fair enough. Now, how are your children emotionally about their dad?"

"They both say they miss him like mad, but there have been no tears. They behave as if they accept his absence. To be honest, we talk about him in daily life quite a bit. They behave almost as if he's just popped out and will be back later, which now I come to think of it is slightly weird."

"Do you think he's been in contact with them?"

"Oh gosh, I really don't know. What do you think?"

"I think from what you've said there is a distinct possibility that there has been or is ongoing contact. Do you think they would agree to speak to me? Would you be happy for me to speak to them?"

"I don't see why not. Take Kate with you and pizza, and then they will tell you anything you want to know!"

Chapter 17

1191 – The Holy Land

Richard the Lionheart continued to march his mighty army south along the coast from Acre towards Jaffa. But conditions had become harsher still: searing temperatures, little water, little or no shade. And still there were the persistent forays by small groups of Muslim soldiers to contend with, a successful tactic that delayed Richard's army. In two days they had scarcely covered ten miles.

After crossing the Belus river, the Christian army made camp. Exhausted, they rested for an entire day before setting off once more towards a place called Haifa. It was now that King Richard divided his army in three. The king led from the front. William, in charge of the Royal Standard, was instructed to ride in the centre of the army. He wondered if this was to confuse the enemy. The king's chosen route now took them across sandy ground which slowed progress considerably. As the day wore on, a mist fell and the rear of the army with its heavy wagons containing supplies and armoury lost contact with the rest of the force. It was then that they were attacked by a large contingent of Saladin's militia who simply appeared from the cover of the dunes. Many supplies, men and horses were lost to the attackers.

As word of the attack reached King Richard, he ordered the middle section of his army to race to the rear. The king himself joined the charge and galloped into the chaos, along with William and many of his fellow Templar and Hospitaller Knights. The fighting was fierce, but eventually their attackers melted back into the dunes, leaving an eerie scene of carnage. The Christian army re-grouped and struggled on until they reached Haifa, where they made camp.

Towards dusk on the second evening, William sat at the entrance to his tent as he watched the sun dip lower and lower in the sky, a rich perfectly circular suspended orange ball. He was transfixed, until Zafir careered around the corner to shatter his peace.

"Master, Master, you must hurry, please. They have Sayf and, whilst I do not care for him, what they are doing is wrong! Please stop it!"

"Slow down, my friend. Who has Sayf and what are they doing to him?" asked William calmly.

"All right, after yesterday's attack, some of the king's personal guard went in search of survivors. They came across Sayf doing what you do, tending to the dying and offering comfort, which is totally out of character for him, but that's what he was doing."

"Sorry, say that again?"

"Sayf, Saladin's nephew, was walking amongst the fallen of both sides offering water and words of reassurance. He was also tending to those who were injured and had started to load them into a cart when he was jumped by the king's guard."

"Are you absolutely sure, Zafir? How do you know this to be true?" William had now got to his feet and was reaching for his sword.

"Because Salma overheard a couple of the king's guard bragging about it in the communal bathing area."

"Go and fetch Salma now, would you, please?"

While Zafir was gone, William went to dress. Instead of putting on his new chainmail, however, he reached for his much-loved and well worn armour.

A breathless Salma arrived. "Salma, it's really important that I understand what the king's guards said about Sayf, please," said William, fixing her with a serious gaze.

"William, my English is not so good, but I heard a group of them laughing and chatting. They called Sayf a Muslim devil, a dog. They boasted how they'd kicked and punched him many, many times and how he was going to die a terrible death."

"Okay, thank you, Salma," said William, gently placing his hand on her shoulder.

"Master, they will kill him horribly." Salma was looking down at the ground.

"Not if I can help it. Salma, Zafir, you will need to move quickly. I must get a message to Saladin. Can you do that?" They nodded. "Tell him that God willing he will see Sayf by daybreak. When the message has been delivered take the horses and the cart and make your way to the port at Jaffa. Zafir, you must take my box with you. Guard it with your life. Wait for me there." Once again Zafir nodded. William shook Zafir's hand and enveloped Salma in his arms for a brief moment. "Until we meet again, my friends."

William made for Thierry's tent where he found the old Knight napping. He shook him. "I apologise, my old friend, for the rude awakening, but I require your help once more. I have learned of a grave injustice to a Muslim soldier. The conventions of warfare have been violated and I cannot let it lie. Please rouse the rest of the Templars and request they make their way to the king's tent with God's speed."

William left a startled and sleepy-looking Thierry and made his way to the king's tent. Inside, it was crammed with rowdy soldiers. It was warm, very warm, and the air was thick with smoke. There was little light. William followed the sound of the baying crowd who surrounded a young man sitting cross-legged on the floor, head bowed. Sayf was barely recognisable, so severe had his beating been. William walked measuredly towards the prisoner, gently pushing his way through the crowd. When he reached him, he knelt. The mob went silent, no doubt intrigued by the appearance of the tall Templar.

It seemed Salma's account was true. William saw that Sayf was indeed bloodied and bruised, one eye closed, his left cheek blackened. There was no fight left in him. It had clearly been punched and kicked out of him.

William put his mouth close to the prisoner's ear and spoke in Arabic, believing it unlikely that those in his immediate vicinity would understand what he was saying.

"Sayf, I am truly sorry for your situation. It is wrong. I will do my best to help you." He could hear some in the crowd ask their neighbours what had been said.

Sayf did not immediately respond but when he did his voice was hoarse. "I have wronged you in the past and I sincerely apologise. But please do not put your life in jeopardy for me. I die knowing I have changed the course of my life and that is enough."

William put a strong hand on the prisoner's shoulder and whispered, "Do not lose faith, Sayf," as he got to his feet. It was at this moment that his Templar brothers arrived with Thierry at their helm.

William turned to the king and his council who were observing from the royal platform to his left. He bowed long and low.

"Your Majesty, I have reason to believe that a great wrong has been done to this man." He pointed towards the prisoner.

Jeers of "dog" and "devil" were shouted from the crowd.

"William, William, surely even you are not going to make a fuss about one little Muslim?" said a smirking king, wagging his finger at the Templar.

Laughter erupted from the crowd.

"Sire, with the deepest respect, this soldier was tending to the injured and the dying on both sides. He was no threat and therefore as per our rules of engagement should have been permitted to continue with his humanitarian work unimpeded."

"William of Hertford, I hear you, but I wonder if you are merely quibbling over semantics," said the king to much applause from his supporters.

"Indeed, no, Sire. Without rules and regulations to guide us, without boundaries, we run the risk of descending into chaos and savagery." The crowd booed loudly but William continued, nevertheless. "We have a long and noble history with compassion at its centre. I do not believe that any Christian soldier truly wishes to be considered a lout or thug. In this instance, the behaviour of a few has tainted the many." The crowd fell silent.

"For goodness' sake, William, why do you care so much about this prisoner?"

"I care for all men, Sire; I care that all men are treated fairly and honourably. It was entirely wrong that this man should have been beaten and spat on and treated like a dog. Those who took it upon themselves to violate the rules of war should be ashamed. It is they who should be punished, not this man before us. A grave injustice has occurred here, a disservice to God, to you and to our cause. '*Let not mercy and truth forsake you; bind them around your neck, write them on the tablet of your heart, and so find favour and high esteem in the sight of God and man.*' Proverbs 3: 3-4."

The tent was eerily quiet. All eyes were on the king, who was scowling. His mood had clearly changed. William wondered if he had gone too far, if he had pushed too hard. He glanced across at Thierry, who was wide-eyed and looked terrified. The king remained silent for a moment before getting to his feet and moving to the edge of the platform.

"I am most interested to know who else here agrees with William of Hertford on this matter? All those who concur, please make yourselves known to me."

It seemed an age before anyone reacted, but then slowly a thunderous noise began to fill the vast tent as the Templar and Hospitaller Knights rhythmically thumped their chests in support.

The king stood motionless, fixing William with his steely gaze. "In that case, William of Hertford, kindly take the prisoner back to his camp with my compliments. Those involved in this man's torture will be dealt with severely."

William bowed to the king, then to his fellow Knights before walking across to Sayf and lifting him onto his shoulder. He was keen to exit before the king had time to change his mind.

Outside, William found his horse and, with the help of some of his fellow Templars, Sayf was lifted onto the front, William nimbly jumped up behind. As he was about to ride out, a mounted Thierry appeared.

"My friend, I will hear no argument. I will ride with you."

169

William nodded and they rode out of the Christian camp for the last time.

Their progress was slow, partly due to the sandy ground and fading light, partly because Sayf kept sliding in and out of consciousness. William was forced to keep hold of him to stop him from falling off. They had gone little more than a mile through heavily wooded terrain when a loud voice boomed out.

"William of Hertford, I mean you no harm. I have been sent by the mighty Saladin. My name is al-Afdal. I come in peace."

Thierry drew his sword.

"al-Afdal is a cousin of mine, a good man," said Sayf weakly.

"Greetings, al-Afdal, please show yourself." As he spoke, William gestured to Thierry to put his sword away.

Out of the gloom a magnificent black Arab horse came into view, ridden by a grinning young man, William guessed in his early twenties, dressed in an embroidered blue and black long line jacket, with plain black leggings, riding boots and a striking turban of smoky blue with a large sapphire jewel at its centre.

"Cousin, praise Allah that you are alive!" said al-Afdal.

"Praise Allah and William of Hertford, for without his intervention I would be a dead man," said Sayf, pain etched across his face.

"The Sultan sends his extreme thanks, William of Hertford, and an offer of assistance. We do not have long; our spies are everywhere, and they report that your king is set on revenge. Apparently, he is aggrieved that you made him look weak and petty in front of his men and, as a consequence, he has ordered his personal guard to apprehend you."

"How can we be sure you are telling the truth?" piped up Thierry.

"Apologies, al-Afdal, this is my mentor and brother Knight, Thierry of Tyre," said William. "He makes a sound point though."

"My motives are purely honourable, I can assure you. What does your heart tell you, William of Hertford?"

William broke into a smile. Rabia's influence was clear. "My heart tells me that you are here to help and for that we are grateful. I am indebted to you for risking your life to save us."

"It is an honour. My father speaks most highly of you, Templar. He refers to you as a noble Knight, a man of God."

"I thank you. I too hold your father in high esteem."

Once Sayf had been secured to William's horse, they rode at speed. al-Afdal took them away from the usual routes, down narrow overgrown tracks, through rocky ravines and wooded areas. After several hours, they stopped briefly to water the horses and check on Sayf, who was noticeably frailer, before once again riding at pace. Just before dawn they reached the outskirts of Saladin's camp. As they made their way through the camp, William noticed their route was lined with Muslim soldiers who bowed as they passed. William took a deep breath, the first proper one, since they had taken flight. His heart slowed to a normal pace and he felt a sense of relief flood his body. He had done the right thing, in the face of much opposition. What lay ahead was unclear. But he was undoubtedly displaced.

The horses came to a halt outside Saladin's tent. William recognised it immediately. And before he had a chance to dismount, the great man himself appeared. He looked thinner and older than William remembered. Waving at William he rushed to his nephew who was slumped on the front of William's horse. He spoke gently in his nephew's ear. They all dismounted and William watched as Sayf was carried away.

"William of Hertford, I thank you with all my heart for returning my kinsman." Saladin took both his hands in his. "May God be with you."

William bowed. "Saladin, may Allah be with you. It's good to see you again."

"Indeed. Much has happened since our last meeting."

"Undeniably it has. May I introduce you to my very good friend and mentor, Thierry of Tyre."

"Thierry of Tyre, you are most welcome. Any friend of William of Hertford is a friend of Saladin." He walked forward and took Thierry's hands in his.

"Thank you, Sultan, you are most kind." William saw that Thierry was doing his best not to stare directly at the supreme leader of the Middle East.

Saladin beckoned the men into his tent. Inside it was cool and airy and, as at William's last visit, the aroma of roses perfumed the air. Bowls of water were brought forth and hands washed. When everyone had taken their fill of bread, cheeses and fruit, it was time to talk.

"Well, William, it seems that you are out of favour with your king. Do not be crestfallen, for you are a courageous man, a man of integrity. Unfortunately, your king falls short when it comes to these particular character traits. He may be bright and brave – what do they call him? the *Lionheart*? – but he is also dysfunctional, a hothead, impetuous, untrustworthy and a murderer. What you do now will define you." Saladin was looking directly at William.

"I thank you for your generous words. It was not my intention to embarrass the king. I did what I felt to be right and I would do it again. However, my actions have clearly resulted in unanticipated consequences. As I see it, I have a number of options. Firstly, I could return and beg the king's forgiveness and hope I catch him on a good day. Secondly, I could ride to the coast and take a ship home to England. Thirdly, I could continue to fight for God, whatever that looks like now. I fear I need to reassess."

"William, I'm not sure I like your first choice. I fear it is doomed to failure. Even if you make it through to the king, he is unlikely to pardon you. It's too risky a venture. Your second option has merit, except that I do not think you have any idea where home now is. Besides, what would you do? Go back to a Monastery and die of boredom? No, I think you should do what you do best, and you may be surprised that I suggest this, but lead your men and fight for your God, in whatever way you now see fit."

William frowned. "I'm sorry, I don't know what you mean by my men. I prefer the term family, for other than Thierry, Zafir, and Salma, there is no one."

A huge grin spread across Saladin's face. "Oh, William of Hertford, you really don't have any idea, do you? Come with me." Saladin led William and Thierry through a maze of tents, to the outer limit of the encampment. In the distance it was just possible to make out a caravan of horses and carts wending their way towards the coast.

"William, it seems that you are much admired. When you left the Christian camp, more than two hundred and fifty Templar and Hospitaller Knights left also as you can see. My spies tell me that they are heading for Jaffa, and we are assisting them to avoid the king's guard. They have voted with their feet; their loyalty is to you. Now do you understand the king's anger?"

William gulped. "Thierry, why do you smile so?"

"Because, William, despite your best efforts to stay in the background, despite your assertions over the years that you are not leader material, quite clearly there are many who disagree."

"Very funny and, whilst I am truly humbled and my heart is bursting with pride, the situation is somewhat a logistical nightmare."

"You will need to get word to Zafir and quickly, so he can make the necessary arrangements," said Thierry, stroking his beard.

"There are two issues to overcome first, my friend. Who to send to Zafir without alarming the poor fellow and how to pay for the arrangements?"

"William of Hertford, may I suggest that you send Lubna, Rabia's maid?" said Saladin. "She is well known to Zafir and he will trust her word. And it would be my honour to provide funds for whatever it is you have planned. I will not accept 'no' for an answer but I do not wish to know what you are going to do with the money."

William did not reply for a minute or two, so busy was he mulling over the situation and weighing up his options. The mere mention of Rabia had set his heart racing. He wondered if she might already be in Jaffa. Would he perhaps get to see her one last time? An intense flush of sadness flooded his body at the thought of life without her. For a moment, he struggled to get his thoughts back on track.

"I thank you for your most generous offer, but what is the catch? Why would you help us, for whichever way you look at it we are the enemy?"

"Oh, William, there is no catch. I admire your nobility of spirit and I respect your character and, whilst we may not share the same beliefs, we have the same moral principles. I'm aware you did all in your power to save my men from slaughter at Acre and now I'm determined to return the favour." Saladin folded his arms across his chest, as if to emphasise his point.

"In that case, I am most grateful and accept on behalf of us all. But I insist your financial support is a loan that we will repay in full, as soon as is practically possible." William bowed to the supreme leader.

"Excellent, excellent. We will make the necessary arrangements. I suggest you rest until dusk. I will send some of my best scouts with you, but you will have to ride hard to avoid the king's guard."

Just then, a courtier approached to request William's presence in Saladin's tent. Inside, William found Sayf conscious and propped up on a mountain of cushions.

"William, I wanted to thank you again for saving my life and to explain to you how I came to change my life. I was so full of hate and bile for all Christians, but particularly you. You see, you epitomised all I had grown to despise. You were popular, intelligent, steadfast, a skilled and brave warrior, but I only saw you as an interloper. I realise now something was missing from my life, call it faith or purpose. I focused on trying to destroy you at all costs. I now bitterly regret my actions and my terrible behaviour towards your friend Robert of St Albans, for he was a good man too. And towards the old woman Salma and my sister Rabia. It was unforgivable. I was blinded by rage and jealously. Do you remember when I tried to kill you at Tyre?"

William nodded.

"Well, after the battle, I sneaked back to the causeway, hid behind an old cart and watched as you and your manservant and Salma systematically walked amongst the quagmire to tend to the injured and dying from both sides. I watched as you cared for a young Muslim soldier just feet away from me. You spoke in Arabic and offered him words of comfort. You stayed with him as his life blood drained away. I overheard you tell him that he mattered and was a brave Knight of Allah, and I was utterly ashamed that this young man had been abandoned by his kind. I wept for him, and I wept for myself, for in that moment I realised that I had completely misjudged you. I vowed that never again would I abandon injured and dying soldiers on either side. I would not be that spoilt impetuous soldier blinded by rage. I pray that, given time, and Allah willing, I can become more like you."

"I thank you for your honesty, Sayf. My heart is filled with gladness to know that the work I started and can no longer continue on the battlefields will endure." William placed a hand on the young man's shoulder.

As William and Thierry mounted their steeds, Saladin once again appeared.

"My friend, many years ago I chanced across an old man who told me something that has stayed with me ever since and I think you might have use for now. He said, *'Peace comes from within, do not seek it without.'* Safe passage, William, and may God be with you."

"I suspect our paths will not cross again. Thank you, Saladin, for everything you've done for me, it's been an honour. May Allah be with you." The two men bowed to each other before William of Hertford urged his horse forward and rode out of the camp into an uncertain future.

Chapter 18

Cyrus and Harriet slept late. The excitement of the night before had taken its toll on them both. They ate a light breakfast before donning their walking boots and coats to walk along the cliff path to the little coastal hamlet of Tresaith. The storm had blown itself out. It was a sunny Saturday in early March. As they strolled, talk turned to Harriet's desperate situation in the storm and how lucky she'd been to survive. They stopped at The Ship Inn for a late lunch, a generous local ploughman's, before re-tracing their steps. There was no sign of Cleo. Harriet's protection officer Chris kept a discreet distance, blissfully unaware of the drama of the night before. Red campions provided a show of pink and blackthorn white, amongst the yellow coastal gorse. The sea was steely blue but still murky after the storm. Cormorants and gulls screeched overhead. A cool breeze darted across the footpath. They spent the rest of the afternoon chatting outside while Cyrus helped Harriet to tidy the cottage garden. Harriet felt an inner calm for the first time in many months.

That evening Harriet cooked a meal of bruschetta topped with aubergine and peppers, melted mozzarella and olives, home-made lasagne, and tiramisu. It was only after they had done eating that talk once more turned to William of Hertford.

"As I couldn't sleep I did a bit of research on the Templars last night," said Harriet, "and discovered that not long after they were established a long list of rules was drawn up that had to be obeyed. These included forsaking wills, fighting bravely, being prepared for death, wearing white to signify they had put the murkier side of life behind them. Being virtuous. I took that to mean they were not allowed sexual relations. They also had to keep their hair short and wear beards; they were not allowed to shave. Swearing and shows of anger were not permitted. Letters and gifts given or received were subject to the approval of the Grand Master. In short, their job appears to have been to protect the Church and fight the opponents of Christianity. I guess you could say the Templars were part soldier part holy man. It all seems very restrictive to me. And I wondered if William had to seek permission to send each letter to his mother."

"Very interesting indeed. I guess that, like many rules, whether they were conscientiously adhered to or not often depended on the circumstances the Knights found themselves in at the time. In a battle scenario I'd expect that the Grand Master had more pressing things to consider than giving permission for letters home."

"Yes, I'm sure you are right." Harriet took a sip of her red wine. "So, tell me more about the map you found in William's bible."

"I can do better than that." Cyrus smiled. "I've brought a scanned copy with me."
Harriet cleared the dishes from the table and Cyrus unfolded the paper, flattening it with his hand.

"Tell me, what do you see, my dear? What are your initial observations?"

Harriet leant over the table to get a closer look at the chart. It was a few moments before she said anything.

"Well, right at the top of the map is the seal we talked about last night, the two Knights on one horse, which one might interpret as the author of the map indicating that he is a Templar, and maybe also that he is connected to the seal. And we now believe that William of Hertford was related to Hugh de Payns, one of the men depicted on the seal. So that would fit in nicely."

"That's good, very good, I thought that too. Please continue." Cyrus was beaming.

"I'd say this is a map of Europe, North Africa and the Middle East or the Holy Land and that, let me see, fifteen maybe sixteen locations are highlighted. Most look like forts or castles, but I can't be sure."

"I think so too. Of course, the only way to be sure would be to take a look in the flesh."

"What, actually visit each site? Look for clues?"

"Well, why not?"

"Why not indeed?" said Harriet, beaming from ear to ear. Then her face became suddenly serious. "Cyrus, I can't. I have absolutely no money to spare. When Nick disappeared, I discovered the family home had been re-mortgaged several times. The bank has since repossessed it. On top of this, Nick cleared out our savings and left hefty debts, which I'm struggling to repay."

"I'm so sorry to learn that, but please don't worry. I have more money than I know what to do with. We can work something out. You are crucial to this quest. I suspect we have much more searching and scouring to do!" Cyrus spoke animatedly.

"Well, thank you, I really appreciate that. We can talk about the detail at a later date. In the meantime, can I ask, do you have any idea as to the purpose of the map?"

"Good question. No, I don't know if it's just the record of a journey, or whether it contains clues to follow, or if it has a message hidden in it. But perhaps we won't know until we follow it. Of course, we don't know in what order the places highlighted were visited."

"True, but it will be fascinating to take a more detailed look and maybe its meaning will become clearer."

"Maybe," said Cyrus, peering at the map close up.

"Do we have any idea of the date of the map?" asked Harriet.

"That's a really good question and the short answer is no, but there are some clues in the letters we have, dates that we know about, so we can start to build a timeline perhaps."

"How do you mean?"

"Well, we know William was left at St Albans Monastery in 1158 as a seven-year-old, so that would mean he was born in 1151. We know he left the Monastery with Robert aged twenty. That would have been in 1171 and we know they were in France training. If we allow a year for training and travel to the Middle East we probably wouldn't be too far off the mark to say they probably arrived in 1172."

"That's brilliant, Cyrus. We just need to do some more research to see if we can identify some of the other significant dates."

"Yes, exactly, we will just keep looking in between our other commitments."

On Monday morning, Harriet was back in the incident room. The old sense of unease had returned, and she was having difficulty concentrating. She had spoken to Derek Wynn about Veronica on her journey home from Wales the night before and was waiting to hear the details of his meeting with the Crown Prosecution Service. She wondered if they would agree to Veronica potentially becoming a participating informant. Harriet's phone sounded. She swiftly picked it up but it wasn't Derek.

"Morning, Harriet, have you got time to meet with Kate Squires and me this morning?" said a cheery sounding Geoff Harvey.

"Hi, Geoff. Of course. Are you going to tell me why?"

"Nope, want to see your face. Meet you in room 201 of the scientific support building at HQ at eleven?"

"You are such a tease! See you then."

Kate Squires greeted Harriet with a little squeal. "It's so lovely to see you, how are you?" She hugged Harriet tightly.

"I'm getting there, thanks, Kate. It's so good to see you too. I've really been enjoying Cyrus's company. He is keeping me both occupied and entertained."

"Cyrus is a wonderful man."

"And he also saved my life." Harriet was laughing.

"He did what?" said Kate, her mouth open.

"It's a long story, but he basically pulled me out of harm's way during a violent storm. If, he hadn't come along when he did, I'd have been a goner."

"What are you talking about?" said Geoff, frowning.

"I made a silly mistake and nearly drowned. We are getting side-tracked. I'll tell you later."

"Okay, but we are both going to hold you to that. So, tell me, has there been any progress locating Cleo?" All remains of a smile had left Kate's face.

"Not really," said Harriet. "She is a constant stress in my life I could really do without."

"What do you mean?" asked Geoff.

"She's playing with my head. She visited my mother a few weeks ago, then I'm positive she was hanging around just outside the farm search area. I saw a figure by the perimeter fence one morning. It was misty but I'm pretty sure it was her and I've seen her drive past the cottage. It would seem she does so most nights, always at different times, always in different cars. Then to top it all, she turned up in Wales while I was there with Cyrus."

"Oh my God, Harriet, no wonder you've been distracted lately. I'm so sorry, and there I've been burdening you with my problems!" Geoff coloured.

"Don't be silly, you have been amazing. You've taken very good care of me."

"She's not going to stop, is she?" said Kate.

"No, she's not, but without saying too much, because I can't yet, there is potentially someone who may be able to help us with Cleo."

"Ooh, very cloak and dagger," said Kate, clapping her hands together.

"Yes, indeed," said Geoff. "Are you ladies ready to talk about the mobile found with Eve?"

"You bet, what have you found?" asked Harriet.

"Well, I don't think Eve can legitimately claim she knew nothing about it," said Geoff. "For a start, her fingerprints are all over it and there is absolutely no trace of David Wilson on it whatsoever."

"Not at all?" asked Harriet.

"No," said Kate. "But it does contain at least twenty text messages between them. The messages are mundane in the main, but what they do suggest is a very different relationship to that portrayed by Eve in her statement."

"I would say that Eve is very definitely in the driving seat," said Geoff. "She is in control. And, most significantly, we can prove that she knows about Elly Bridgeman, because in a text she instructs David to and I quote, *'Get shot of that bloody tart upstairs'*. To which he replies: *'It's in hand, don't be such a jealous bitch, she's just a distraction and why should you care, you've got what you wanted'*. To which she replies: *'Hurry up and get me out of this awful place, I can't stand it'*."

"Harriet, you were right to trust your gut instinct," said Kate. "Eve Wilson is up to her neck in this."

"This is really good work, both of you. I'm just trying to think through our next move. I'm trying to think back to when I saw Eve at the hospital and asked her about what happened. We need to handle this information extremely carefully, draw up timelines, work out when and what was said by text. Compare statements as well as the interview transcripts with David Wilson and draw up a list of questions to put to both of them. We also need to look at the forensic evidence again. If we are clever, we can trip them up and get to the truth. Can I just clarify, did Eve use the phone to make calls?"

"There's no evidence of it being used as a phone, there are only text messages between the two," said Kate.

"Why would she do that?" asked Harriet.

"Well, I suspect that Eve had no intention of the phone's existence ever being known. I'm sure the plan was to delete all activity and throw the phones. Perhaps Eve was concerned that Elly Bridgeman might overhear any conversations between them?" suggested Kate.

"Perhaps," said Harriet frowning. "It was an almighty cock-up as far as Eve is concerned though. I wonder, Geoff, can you get the hospital to provide details of her blood work? When she was found she was unconscious – why was that?"

Geoff nodded.

"When I was at the hospital with Eve, I asked her some questions, just to try to get my head around what had happened. I asked her if she was in the tiny room for the entire time she was incarcerated. She hesitated, which at the time I thought was odd, then she provided lots of detail about how she loathed David and how he was mentally ill. When I thanked her for the insight, she insisted on providing yet more information, which now I come to think of was peculiar. Hang on a minute, I just need to check my notes."

Geoff made coffee, while Harriet dived into her handbag for her notebook.

"Oh, good God!"

"What? What?" said Kate who was swiftly joined by Geoff.

"She actually said that in some ways she felt fortunate as although David was rough, he did not really assault her physically or sexually *like the other poor girl*. I think she may have been referring to Elly Bridgeman. I think we can safely say she knew all about her."

"Bloody hell, Harriet, you need to speak to Peter Brookes and Derek

184

Wynn," said Geoff.

"No, *we* need to speak to them. Come on, now's as good a time as any."

As luck would have it, Derek and Peter Brookes were meeting in Derek's office at police headquarters.

"Good to see you all, please come in," said Derek, opening the door to his office.

"Apologies for the invasion, but we need to speak to you both about some crucial developments in Operation Juliet. I'm going to ask Geoff and Kate to bring you up to speed." Harriet took the seat offered to her.

Geoff and Kate outlined what they'd discovered, detailing the intelligence that had been gleaned from the mobile found with Eve.

"Bloody hell," said Peter Brookes. "This really is explosive and changes everything. We need to alter the course of the investigation. From now on, Eve will need to be treated as a suspect and not a victim."

"Yes, indeed. Under these circumstances, Harriet, what is your initial view of what's required?" asked Derek.

"Well, apart from the obvious, which includes a complete review of all statements and interviews to date and a thorough forensic review, I think it would be sensible to undertake some discreet enquiries into Eve Wilson's movements. Given the mobile intelligence, I would say we have enough to apply for surveillance on her. I'd like to see what she does. Also, I think we need to speak to the prison holding David Wilson to see if he's had any visitors and who his phone calls have been from. He's currently on remand, and I guess he will have realised by now that there is a strong likelihood he will be convicted for the murders of Philip and Archie Wilson. I would also imagine that he might be willing to implicate Eve, if he thinks he is likely to benefit in some way for his cooperation. Perhaps an early 'What if' conversation with CPS might be in order?"

Derek Wynn nodded.

"Also, I've been thinking that the murder of Philip might have been partly about money, principally life insurance. If Eve doesn't know we are suspicious, the family liaison officer could probably find out if she's actively making enquiries into this, without alarming her. In addition, I've asked Geoff to find out from the hospital why Eve was unconscious when we found her. We are hoping her blood work might shed some light on this. The current thinking is that we were never supposed to find the phone, so Eve is somewhat on the back foot. But she is far from stupid, so it won't be long before she will expect to have to account for it. In the light of this we don't have long to pull this together."

"I couldn't agree with you more, Harriet," said Peter Brookes. "I think we have an opportunity here to play David and Eve off against each other. And don't forget that we have other victims too who as of this morning remain unidentified. It's possible that if Eve talks she may tell us more about Elly Bridgeman and possibly the three other female victims found at the farm."

"Yes, I've been thinking about this quite a lot recently, but I've hit a bit of a brick wall. Potentially the victim found in the boot of Eve Wilson's car could have died at the hands of David Wilson, as the timeline fits. In other words, she died whilst he was still at large. However, I saw the initial forensic report for the skeletal victim found with the remnants of black trousers and a purple jumper, this morning. It's estimated that this is a recent re-burial, but that the death occurred potentially thirty years ago. This is concerning for obvious reasons, as David Wilson would have been a young boy then, too young. And then there's the final victim, the body that showed no signs of decomposition. Well, the forensic report is adamant that the death occurred within a seventy-two-hour window of the body being found, which means David Wilson could not be the murderer because we had him in custody at the time."

"Blimey. Shit. So, are you saying we are looking at a second offender?" asked Geoff Harvey.

"I suppose I am saying that, yes. Actually, potentially a further two offenders." Harriet sighed loudly.

No one said anything for several minutes as they tried to process Harriet's words.

"This is extraordinary work, everyone, but time is of the essence," said Derek Wynn. "I'm minded to call a full incident room briefing to get urgent actions allocated to the teams. We very much need to drive this forward, before Eve and/or David realise we are onto them. If we are lucky, we will be able to work it so that they implicate each other."

That same afternoon, everyone working on Operation Juliet gathered together and were told about the new information. Harriet's conversation in the hospital with Eve that led her to be suspicious, the tests on the mobile found with Eve and the discovery of her fingerprints all over it. The nature of the texts between David and Eve which clearly illustrated Eve was the one in control.

"So, Eve Wilson will now be treated as a suspect rather than a victim," said Peter Brookes. "Jonesy, I understand you have something for us?"

"I do indeed," said DS Paul Jones. "I was asked by DS Harvey to liaise with the hospital regarding Eve's blood work and it proved most interesting. It would appear that she may have been suffering from the effects of an overdose of diazepam. Typical signs of this are deep sleep and slowed breathing, which is exactly the state we found her in. I think it's possible she accidentally overdosed, rendering herself incapable. I've thought about why she might have been taking this and it was probably to deal with the cramped cold conditions she was in. But I still think it's unlikely she was there for the entire duration of the staged abduction. It's possible she got confused and overmedicated. It would perhaps explain how we found the mobile phone, for she was simply too medicated to hide or dispose of it."

"That would definitely make sense," said Harriet. "I think it's possible that she meticulously planned this, over a period of time. It was out of character for her to make such an error. The diazepam would explain how this occurred. I think I would like to look into her life before she married Philip Wilson. I'm wondering if she is in fact an accomplished actress."

"I agree, take a look and report back," said Derek Wynn, turning back to address the room. "Okay, so now I'd like to move onto the victims. Steven, any updates?"

Steven Leach leapt up and moved to the front of the room carrying a bundle of papers. "Okay, so Victim number one, the female found in the boot of Eve Wilson's submerged car, was strangled before being placed in the car. At the moment we are looking for forensics on the body to link the crime to David Wilson but the body was submerged in water for some time, which makes it more problematic. David remains the prime suspect, however. The problem I have, and I've discussed it with DS Jones, is that this killing has all the hallmarks of someone who has killed before and by this I mean it appears to have been calculated and well planned which suggests it was not his first and, as you will hear, it's unlikely that the other two victims died at David's hands. First-time killers routinely make mistakes and leave clues and there are none. Based on this, I think there may be at least another body he's responsible for, somewhere on the site." At this everyone started talking at once. Derek Wynn was forced to bang on a table to restore order.

"In short, I would like permission to take another look at the farm site."

"Permission given; I would like Dave Jones to work with you on this as well. Please carry on." said Derek.

"Okay, thank you. Now Victim number two – the skeleton buried with remnants of black trousers and a purple jumper. The evidence suggests that this victim was re-buried recently but died about thirty years ago." Again, the room erupted. And again, Derek had to restore order.

"Sorry to interrupt, but wasn't there also a black handbag found in the grave? Anything from that?" asked DS Harvey.

"Yes, well remembered, Geoff. It was extremely degraded. We are still working on it, but I'm not hopeful of finding anything significant." Steven paused for a moment. "I get that this is all very unsettling. What does it mean? Well, we aren't sure as yet but suffice to say we will be re-examining the evidence. What of Victim number three? Well, the forensics tell us that the victim had been dead for less than seventy-two hours. And this is significant because David Wilson was in custody when this young lady lost her life."

This time there was stunned silence from the room as staff looked at each other in disbelief.

"So we need to check our findings again, and try to discover who is responsible, because it wasn't David Wilson." Steven Leach checked his notebook. "That's all from me."

"Thank you, Steven," said Peter Brookes. "You have given us much to think about. I think I speak for everyone when I say that this case is becoming more and more complex, but I still believe we can solve it. Keep up the good work. Remember we are a team, keep talking to each other. It is the little details that so often crack a case open."

After the briefing Harriet was deep in conversation with Steven Leach when she received a tap on her shoulder. She turned her head to see Derek and Paul Jones standing behind her.

Derek cleared his throat. "Harriet, do you have a minute?" he asked gently. "Would you come to my office for a minute? Steven, you should come too."

Once the door was closed, Derek indicated to Harriet to take a seat. "Harriet, we thought long and hard about whether to raise this with you, but we are not in the business of hiding information and besides I don't think you would forgive us."

"What's going on?" asked Harriet, looking from Derek to Paul Jones and back again.

"Well, earlier this morning a bouquet of flowers and a box of chocolates were delivered for you at the front desk," said Paul. "Luckily the receptionist remembered the directive to contact me regarding all deliveries addressed to you. So, I collected the said items and took them to the lab. As I was examining the flowers for a card, something made me glance at the box of chocolates. You see I was sure it moved."

"Oh my God, I think I know what you're going to say next," said Harriet, wringing her hands. "Go on."

"Well, I called for back-up, and very carefully we opened the chocolate box to find an extremely lively..."

"And no doubt deadly, black mamba snake," said Harriet in a whisper.

"Yes, indeed," said Paul.

"Sorry? Did you just say a black mamba?" interrupted Steven Leach.

"Yep. Cleo Morris liked to assassinate her victims using black mamba venom. To enable her to do so without arousing suspicion, she farmed them."

At this Leach pulled a face and shivered involuntarily.

"Fucking Cleo." Harriet coloured; her top lip was moist with perspiration.

Chapter 19

Feeling more unsettled than she cared to admit by Cleo's latest stunt, Harriet arranged to work from home for the rest of the afternoon. She kept herself busy briefing a couple of detectives on her team. She had asked them to drive to Swindon, as she was keen to know more about Eve Wilson's life before she moved in with Philip. As the afternoon progressed, bits of information started to filter back that began to paint a significantly different Eve to the one she had so carefully cultivated over the years. Timid, church-going Eve was described by one former employer as 'loud, flirty, unreliable, and always broke' and by another as 'a good time girl'. A former friend described her as 'the ultimate party girl, always drunk, always living beyond her means, always thrill seeking'.

A call came through on Harriet's mobile and she glanced at the screen to see it was Mike Taylor.

"How's my favourite detective?" he said.

"Hi, Mike. To be honest, I've been better."

"Well, I'm not bloody surprised. Derek asked me to call you to tell you that he's tasked me with looking into Cleo's latest stunt but also he's asked me to review everything we have on her."

"Well, she's doing a fantastic job of wearing me down. To begin with I was terrified. Now, although she gives me the creeps, I'm angry – no, furious – that she's constantly interrupting my life."

"I completely understand that. But I promise you I will do

192

everything I can to find her."

"I know you will. Thanks, Mike. I am grateful, you know."

"Grateful enough to make an old friend a cup of tea?" The doorbell sounded.

Harriet peered through the viewer to see a beaming Mike, holding a bag of doughnuts.

"My favourite," said Harriet, opening the front door and licking her lips. They hugged warmly, before sauntering into the kitchen.

"I haven't just come to drink your tea," said Mike when they were settled at the table. "I'm also the bearer of some good news."

"You are?" Harriet wiped doughnut sugar from her mouth.

"Yes, I think you'll like this. CPS has agreed to Veronica Morris becoming a participating informant but, as you would expect, they have laid down some conditions. The first is that only a handful of officers are to know about this. The second is that she is to have no contact with you. This is primarily to protect you, just in case she wittingly or unwittingly delivers you into the hands of Cleo. I will run her and report directly to Derek Wynn. Don't pull that face, Derek has already given me the lecture about her being a classy educated woman who will react badly to my rough diamond routine. So, I have promised to be professional at all times."

"Ha, ha, how are you going to manage, Mike?" Harriet could not keep a straight face.

"What do you mean? Okay, yes, it's going to be bloody purgatory." Mike stuck his tongue out.

"And the other conditions?"

"She cannot travel anywhere other than locally without first running it past me. And I will need to travel with her. CPS will look at the case against her in relation to any offences she's committed, the obvious being assisting an offender and perverting the course of justice, with a view to prosecuting her. But they have said there is strong mitigation in this case and indicated that, subject to there being no further surprises, they could be persuaded to push for a suspended sentence. Lastly, as you requested, she must agree to explain in person to Henry and Kate Squires the circumstances of Ella Squires' death."

"Oh, gosh, I really hope that goes well, and that they aren't too angry and upset. I hope Kate won't be offended that I did not tell her immediately I found out. Will Cyrus be present?"

"Yes, don't worry, Cyrus will be there, along with Derek. And I'm sure Kate will be fine, just relieved to find out the truth at long last. Don't stress about it."

"Okay, thanks, Mike."

Just then Harriet's phone pinged. She glanced at it. A WhatsApp message from the detectives in Swindon containing a photo. Harriet clicked on it and gulped.

"Everything alright?" asked Mike.

"Yes, this is a photo of Eve Wilson sitting on the lap of a man who I'm pretty sure is David Wilson. It was taken about ten years ago."

"He's the geezer on remand for his twin brother's murder, isn't he?"

"That's right. They seem pretty close in the photo. I'm beginning to think Eve has been economical with the truth around the extent of her relationship with David Wilson. It would perhaps explain how she was able to involve him in the murder of his brother."

"Interesting."

"It is. I wish you were working on it with us, as it's the sort of case that just keeps giving!"

Harriet spent another couple of days working from home. She still felt emotional and could not trust herself to hold it together. Late in the afternoon on the second day, there was a knock at the door. Harriet checked the monitor in the kitchen and was alarmed to see Cyrus, Kate and Henry Squires standing outside. She did not feel like dealing with a scene and, for an instant, she considered hiding but then thought better of it, opening the front door to her unexpected guests.

"Dearest Harriet, if we are not intruding, can we come in a for a minute or so?" asked Cyrus.

"Of course, please do." Harriet was searching their faces for clues. To her relief both Henry and Kate were smiling.

Immediately the front door closed, Kate flung her arms around Harriet, holding her tight.

"Thank you, thank you from the bottom of my heart. Losing Mum was hard enough, but not knowing what happened was far worse, always there in the background, and unresolved until now."

"I'm only sorry that I was unable to tell you immediately I found out, but I'm sure you understand that Veronica's story needed to be corroborated?" said Harriet.

"I do, it's fine, really it is!" said Kate. "I completely understand. Now where are my favourite Lacey offspring?"

Harriet pointed upstairs, and Kate went in search of them.

Henry now stepped forward. He took Harriet's hands in his and looked directly into her eyes. She found herself catching her breath. She could feel her heart beating faster than usual and, although she wasn't exactly uncomfortable, she felt unable to move, completely mesmerised by his gaze. As she waited for him to say something, she took in his scent, and found herself thinking it was utterly compelling.

"Like Kate, I cannot thank you enough. It's hard to describe the agony of losing your soul mate, but to lose Ella in such a violent way and not to know the circumstances of her death was even more torturous. I feel as if a massive weight has been lifted from my shoulders. Despite not wanting to, I absolutely believe Veronica's account of events. It was clearly difficult for her to relive it. Her pain and sense of guilt were clear for all to see. As a father myself, I empathise with her predicament. And I cannot put my hand on my heart and say I would have done differently had I been in her shoes. The important thing now is to apprehend Cleo."

Still holding his gaze, Harriet squeezed his hands but before she could say anything, there was a thunderous sound as Kate, Ben and Amelia bounded into view laughing and joking.

"I think pizza is in order," said an animated Kate.

"Oh, please, please, Mum, can we, can we get pizza in?" pleaded Amelia.

Harriet laughed. "That sounds like a very good idea. Let's see if Derek and Mike are also free to join us, shall we?"

"Yes!" said Ben punching the air. "A pizza party."

Harriet turned to Cyrus and Henry. "My children are easily pleased. Would you care to join us for this culinary feast?"

Both men nodded enthusiastically.

"Good, while I make some calls, Ben and Amelia, please get our guests some drinks." As Harriet moved to one side to use her mobile, she glanced across the room at her children happily chatting and laughing away with their guests. She was proud of her children, for their resilience but also for their zest for life despite all the upheaval of the last year.

It was late when everyone left, but it had been great fun and long overdue. Cyrus stayed behind to help Harriet clear up and talk immediately turned to William of Hertford.

"I have been bursting all evening to tell you about my most recent enquiries. I have managed to track down the curator of the château where Hugh de Payns was lord. It seems that after William of Hertford's father died suddenly and unexpectedly, his mother, Arianne, left Hertford and England with her remaining children and moved back to the family estate in Montigney-les-Monts, a small village twenty-three kilometres from Troyes."

"Good work, Cyrus."

"There's more. The current château stands on the site of the original building, and there is an extensive family library. The curator is a lovely young man called Auguste and he has been researching it for us. I asked him to look specifically at the 1100s."

"And has he found anything relevant?"

"He has, he actually has! A bundle of letters from William to his mother. Your suggestion that we look here was inspired, Harriet."

"Oh, this is fantastic. What do they say, Cyrus? Do they help us at all?"

"Well, I'm waiting for them to be translated, and then I thought we could study them together. I should have them back in the next few days."

"Cyrus, I'm so excited, I can't wait. I know I've said this before, but there is just something compelling about William's story and I know I shouldn't get ahead of myself but I have a gut feeling that there is something significant for us to discover."

"I totally agree. On another matter, my quest to trace Nick, I can report that I have now spoken to both Ben and Amelia and they are indeed in touch with their father. They didn't tell you because they didn't want you to stop the contact, nor did they want to put you in a difficult position, and they did not want to hurt your feelings."

Harriet said nothing for a second or two. "I would never stop them having contact with their father, but I respect their thoughtfulness, though knowing they are in contact does present a dilemma for me. Do I tell Derek Wynn or not?"

"Is that a rhetorical question? Or do you want my opinion?"

"No, I want to know what you think."

"Absolutely yes, you should tell him."

"So, do you know where Nick is and what he's doing?"

"I will do shortly."

"Thank you, Cyrus." After Cyrus had left, Harriet sat in her favourite armchair. It had been her father's and she cherished it. She did not mind that Ben and Amelia were in contact with their father, but she could not see the situation working out well. She would soon have the opportunity to speak to Nick face to face. She wondered how that might go: would he be angry, resentful, would there be any remorse? And, more to the point, she wondered how would she react.

Chapter 20

Present day

Finally, after many long hours of work, they were ready to interview David and Eve Wilson. The plan was simple, they were to be spoken to simultaneously by experienced detectives.

Geoff Harvey took the lead in David's interview. He had a well laid out plan. As David had previously been interviewed and charged with offences, Geoff had to ensure he stuck to new lines of enquiry. Peter Brookes took the lead in the questioning of Eve. Derek Wynn, SIO, had decided that Harriet should not be present at either. In his words she was their "secret weapon" and, when he was asked to explain this, he simply said, "Harriet has the unique ability to get under people's skin". Harriet had laughed along with everyone else but later worried that Derek might not have meant this as a compliment.

David's interview took place at Belmarsh Prison where he'd been remanded, Eve's at Church Lane Police Station. It was about three o'clock in the afternoon when the teams returned. Derek lost no time in convening a debrief. Harriet, Paul Jones and Steven Leach were included in this.

"I apologise for dragging you all straight into a meeting, but time is of the essence and I am keen to discover how you got on. Geoff, can you feedback first, please?"

"Yes, of course. I'd like to start by saying that this was one of the most compelling interviews I've ever been involved with. Quite apart from the surprise of discovering David was keen to talk rather than stick to a 'no comment' stance. I think he genuinely wanted to unburden himself. It's probably best if I highlight his key revelations.

"I started by asking him about his relationship with Eve, how had they met, how long had they known each other, and so on. He told us they'd met as teenagers, at school and had a short but passionate sexual relationship. He said she was a 'nutter', full of life and fun, made him laugh, took his mind off his home life. He was reluctant to talk about his childhood, other than to say it was difficult. When pushed, he said his mum had left suddenly when he was about eight years old, his dad never had any money, was bad tempered and violent and spent any money he did have on booze. He was pretty matter-of-fact about how he and his siblings were left to their own devices and said he did not attend school for about two years. They lived at the farm until they were about ten when his mother's parents intervened and took them in. His father died a year later. When I told him Eve had claimed she left him for Philip, he banged the table in anger and called her a liar. He was adamant that she'd gone out with Philip first, but complained he was boring, before swapping allegiance to him. When I asked him why their relationship ended, he blushed and scowled before saying she simply found someone else. He would not say whom. They met again years later in Swindon. He was working in a call centre; she was working in a series of cafés and bars. They hung out together for a while."

"What's your opinion of David's feelings towards Eve?" asked Harriet.

"I would say that without a doubt he's in love with her, always has been."

"And therefore, vulnerable to her charms?"

"Oh yes."

"But to the extent you think he would have risked everything to kill for her?" asked Derek.

"Yes, I would say so. In fact, he pretty much said so later in the interview, after we'd told him about the discovery of her mobile phone and its contents."

"Are we talking here about a love triangle?" asked Peter Brookes.

"Not in the normal sense. I don't think Philip Wilson had any knowledge of the relationship between his twin and his wife. From everything we do know about him he was a kind, decent, hard-working man with limited aspirations who wanted nothing more than to raise a family. I think he was blind – no that's not the right word, clueless – to what was going on under his nose."

"I'm sorry, Geoff, did you say that David's mother left suddenly?" asked Harriet.

"I did."

"Okay, maybe I'm reading too much into this but, with my domestic abuse hat on, what do we know about this family? Has anyone looked for old reports relating to them? Was David's mother reported as a missing person?"

"That's a good point, Harriet, I will get this actioned right away," said Derek. "Just to be clear, are you suggesting that Mrs Wilson, David's mother, may have come to some harm at the hands of her husband?"

"I think we should at least pursue this line of enquiry, if only to eliminate it. Forensically, Paul and Steven, is it at all possible to harvest DNA specifically from the skeleton found with the remnants of the black trousers and purple jumper and compare it to David's?"

"Theoretically, it should be reasonably straightforward," said Paul. "However, this body was moved from its original resting place, for whatever reason. It would be easier if it hadn't. Without being too gruesome, the original site is likely to be richer in terms of DNA samples."

"Okay, please organise for these tests to be carried out urgently." Derek wrote a note in his folder. "Please continue, Geoff."

"Okay, well, perhaps we should stay with the topic of the victims found at the farm. We did not talk about the body found in the boot of the submerged car, for as you know, despite not finding any DNA on the body in respect of David, we had CCTV footage of him driving the vehicle, his blood in the car from his bloody nose, plus, the vehicle was found in the pond of his family farm. With that level of circumstantial evidence, he was charged with that murder. But when I asked him if he knew anything about the skeleton and why it had been moved, he grinned and just said, "Perhaps". He would not be drawn further. But if you are right, Paul, about David having killed more than once, it's possible that the original resting place for the lady with the purple jumper was re-used for another body, although why that would be I have no idea."

"To dig a deep enough trench to bury a body takes time and effort," said Steven. "If there is one that has already been dug, you can re-use it. And the grave in which the skeleton was found was remarkably shallow, quite simply because it didn't need to be deep."

"So, reading between the lines, Geoff, do you think there is another victim of David's at the farm to be found?" asked Derek.

"I do, and I did ask him if he would tell us where to look. Again, he grinned and said, *'an apple never falls far from the tree'*. I have no idea what that means."

While Geoff was speaking Paul Jones and Steven Leach were busy poring over aerial photographs of the site.

"I think I know where to look for this body," said Paul Jones.

"Where?" asked Geoff.

"In the vicinity of the large apple tree which stands in what was the farmhouse garden. The garden is totally overgrown. We will need a digger."

"Definitely worth a look," said Derek.

"I then asked him about the third body, the one that he could not have been responsible for. I asked if he had any idea whose work it might be, and asked if he'd been running with an accomplice? David said nothing for a minute or two, as if he were carefully thinking through his response, then he said, *'they made a wish and three came true'*. He refused to say any more on the matter, and I have no idea what he meant."

"How bizarre, what does that mean? Anyone?" asked Derek. The room was silent.

"Lastly, the interview focused on the murder of Eve's husband and David's brother. Now as you know, David has been charged with this, so my line of questioning was around Eve's involvement and to my surprise David was quite forthcoming. Harriet, you were right to suspect money as the prime motivation, specifically life insurance. David says Eve persuaded Philip to take out a hefty life insurance policy on the grounds that the family he so adored would be financially secure should anything happen to him. That was about a year before his death. Eve, he said, has always lived beyond her means. She persuaded David to help her get rid of Philip by offering him half of the life insurance. David said he was never close to Philip, who was the quiet one, always had his head in a book, a studious child. David agreed to help Eve as he was desperate for the money to cover huge gambling debts. He also said that Eve promised they would start a new life together and he was powerless to resist her. But as soon as the deed was done things began to fall apart between them, and their physical relationship ended. His description of the actual murder contradicts Eve's version of events. I won't say anything further about this now, I'd like to hear what Eve has to say about it first."

"Essentially, do you believe his account?" asked Derek.

"I do, sir. David is childlike, he is emotionally immature, and damaged. I think he was hoodwinked by Eve, who is bright, calculating and determined. That's not to say that he isn't responsible for his actions."

"Interesting, very interesting. Does anyone else have any questions for Geoff before we move on to Eve's interview?" asked Derek.

"I'm just wondering why he chose to be so accommodating when he wasn't actually offered a deal of any kind? What was in it for him?" asked Harriet.

"I know, that's been troubling me too. Perhaps he sees it as an opportunity to ensure that Eve doesn't get away with her part in the sorry saga?" suggested Geoff.

"Perhaps," said Harriet, frowning.

"Okay, Pete, let's move onto Eve's interview. How did you get on?" asked Derek.

"From the word go, it was a disaster in terms of information gathering. Eve completely stonewalled us. 'No comment' was her answer throughout. She showed no emotion whatsoever. Despite my best efforts, I could not get her to engage."

"That's really disappointing but not wholly unexpected," said Derek, turning to Harriet. "How'd you like to have a go? I have a gut feeling you will be able to get to her to talk. It can be about anything to start with: try to get her to divert from this 'no comment' position she's been sticking to. You're ideally placed, as you've already spoken to her and also looked into her background. Push her buttons. See if you can get a reaction."

"No pressure then!" said Harriet, chewing her thumb nail.

"It's nothing you can't handle." Derek winked. "Pete, before you go home for the day, I'd like you to work with Harriet to put together an interview plan for the morning. I'm going to invite Eve in for another interview under caution at 9 am."

"What if she refuses?" asked Peter Brookes.

"Then I'll have to decide if we have sufficient to arrest her."

Early next morning Harriet was busy applying her make-up when her work mobile sprang into action. Grabbing it from her bedside table she saw it was Derek Wynn.

"I'm so sorry to ring you at home, but we have a huge fucking problem."

Derek Wynn rarely swore.

"Really? What's happened?" asked Harriet, aware of a sinking feeling in the pit of her stomach.

"David Wilson topped himself in his cell in the early hours of this morning."

"Shit. Shit!"

"Exactly."

"How?"

"It seems he plaited his bed sheets into a noose, tied this to the window bars, as high as he could reach and then sat down. He was found lifeless at about 7 am."

"Oh my God. I understand why he was held on remand in Belmarsh, because of the seriousness of the offences and because of the press interest surrounding the case, but why wasn't he checked during the night?"

"Because there was absolutely no indication that he was a suicide risk. He was not considered vulnerable, he displayed no suicidal tendencies of any kind, there were no signs to indicate staff needed to be concerned."

"Do you have any more detail?"

"The specifics are somewhat sketchy at the moment; I'll know more later. What I have been told is that when his body was discovered, the Code Blue alarm was activated, as is the protocol, and the duty nurse informed, along with response officers. They attended and David's body was cut down immediately. Unfortunately, there was no CPR to be done. He'd been dead for a while. His body had a grey hue to it, and his eyes were bulging and bloodshot. The duty nurse confirmed life extinct and called an ambulance. The cell has been sealed off, for further forensic examination."

"A pretty gruesome scene. I don't suppose he left a note?"

"Well, not in the usual sense. He cut himself with a razor blade he'd managed to smuggle into his cell and wrote a cryptic message in his blood on the wall."

"What did it say?" Harriet shifted to the edge of the bed.

"'*Two down, one to go.*' Does that mean anything to you?"

"Not really, unless of course he was referring to Eve as the third. Philip, David, Eve?"

"Maybe."

"Where does this leave us now, in terms of the interview with Eve?" asked Harriet.

Derek didn't immediately reply.

"I think we continue as planned. Don't tell Eve about David unless you feel you have to."

"Okay, I'll give it my best shot, but I'm not convinced she will take the bait. She's far cleverer than she portrays."

"But, I suspect, not as clever as her interviewer. Harriet, I have complete faith in you. Good luck."

Chapter 21

Eve Wilson was clearly grumpy. Although she'd agreed to a second interview, Harriet could tell by her demeanour she did not want to be there. But Harriet guessed that she had not dared to refuse as she needed to establish how much the police knew and potentially how much trouble she might be in.

Harriet's starting point was to strike up a friendly conversation, to check facts, not to challenge Eve's story until she was ready. She started by asking after Eve's little daughter, Chloe, and enquiring as to how she herself was feeling and whether she had enough support around her. Eve lapped this up and very soon the clenched hands had released and she was sitting back in her chair sipping some water. Next, Harriet engineered the conversation around to casually re-checking facts, and again Eve was happy to oblige as the interview had the feeling of a cosy chat.

Gradually, Harriet began to talk about David Wilson, explaining that there were some discrepancies between his account and Eve's and, much to Harriet's relief, Eve appeared happy to chat, and did not revert to her 'no comment' stance of the day before. Clearly curiosity had got the better of her.

"Eve, David was adamant that as a teenager you went out with Philip first, dumping him for David."

"What does it matter what order it was in?"

"It seemed to matter to David very much. He was clearly besotted

208

with you, described you as a 'nutter', full of life and fun."

Eve's face broke into a smile. "Yeah, we were a bit mad together, just childish stuff, until I met someone else…"

"Ah, yes, I was about to come onto that. Who was that?"

A flicker of something crossed Eve's face – was it panic?

"I'd rather not say."

"David wouldn't either."

Eve's face cracked into a smile.

"David clearly had extremely strong feelings for you."

Eve said nothing.

"I'm curious to understand what led to David's behaviour becoming, how should I put it…?"

"Sexually deviant?"

"Well, I suppose that's as good a description as any, yes, becoming sexually deviant. You've known him a long time. Are you able to shed any light on this?"

"He's always been a bit weird. When I first went out with him, he was exciting, naughty, we would often bilk together. You know what I mean? Run out of cafés without paying, steal milk off doorsteps, not pay for petrol for his motorbike. Don't get me wrong, he could be charming, they could all be charming, but when it came to sex he was rough. He used to hit me, slap me, and he would never look at me, sex was always from behind, if you know what I mean?"

Harriet nodded.

"I quite liked rough sex. It made me feel alive."

"Where do you think David learned that behaviour?" asked Harriet.

"I'm guessing his father. He was a very good-looking man, but a nasty, vicious individual. There were always young women at the farm. He was violent towards the boys. He often hit them. I think he had a profound hold over David in particular. But, having said that, David was absolutely devastated when his mother left, kept a photo of her in his wallet. Sometimes when he got drunk, he would get it out and weep, proper cry over it. To be honest, drink and David did not go well together. His character would change, he'd often become volatile, excitable and violent. I would always make sure I left as soon as he started to cry."

"When you say he became volatile and violent, can you elaborate at all?"

"Yeah, he would become agitated and start swearing and shouting and saying things like 'all women are sluts and slags'. Once or twice he put his hands around my throat and squeezed really tight. On one occasion, I had to kick him in the balls and make a run for it."

"What about Philip's character?" asked Harriet.

"Well, Philip was different – he was always reading. I'm not sure he was aware of what was going on, certainly he wasn't worldly wise. To be honest he was boring, loved birdwatching, golf and walking in the park. When I went out with him as a teenager, it was walks to the park for ice-cream and awkward fumbling, if you know what I mean?"

"So, you went from Philip to David and then moved on again."

"Got my heart broken in the process, though."

Harriet noticed two things: Eve had not contradicted her this time, so Harriet assumed David had been correct that Eve had gone out with Philip before moving onto him. And, secondly, as she watched Eve, she could see a distant look in her eyes, a real sadness, which seemed to fill the room.

"Who was he, Eve?"

"I thought he was the one." Eve's face was strained, drained of colour; beads of sweat had formed across her top lip. Harriet noticed her voice had begun to falter. As much as Harriet disliked Eve, she couldn't help but feel sympathy for her obvious pain. She guessed that, whoever the guy was, he had well and truly broken Eve's young heart, and she had never recovered.

"Do you ever see him?"

"No. Well, I mean, sometimes. I didn't for a long time, several years, but then about a year ago he reappeared in the area. Completely blanked me, though, as if I'd never existed."

"That must have made you sad."

"I was devastated. I still don't know why our relationship ended."

"What's his name?" asked Harriet.

A weird little smile spread across Eve's face, as if to say I know and I'm not telling.

"I'm not prepared to say. I'm not sure why you are so interested anyway. I went out with many boys in my teenage years."

As Eve began to talk about her past love life, in more detail than Harriet cared to dwell on, Harriet found herself looking at her scribbled notes and something caught her eye, something Eve had said earlier. *They could all be charming.* And suddenly she had a thought, which would not wait, she just had to check it out.

"Eve, I'm so sorry to interrupt you," said Harriet, deliberately looking at her mobile. "But I'm going to have to stop the interview briefly.

The time is now 1000hrs."

Mr Moses, Eve's solicitor, a rather overweight and dishevelled man in his late fifties, looked startled, for he had just awoken from a nap.

"Eve, Mr Moses, why don't you grab a coffee? I'm afraid we need to have a short break, as I'm needed elsewhere."

"Sounds intriguing," said Eve, evidently perfectly happy with the arrangements.

Harriet left Eve and Mr Moses in the care of a colleague, while she made her way to the exhibits store for Operation Juliet. She soon found what she was looking for and signed out several photos which she took back to her desk in the incident room. Carefully, she laid them out on her desk.

"Oh, good God!" she exclaimed, staring at the last photo in her hand.

Before anyone could ask her what was up, she hastily grabbed the photos, and left, making her way down the corridor to a door marked SIO. Harriet knocked loudly, but did not wait to be invited in.

"Sir, I'm so sorry to barge in like this, but I urgently need to speak with you."

"It's no problem. Peter and I had pretty much finished." Derek indicated to Harriet to take a seat. Peter Brookes smiled and stood up.

"Peter, I think you should hear this too."
Peter sat back down.

"Ready when you are," said Derek.

"Right, well, I've stopped Eve's interview. She's gone for a coffee. I did so because she said something early on about the Wilson boys which I didn't immediately register. However, I subsequently glanced at my notes and realised its importance, and I quote: *'they could all be charming'*."

Derek and Peter looked confused, confirming to Harriet that they did not yet understand the significance.

"That is not a phrase you use when talking about two individuals. You would most likely say *'they could both be charming'*. Anyway, I suddenly remembered that whilst conducting a Section 18 search of David Wilson's address following his arrest, we found some old faded photos and correspondence relating to Rock Farm which we hadn't yet got around to studying in any detail. Well, amongst the photos is this one." Harriet held it up. It showed a smiling young couple with their hands on the shoulders of not one, not two, but three identical little boys.

"Oh, bloody hell. Triplets?" asked a wide-eyed Derek.

"Yes, it really looks like it," replied Harriet.

"Good grief, that could have a significant impact on the case." Peter had got to his feet.

"I know! And I'm now thinking that David's cryptic message in blood might refer to this. *'Two down, one to go.'*"

"Phenomenally good work, Harriet," said Derek.

"Yes, absolutely. Are you going to ask Eve about the third brother?" asked Peter Brookes.

"I doubt she will tell us; I've already established he broke her heart. So far she is refusing to divulge his name."

"Fair enough," replied Peter.

"I do need a favour, however. Can you get a team to scour the rest of the photos and paperwork for any more clues and get someone to go to the registry office to look through births, marriages and death certificates please?"

Derek nodded.

"Oh, and there is something else. Eve has suggested that David was profoundly affected by his mother's sudden departure and never recovered from her loss. Apparently he kept a photo of her in his wallet. Can we get our prison liaison officer to contact the prison to see if they can locate it for us?"

"Will do. And I think we should call a briefing as soon as possible, with scenes of crime. I suspect that this information will increase their workload greatly." Derek got up from his desk, stretched and walked to the window.

"By the way, Cleo is outside. I've just spotted her staring up at the window," said Harriet.

"What the hell?" Derek scanned the crowded pavement below and, sure enough, there she was by a lamppost. Peter Brookes joined him. Derek reached for his radio and in no time officers were dispatched to effect an arrest.

"How have you managed to stay so composed?" asked Derek.

"I don't really know. Maybe I'm just getting tired of her constant games. Maybe I no longer want to play. You know you won't get her? She's wily. I bet she's already disappeared." Harriet waved at them as she exited the office.

A short time later Derek was informed that officers had indeed been unable to locate the suspect.

"How did Harriet know that would be the result?" he asked Peter.

"Well, I guess after all this time, and their history, they know each other pretty well."

The interview re-commenced less than an hour after it had been halted. Harriet continued to clarify points from Eve's statements.

"In your first statement," said Harriet, "you said David killed Philip out of the blue, that you had no idea he was planning it, that you were as surprised as poor Philip and that you were taken against your will and imprisoned in the dark for days with no contact."

"Yes, that's right. David is a very disturbed individual."

"The thing is, Eve, I'm having a hard time believing that David was capable of organising Philip's death. It was meticulously planned. David was unreliable and disorganised except for his flat, which he kept obsessively clean, almost sterile. And it's very clear that you were communicating with David during the days that followed Philip's death."

"Oh, he's so lying if he told you that. He's a devious man. And you've no proof of any contact. I've told you that was not my mobile phone you found."

"The thing is, Eve, your fingerprints are all over the phone, and there are numerous text messages between you. In interview David gave us a credible account of events, the details of which we are now checking. He also confirmed what I'd long suspected that, far from being incarcerated at Rock Farm for the entire time, you spent some considerable time at his flat."

Aware that Eve was glaring at her with arms folded across her chest, Harriet guessed the interview was about to enter a new phase.

"You see, Eve, I don't think David was lying in interview. I think he was unburdening himself. Ever since he was a teenager, he has loved you with a passion, even though you were in love with his brother."

"I was never in love with boring Philip," spat Eve.

"I wasn't talking about Philip."

"What, Joe? Damn it. Fuck it!"

"Yes, indeed."

Eve leapt to her feet and slammed both hands down on the desk. "You fucking bitch, you absolute fucking bitch."

"Mrs Wilson, can I have a word?" said Mr Moses, his voice higher in pitch than normal.

"No, you fucking can't." Mr Moses sat back down, retreating into his notebook, as sweat patches appeared on his light grey jacket.

"I'm not saying another word to you, you fucking cow."

"According to David, things went down a little differently than you would have us believe. David attests that, far from trying to help poor Philip, you were fighting with him to prevent him stemming the flow of blood from his neck and it was your shouting that woke up Archie. David maintains Archie's death was a mistake. He was trying to keep him quiet and used too much force, resulting in his suffocation. He says he panicked and the pair of you fought in the kitchen, during which you elbowed him in the nose, causing a nosebleed."

"Fucking lies from an absolute imbecile. There's no way you can prove this rubbish."

"All his adult life David has done as you asked, believing that one day you would have a future together, that is until he realised you'd got what you wanted with Philip's death. Now, you counted on David remaining loyal, but long hours on remand helped the penny to drop. He figured out that you were going to let him take the blame. When you failed to visit him as promised, he realised you never intended him to see a single penny of the share of the life insurance you'd promised him." Harriet sat back in her chair.

Eve had her hands on her hips and her face was flushed. Was she hot or was this fury? Harriet wondered.

"So, here's what I know about you, Eve Wilson. Far from being the devout Christian wife and patient teaching assistant you've portrayed with such aplomb, you are in fact an atheist, a party girl. You have no time for children, you like the high life and have routinely lived beyond your means. You've never been interested in settling down, you simply saw Philip as a meal ticket, a means to an end, an opportunity to make money. I'll give you one thing, though; you are a truly accomplished actress." As Harriet stopped speaking Eve swung at her, with a clenched fist, but Harriet was too quick and managed to block her hand in mid-air.

"You think you're so fucking clever, but you're not. No court is going to believe socially awkward David. He will make a terrible witness." Eve was screaming at the top of her voice.

"Eve May Wilson, I'm arresting you for your involvement in the murder of Philip Wilson. You do not have to say anything. But it may harm your defence if you do not mention when questioned anything you later rely on in court. Do you understand?"

"You can fuck right off. You'll see, David will take the blame. He loves me, me! Do you understand?" Eve had a defiant look about her.

"I have no doubt that he loved you but, unfortunately, Eve, we will never know the nature or extent of his evidence, because he was found dead this morning."

Eve let out a howl before punching the wall repetitively. Despite her diminutive size, it took several officers to restrain her. Were the tears for David or her? Harriet pondered.

Harriet wasted no time in seeking out Derek Wynn. She found him in his office. It took over an hour to update him. They discussed the way forward, deciding that a full incident room briefing should be convened as soon as possible in order to understand where they were with the multitude of enquiries and indeed what was still outstanding. Harriet told him she was pretty sure there would be further charges for Eve which would probably include attempting to pervert the course of justice.

Just as Harriet was about to leave his office, she turned back to face him. "Derek, there's something I need to tell you."

"That sounds ominous."

"I suppose in a way it is. I've recently learned from Cyrus Hart that my children are in contact with their father. I understand Nick sends them postcards from abroad, and sometimes includes a return address, but it seems he is always on the move. The children didn't tell me because they didn't want me to stop the contact nor did they want me to be compromised."

"Blimey, well, that seems incredibly thoughtful of Ben and Amelia. Thank you for sharing this with me. Do you have any objections if I take a look at the postcards?'

"No, that would be fine. Thanks for your kind and measured response. My life is complicated enough and I thought you might at best find this irritating, at worst see it as a serious issue. Just so that you know, I've asked Cyrus to try to locate Nick. I will of course keep you in the loop."

Chapter 22

Present day

Next evening Cyrus prepared dinner for Harriet and Henry in his state-of-the-art kitchen. His house was not what Harriet had expected. From the outside it was a character Edwardian townhouse; inside, however, it was modern and light and extremely stylish. Lots of glass and light, decorated in subtle shades of grey. It was beautifully styled, with large comfy sofas and lamps, paintings and artwork in every room, but in no way was it overcrowded. Harriet was in good spirits and, although she would never admit it, extremely pleased to see Henry again.

After a delicious dinner consisting of heritage tomato salad, fillet steak with a peppercorn sauce and triple cooked chips and a home-made sherry trifle, they moved into the library, where Cyrus proceeded to pour three large brandies and light an enormous cigar. The talk naturally turned to his quest.

"I'm so excited to share the transcripts of the letters found at Montigney-les-Monts with you both," he said as he distributed a wad of letters between them. There was silence as they read their way through what amounted to fifteen letters in all. Harriet was the first to speak.

"These give a breathtaking insight into William and his world. They shed light on some of the challenges he and his fellow Knights faced. You start to get a real feel for his life and his struggles. And there are tantalising references to individuals he clearly had extremely strong feelings for, such as his manservant, Zafir, the old woman, Salma, his mentor and friend

Thierry of Tyre and the mysterious Rabia. Does anyone else think he had feelings for Rabia?"

"Absolutely," said a smiling Henry. "He mentions Rabia far too often in his letters for there not to be a deep connection. Friendship or attraction perhaps? But, at the same time, I get the feeling that this friendship caused him some inner turmoil."

"I totally agree," said Harriet.

"Everything we've learned so far about William of Hertford," said Cyrus, "leads me to believe he was a man of God, a man of honour and integrity. I do not believe that at the time these letters were written there was anything more than a deep respect and friendship between William and Rabia."

"I agree with you, mate," said Henry. "I think there is wistfulness and reflectiveness to his later letters but, frustratingly for us, it's unlikely we will ever know the truth."

"Yes, but I also detect a guardedness, perhaps even antipathy, towards King Richard the Lionheart," said Harriet.

"Do you think so? I missed that; can you show me?" Cyrus moved to the edge of his chair.

"Yes, sure, just a minute, let me see... ah yes, here it is. In June 1191 in a letter to his mother, William describes how he struggled to be energised by the king's call to arms for the third crusade. He mentions feeling wearier than he's ever done. He also tells her that years of terrible suffering not just for those fighting in the crusades but also for the local population have taken their toll. And then he says that with the experience of age he's recognised that life, indeed faith, is complicated. Man, he says, has a nasty habit of manipulating faith for his own ends. I took it, perhaps mistakenly, to mean that he was criticising the king."

"Fascinating." Cyrus jumped to his feet. "Of course, one should remember that by this time William had been fighting in the crusades for nearly twenty years. And then along comes this upstart, the new King of England, young, fresh-faced, inexperienced and perhaps overconfident. It must have been galling in the extreme to hear him boast about his ambitious plans." Cyrus drew heavily on his cigar.

"I couldn't agree more with you, Cyrus," said Henry.

"Of course, what these letters don't help with in any way is deciphering the map. So, I've been wondering if it's worth travelling to France, to Troyes and then on to Payns, which is about ten kilometres from there, to the ancestral home in Montigney-les-Monts to see if we can uncover anything else to help us."

"I think that's a really good plan, Cyrus, but I'm really sorry, I can't come with you at the moment. I'm up to my eyes in this murder case. I'm not sure what your commitments are, Henry? Maybe if you're free you could go ahead with Cyrus and then I could join you both when I'm able to in a couple of weeks."

"I think I could probably make time in my schedule. After all, I haven't taken any leave for at least a year. That's a great idea. What do you think, Cyrus?"

"I can't wait, old man. I'm so excited. Who knows where this may lead?"

"Indeed." A smiling Henry locked eyes with Harriet who was unable, or truth be told, unwilling to break contact but then Cyrus stood up and began to pour more brandy and the moment was gone.

"Oh, not for me, thank you, Cyrus." Harriet got to her feet. "I'm going to have to take my leave. There's an important briefing tomorrow morning that I need to prepare for. Thank you both for a wonderful evening."

In the back of the taxi on the way home, Harriet wondered if there had been any significance to Henry's gaze. Perhaps she had misunderstood? After all, it had been a while since she'd been aware of any man looking at her in that way. In fact, now she came to think of it, she couldn't ever remember a time when Nick had. And even Derek Wynn's attention had definitely been less passionate than tonight's encounter had felt. Perhaps Henry was just intrigued? Or could it be that he was attracted to her? Harriet felt herself blush in the darkness of the taxi's rear seat.

Next morning, the briefing started early, just before 8am. Derek Wynn made sure everyone had tea or coffee before commencing and spent an hour bringing everyone up to speed, summarising the latest developments. It was possible to hear a pin drop, so compelling was the subject matter. But there were two occasions when the room ignited into chaos: first when the SIO mentioned David Wilson's suicide and second when they were told that David and Philip Wilson were in fact triplets, that there was a third brother, Joseph, or Joe, the name Eve Wilson used for him.

"Okay, everyone, I now want to move on. I'd like to concentrate on the identification of the deceased found at Rock Farm and, to this end, I'd like scenes of crime to fill us all in, please. Can I ask that you summarise at this stage as we have much ground to cover and will have the opportunity to look at everything in greater detail later?"

Steven Leach and Paul Jones nodded, then got to their feet and made their way to the front of the room.

"Over the last few days," said Steven, "we have been looking at an area of overgrown garden at Rock Farm and within the vicinity of the old apple tree we found the body of a female. We have since identified her as one Caroline James, aged twenty-five, five foot six inches tall, brunette, and of slight build. A postwoman from Stevenage. Early tests estimate that she died from head trauma and has been dead a matter of weeks but definitely less than three months. Her next of kin have been informed."

"We are pretty certain that Caroline was the victim of David Wilson," said Paul Jones. "We found his DNA under her fingernails. We are working on the assumption that the female skeleton found behind the barn or old milking parlour in the shallow grave was moved there from the apple tree grave to make room for Caroline. We think David needed to hide the body hastily due to the huge police operation surrounding the murder of his brother Philip and disappearance of Eve. It took far less effort to dig a shallow grave for the skeleton than for a freshly killed corpse. And there is evidence of soil transfer between the two sites."

"Sorry to interrupt, but you said you found David's DNA under Caroline's fingernails? How do you know the DNA didn't belong to his brother, Joseph?" asked Harriet.

"That's a very good point and I'll try to explain. Identical triplets come from a monozygotic pregnancy, that's three foetuses resulting from one egg. It is extremely rare and results when the original egg splits and then one of the resultant cells splits again. The resulting children do not have matching fingerprints, but they do share the same genetic blueprint, so, to a standard DNA test they are indistinguishable. However, the chemical structure of DNA can change, and this affects how active certain genes are based on diet and lifestyle differences, so identical triplets who have lived different lifestyles can be genetically distinguished. Basically, the way the gene is expressed is altered without altering the underlying genetic sequence. Now, we know that David did not exercise, drank heavily and ate a diet high in fat and processed foods. We are pretty confident that he was responsible for Caroline's death. Further ongoing tests should confirm this. In respect of the most recent victim, who died whilst David was in police custody, we found DNA which had the same genetic sequence, but showed significant lifestyle differences. The offender is extremely fit, vegetarian and has recently lived in the far east. We are working on the assumption that the offender was Joseph Wilson. Again, more detailed tests should endorse this."

"Bloody hell," said Harriet. "It's absolutely amazing that you can tell all that."

"Outstanding," said Derek, as the room ignited in clapping and cheering for Steven and Paul.

"Thank you, thank you all, but this was very much a team effort, not just Steven and me but a whole team." Paul Jones was smiling.

"There is more to tell you," said Steven Leach. "We have managed to identify the skeletal remains."
The room went deathly quiet.

"Using David Wilson's DNA and also Philip's, we were able to establish without doubt that the skeleton is that of their mother, Josephine Wilson née Arkwright. Cause of death was blunt force trauma to the head;

in other words, she was hit very hard with an unknown object. We estimate she's been dead for approximately twenty-five years."

"That's really good work," said Derek Wynn. "Despite extensive searches with the NHS and social services and of course old police records, we've not been able to find records to corroborate our belief that Josephine Wilson was subject to domestic violence. Too much time has elapsed for any records to still be in existence. But both Eve and David have confirmed in interview that Mr Wilson senior was a violent man who drank heavily. On the balance of probabilities, I think it's likely she met her death at the hands of her abusive husband."

"And there is something else extraordinary," said Paul Jones. "Yesterday, our prison liaison officer handed over the photo David kept of his mother in his wallet and, well, she appears to be wearing the exact same outfit she had on at time of death. Black trousers or slacks and a purple jumper."

"Oh my God." Harriet put her hand over her mouth.

"So, just to summarise," said Peter Brookes. "We believe David Wilson was responsible for the murders of Philip Wilson, Archie Wilson, Caroline James and the body found in the boot of Eve's Ford Fiesta. By the way, have we managed to identify her yet?"

"I believe we have. Paul, can you help?" asked Derek Wynn.

"I can. This was one Vera Cook, aged twenty-seven, a local woman, and a chef by trade. She worked at the Red Lion Inn. We haven't been able to trace any family yet, though. She was approximately five foot five, of slight or slender build, with shoulder length, wavy brunette hair."

"That's good work," said Derek Wynn. "Note to myself to get a team to make enquiries at the Red Lion."

"So that just leaves the other female found behind the barn or milking parlour, believed to be the victim of Joseph Wilson," said Peter Brookes.

"The identification of this body has proved slightly tricky," said Steven Leach. "We think she may have been a French girl by the name of Florence Ballard, who was working locally at the Lotus Wine Bar in town. We are waiting for identification confirmation from the French authorities."

"Good work," said Derek Wynn. "Well, once you have that, let me know, will you? so we can make enquiries at the wine bar."

Steven Leach nodded.

"Can I just ask, is it possible to say how she died?" asked Harriet.

"Caroline James, Vera Cook and Florence Ballard all suffered the same or similar fate to Josephine Wilson, blunt force trauma to the head," said DS Paul Jones. "And it's worth noting that they all bear an uncanny similarity to each other in terms of age, build and hair colouring."

"It's an awful thought but do you think it's possible David and Joseph Wilson were present when their father killed their mother? How common is it for an identical MO to be employed by different killers?" asked Harriet.

"In my experience, not common at all," said Paul Jones. "I think it's highly likely those two eight-year-old boys witnessed the violent death of their mother and suffered significant trauma as a result."

The room was silent for a moment as everyone tried to process this.

"There is one further matter Steven and I would like to bring to your attention," said Paul Jones. "It's rather explosive. Whilst analysing David

Wilson's mobile we found the following clip of video hidden in a file. It should come up on the big screen at any moment. I must warn you it makes grim viewing. Geoff, will you talk everyone through it please?"

"David Wilson must have been standing by the door between the kitchen and lounge as he filmed Eve struggling with Philip on the kitchen floor," said Geoff. "You will notice that, far from trying to stem the flow of blood from his neck as she's claimed on numerous occasions, she is in fact fighting with him and appears to be trying to prevent him from staunching the flow himself. Watch carefully now. As Philip is gasping for breath you can see and hear Eve screaming at him. *Just die, just bloody die!'* I can honestly say that this is one of the most chilling and horrific clips I've ever seen. David Wilson clearly decided he needed an insurance policy: if he was going down, Eve was going down with him. I may have misjudged his capacity to look after himself."

"Thank you, Geoff, thank you, Paul and Steven, your briefing has been enlightening, disturbing and extremely useful," said Derek Wynn. "Before we move on, is there anything else you'd like to add?"
Paul and Steven shook their heads, and quietly returned to their seats.

"In that case, I suggest we all take a minute's silence to remember the victims and their families." Derek Wynn got to his feet; and was immediately joined by everyone else.

Harriet got home close to six that evening to find Ben and Amelia sitting together in the courtyard in the sunshine. On spotting her, they jumped up and greeted her with warm hugs. Ben then disappeared into the kitchen only to re-appear a few minutes later with a glass of white wine.

"Thank you, son, you are a life-saver. Would you like a lager?"

"Thanks, Mum, I would. No more exams!"

"Amelia, would you like a small white wine spritzer?"

"Oh, yeah, that would be great. Can I have an umbrella and cocktail cherry in it?"

Harriet laughed and nodded. She was filled with a mixture of happiness and pride in her children.

"Amelia, something smells delicious. What is it?"

"Roasted vegetables. We're going to have them with couscous."

"That sounds delicious. It's so kind of you."

"You're welcome."

"That sounds decidedly meat-free to me," said Ben, pulling one of his faces.

"Well, it is, but I've put a couple of pork chops and French fries in the oven for you."

"Have you really?"

"Yes."

"You're an alright sister, you are."

Amelia beamed.

After dinner, Ben helped Harriet to wash up and put away the dishes.

"Mum, you know that map you and Cyrus have been obsessing over? Amelia and I were looking at your copy earlier, and we both think it really looks like the map of Odysseus's quest to reach home after some war, might have been the Trojan war. Anyway, it was immortalised in Homer's poem *The Odyssey.*"

"Really? I'm not that familiar with Homer's work. What I mean is, I know of it, but I can't say I've ever studied it. Have you got a copy somewhere?"

"I think one of us has, we both studied it at school. Hang on a minute."

By the time Harriet had re-filled her wine glass, Ben returned with a rather dog-eared textbook in his hand.

"So, can you give me the gist of the story of Odysseus?" Harriet asked.

"Amelia! Come here a minute, will you?" shouted Ben in the direction of the stairs. Thunderous footsteps followed.

"What?"

"Can you quickly and briefly give Mum the basic story of Homer's *Odyssey*? Cos I can't remember it."

"Yeah, sure. So, it's an epic poem written by Homer, about Odysseus' ten-year fight, or maybe struggle is a better word, to get back to his home on the island of Ithaca, after the Trojan war. Unfortunately for him he has to battle supernatural creatures and also face the anger of the gods. While he is trying to get home, his wife, Penelope, and his son, are faced with numerous suitors who are fighting each other for Penelope's hand and the throne. They manage to stall the suitors long enough for Odysseus to return and reinstate his authority."

"Well, thank you very much young lady, expertly explained."

Harriet and Ben sat at the kitchen table to compare the maps.

"Bloody hell. Bloody hell! Ben, you and Amelia are truly amazing. I think you are absolutely right. The trick will be to work out where each of the places on Homer's map actually is. I wonder if William followed it to the letter, or just used it as a guide."

"Or maybe, Mum, it's a red herring."

"Yes, maybe."

"Why don't we compare the two maps, and try to work out where Odysseus and potentially William went?" Ben cleared the table of junk.

"That's a brilliant idea. Okay, where do both maps start?" asked Harriet.

"Well, the first location is Troy, which would make sense if Odysseus had been fighting in the Trojan war. He then sails to Ismarus, which is where? Do you know, Mum?"

"Somewhere in Greece, I think. Hang on a minute, I'll look on the laptop. Okay, it is on the Aegean coast off Thrace. Where did he go next?"

"To somewhere called the Lotus-Eaters. Let's see, the laptop map seems to indicate somewhere in Tunisia. And then to Sicily where he encountered the Cyclops, then to a place called God of the Winds. But God knows where that is." Ben chuckled.

"God might not know, but Google maps might." Harriet giggled. "Let me see, okay, it's not far from Sardinia. Perhaps it was a small island that no longer exists? What do you think?"

Ben screwed up his face and studied all three maps closely. "Possibly. It's really hard to tell."

"Okay, let's leave that for now. Where to next?"

"Looks like somewhere in Italy on the west coast. Then the seventh location is definitely Corsica. The eighth place on the map is on the coast of France, a place called the Land of the Dead."

"Sorry, say that again?"

"The coast of France at a place that looks like it could possibly be

Monaco, or somewhere along the coastline near there."

Harriet took in a sharp intake of breath.

"Mum, what's up?"

"I have absolutely no proof, but I think William may have travelled to see his mother. Oh, Ben, this is so exciting! How far is Monaco from Troyes?"

"Give me a second. It's approximately 550 miles. That's a bloody long way by horse, Mum."

"It is, but William was a determined individual and seemed to have had an extraordinary bond with his mother, Arianne. Where to now?"

"It would seem to Sardinia and then across to Italy again, but this time towards the bottom, maybe one of the coastal ports like Vibo Valentia. Then it appears one of the small islands off the coast of Sicily was the next destination, before the tip of the Italian peninsula. It's really not clear, but it could potentially have been Malta or Gozo. Then they sail to the Tunisian coast again, perhaps to Sousse."

"It that nearly the end of the journey?" asked Harriet who was busy scribbling away.

"Nearly. There is a penultimate stop which looks like Corfu, before Ithaca, Odysseus's home."

"What an absolutely incredible if not highly complex journey. The route doesn't immediately make sense as far as William is concerned. But as you say, he may never have travelled the route at all. Or perhaps he did as a means to evade capture? I don't suppose we will ever know, too much time has elapsed. But at any rate, I can't wait to email Cyrus and Henry. You are so clever, Ben."

"Thanks, Mum, that was actually good fun. You know, there may well be other clues contained on William's map."

"I think you could well be right, Ben."

Chapter 23

A week later, the summer holidays were upon them and Harriet found herself waving Ben and Amelia and their friends off on their train journey to Annie in Sheffield. They were beside themselves with excitement. Ben and his best friends Joe and Matt were to camp in one of Annie's meadows and Amelia and her friend Rosie were going to stay in Annie's annex. Harriet would join them in a couple of weeks.

Before Harriet left for Luton airport for her flight to France, she was summoned to Derek Wynn's office.

"I know you will, but please be extremely careful in France. I have to say that I'm really concerned about Cleo. However, unfortunately, there is no way that I can sanction your protection officers joining you there."

"Derek, don't worry, I'll be extremely vigilant. I feel calmer about Cleo than I have for quite some time. I have no doubt that I will be able to deal with whatever she tries, should she appear."

"Yes, well, don't be complacent because she sure as hell won't be."

"I'll be fine. It's not as if I'm going to be there by myself. I'll be with Cyrus and Henry."

"I know, but I care about you!"

"I know you do. Thank you."

Henry and Cyrus were at Paris-Vatry airport to meet Harriet. As soon as she caught sight of Henry, she felt herself catch her breath and had to give herself a talking to for behaving like a besotted teenager. The problem was that she could not stop thinking about the man. When she was in his company she felt optimistic and happy and could not stop smiling. She wondered if there was something wrong with her. But it was simple really: she just found him captivating.

The sixty-three kilometre drive to Troyes seemed to take no time at all, for Cyrus and Henry had many questions about Harriet and Ben's breakthrough with William's map. As the taxi entered the old part of town Harriet became transfixed by the narrow cobbled streets lined with colourful half-timbered buildings. Her mind drifted to William of Hertford. She wondered if this part of Troyes had been much different in his day, and if indeed he had ever visited. Just then the taxi turned a corner and came to a halt. As Harriet got out of the taxi her face broke into a wide grin.

"The Hotel La Maison de Rhodes," said Cyrus, smiling. "I thought you'd like it; the building dates from the twelfth century and was originally a convent before becoming a Canon's residence. Where the gardens are now was originally a cemetery for the church of Saint Dennis, which no longer exists."

"Oh, Cyrus, it's incredible. Look at all the external timber work, look at the patterns on the plaster, the windows, the stairways!"

Henry and Cyrus were laughing. "I totally agree," said Henry. "It is absolutely beautiful. When you say twelfth century, Cyrus, is that William's period you're referring to?"

"Yes, William was alive in the twelfth century."

"Ah, perfect."

"Indeed, it is! I'm so excited, I really feel we may be on the brink of a breakthrough. Now, come on, young lady, let's get you booked in."

Harriet and Henry exchanged smiles at Cyrus's infectious enthusiasm. But as they made for Reception Harriet stopped in her tracks.

"Cyrus, I can't possibly afford to stay here." Harriet blushed.

"Harriet, you are my guest, I absolutely insist. I am an old man with far too much money. It's my treat. And besides we simply have to stay in the same place in order to keep you safe. I've had my orders!"

"Derek Wynn?"

Cyrus nodded and laughed loudly.

"Well, you are too kind. I feel very humbled by your generosity. But for the record you know I really can look after myself."

"We know you can. But please just indulge Cyrus or he will be impossible to live with." Henry winked at her.

"At least let me buy you both lunch?" said Harriet.

"Now, that sounds perfect." Cyrus linked arms with Harriet and led her into the Reception area.

On entering her room Harriet let out a little squeal. She could not remember ever setting foot in such an exquisite chamber. Light, airy, fragranced by the jasmine in the courtyard outside. The walls, the bed linen, the towels were all soft and of a beautiful magnolia hue. In the centre of the room stood a round table containing a bowl of summer roses. The wooden beams, the bedstead and floor had all been limed. And in her bedroom she had not only a state-of-the-art en suite but also the largest free standing bath she'd ever set eyes on.

"I honestly feel like a princess," she declared, noticing Henry leaning on the door frame watching her. She grinned at him with true unadulterated delight.

Half an hour later, they were seated in a little pavement café with round tables set with red and white checked tablecloths and napkins and large red umbrellas to shield customers from the afternoon sun. Try as she might Harriet could not stop smiling. What a perfect start to her trip, she thought, as she sipped a glass of red wine and watched a group of animated tourists wander past.

Cyrus and Henry were in boisterous mood and amused her with tales of their endeavours. Lunch consisted of three courses, expertly ordered in fluent French by Cyrus. A home-made terrine with onion chutney, local guinea fowl in pastry with potato gratin and crème brulée.

"So, we decided to follow Auguste's suggestion," said Henry, "and visit Troyes Media Library. You will recall Auguste is the librarian at the family château. The library is a really modern example of twentieth-century architecture and yet it holds some of the most important medieval ecclesiastical documents and books including a collection that once belonged to Henry I and his wife, Marie, Countess of Champagne."

"Yes, yes, but guess what, Harriet?" said a very excited Cyrus.

"What?"

"The collection dates from the twelfth century!" said Cyrus with a mouthful of guinea fowl.

"Does it really?" The two men nodded. "That's truly amazing. So, have you found anything about William or his mother yet?"

"Ah, well, no, not yet, but I really think we will." Cyrus was beaming.

"I suggest we go back there this afternoon and continue our search," said Henry.

"Good idea. However, I think I need to stop boozing if we are going to do that." Harriet laughed.

Later that afternoon, Harriet, Cyrus and Henry re-commenced their search for some reference to William or his mother, Arianne. For several hours they laboured. It was approaching five o'clock when Cyrus suddenly jumped to his feet, book in hand.

"You two, I think I've found something! Look here." He beckoned them across. "Two references to Arianne of Troyes and her son, William of Hertford, being received at court in 1193."

"I'm not sure I understand. What court?" asked Harriet.

"It's complicated. I'll try to summarise. Marie was the eldest daughter of King Louis VII of France and Duchess Eleanor of Aquitaine. When their marriage was annulled in 1152 custody of Marie went to her father. Her mother, as an aside, went on to marry King Henry II and became Queen of England. They had children and thus Marie had many half-siblings including King Philip II of France and Richard I or Richard the Lionheart as he is often referred to."

"No? Really?" Harriet leaned in closer.

"Yes. Marie was Richard's half-sister. It's fascinating, isn't it?"

"It is. So, Marie was a princess?"

"Yes, but when she married Henry I, Count of Champagne, in 1164 she also became a Countess. When Henry left for a pilgrimage of the Holy Land and later to fight in the crusades, she remained behind to rule the county and hold court. Troyes is in Champagne, and as Arianne was from an aristocratic family their paths would undoubtedly have crossed at court."

"Do you know what this means? It means that we have documented proof William of Hertford was alive in 1193 and journeyed from the Middle

East to Champagne in France. When Ben and I were comparing William's map with that of Odysseus's we discovered that both maps showed a stop-off in the vicinity of Monaco. I think it's highly likely that William rode north to Troyes to see Arianne."

"That sounds entirely plausible to me," said Cyrus.

Later that evening following dinner at the hotel, the three researchers wandered into medieval Troyes, stopping off at a pavement café to drink coffee and brandies. It was also here that Cyrus enjoyed one of his trademark cigars.

"Over your left shoulder, Cyrus, are a couple of males in dark suits sitting at a table," Harriet said in a whisper. "Don't look, it will be obvious we've clocked them. I noticed them at lunch, they were also in the library, and now they are here. That's too much of a coincidence for me."

"Any idea what they may want with us?" whispered Henry, leaning in towards Harriet.

"A wild guess would be that they know about the map. Is it possible, Cyrus, that its existence is known outside our circle?"

Cyrus frowned and drew heavily on his cigar, sending a plume of smoke out into the warm night air.

"Yes, it's entirely possible. Before I asked for your help, Harriet, I approached an old army friend, retired Colonel Tim Brice. Tim is a scholar of medieval history, but he is also a fanatic. It wasn't until I'd confided in him that I discovered his obsession with the Knights Templar. In one conversation, he divulged his membership of an organisation consisting of like-minded individuals who are convinced they are descended from original twelfth-century Templars. To be honest, I decided to take a step back and keep my distance at this point. Despite what the experts say about there being no evidence of the existence of extreme Templar organisations, I'm afraid I beg to differ. They are dark and underground, and I don't want to think about what their long-term goals are." Cyrus took a large gulp of brandy.

Harriet wondered if Cyrus had told them everything, for he seemed a little rattled. She would pursue this with him again at a later date.

"What do you think we should do about them?" asked Henry.

"I think for the time being we should pretend we are unaware of them and see if they pop up again," said Cyrus.

"What about confronting them?" suggested Harriet.

"What, directly?" asked Henry.

"What do you have in mind?" asked Cyrus, leaning in.

Next morning, Cyrus and Henry wandered into the church of Sainte Madeleine, probably the oldest church left standing in Troyes. They ambled around the building, pausing to admire its famous rood screen, dividing the nave from the choir, now made of stone but originally of wood. They made a point of talking loudly about how important it was.

"Gentlemen, may I ask your interest in my friends over there?" asked Harriet, as she approached two suited males closely observing Cyrus and Henry from a nearby stone pillar. For a moment, they stood rooted to the spot, before walking off in the direction of the main entrance. Harriet walked with them.

"Have you nothing to say?" she asked. "Well, let me give you a bit of advice. Back off."

The two men studiously avoided eye contact and stared ahead as they darted out of the church.

Cyrus and Henry joined Harriet.

"What did they say?" asked Henry.

"Absolutely nothing. They would not engage. But I did surprise them. And, they have been warned off. I also got a good look at them. Both are late thirties, clean shaven, with short dark brown hair, and of slim build. One is slightly taller than the other. I'd say six foot and six foot two. They smelt of aftershave, stale alcohol and French cigarettes. If I didn't think this sounded ridiculous I'd say they were French Secret Service."

"Oh, good God, Harriet! Do you think they'll be back?" Henry looked concerned.

"Only time will tell." Harriet winked at Henry and took Cyrus's arm as they left Sainte Madeleine and walked back into the sunshine.

"Harriet Lacey, you are incorrigible," said Henry under his breath.

"I'll take that as a compliment."

Henry couldn't help but laugh.

Despite them having been warned, Henry spotted the men the following day although the suits had gone and been replaced with jeans and t-shirts. Their trademark sunglasses, however, were still very much in evidence.

On the way to the library that morning, the sleuths decided to stop at a pavement café to discuss how best to rid themselves of their unwanted surveillance. They were sitting in companionable silence in the sunshine mulling over the options when the peace was shattered by a loud male voice behind Harriet.

"Fuck me."

"Well, I don't even need to turn around to know who that is." Harriet got to her feet. "Mike, how lovely to see you. Are you alright?"

"Stubbed me bleeding toe. I'll live."

Harriet gave him a warm hug and Henry grabbed a spare chair from a nearby table. Once Harriet had reacquainted Mike with Cyrus and Henry they sat in silence for a moment or two. Seemingly no one wanted to talk about the significance of Mike's presence.

"Okay, I know I'm not the only one thinking this," said Henry. "But if Mike's here in Troyes that means Veronica's here, and if Veronica's here..."

"Then Cleo is also," Harriet finished.

"Oh, bloody hell, what are we going to do?" Cyrus's brow was furrowed.

"Look, me old muckers, there's no point in panicking. I'm keeping a very close eye on Veronica, and where Veronica goes Cleo almost certainly does too. Albeit in the shadows."

"Where's Veronica now?" asked Henry.

Mike looked at his phone. "She's in the Gucci shop about half a mile from here and, let me see, ah yes, she's currently looking at a pink handbag."

"Let me see." Harriet took Mike's phone. "Oh my God, you're filming her! I take it she's agreed to this?"

"She most certainly has." Mike pretended to look disgruntled.

"Okay, I've got an idea. How friendly is Veronica? What I'm trying to get at is would she agree to help us shake off the two blokes sitting at the table under the town clock, over there?"

"Bloody hell, I thought you lot were over here on a jolly, doing a bit of detective work in between drinking wine and enjoying the sunshine."

"Well, that's what we thought too, old man." Cyrus looked glum. "But it appears we've attracted some unwanted attention. My fault, I fear, but that's another story."

"To be honest, I think Veronica would relish the opportunity to do something other than shop!" said Mike. "And it would also potentially be a great way to keep tabs on Cleo. I'll talk to her over lunch and get back to you."

"Thanks, Mike. Who does Cleo think you are, Mike?"

Mike laughed loudly, before answering. "Unbelievably, Veronica has told Cleo she is having an affair with me and I'm her rich North London bloke. Apparently, I'm loaded."

It was Harriet's turn to laugh now. "Sorry, Mike, but that is funny and is it even conceivable that Veronica would have an affair?"

"Ha, ha! Yes, no need to fret, her husband has had numerous affairs over the years. Cleo has often urged her mother to ditch him. I understand Cleo thinks this is the best move her old mum's made in a very long time. So, we are booked into a very chic hotel with an interconnecting door. Which will remain locked, because I am already spoken for, as you know, Harriet."

"Yes, I know but, really, the webs we weave!"

"Right, well I'd better re-join 'my love' and talk to her. I'm sure she will help. But from now on no more cosy chats in public for us. See you all anon." With that Mike melted into the crowd.

Later that afternoon when Harriet returned to the hotel, she received two key texts: one, although she did not know it, would turn the quest around. The first, however, was from Mike it simply read:

'*Veronica on board, in fact quite excited about the prospect of leading your friends a merry dance. I await further instructions. PS from Veronica: Cleo is frustrated that you are rarely alone. From me: Keep it that way!*'

Harriet smiled but her stomach was churning.

The second text was from Ben:

'*Mum, just a thought, was talking to the boys about your map and the symbols around the edge. Matt says that the Templars were well known for communicating in code and he thinks there are apps you can use to help decipher the symbols. Don't know any more than that, but worth looking at? PS: having an amazing time!*'

Harriet could not contain her excitement and went in search of Henry and Cyrus. She found Cyrus sitting in the hotel garden sipping a cup of tea.

"Cyrus, you look like you have the weight of the world on your shoulders. What's up?"

"Oh, nothing, my dear, other than I feel I'm responsible for the unwanted attention we are receiving."

"Don't be silly. Come on, what's really bothering you? I haven't known you long, but you are clearly a man who is normally forthright and self-confident, so what has happened? You're not your normal self. Has Colonel Tim Brice been threatening you?"

"How in heaven's name did you know?"

"Call it a bit of woman's intuition and a bit of detective skill." Harriet sat down and placed a reassuring hand on Cyrus's arm.

Cyrus picked up his mobile phone and handed it to Harriet. "There are six, no, seven text messages under the name Tim."

As Harriet read her eyes widened and her jaw dropped. "Cyrus, this is unacceptable. Tim Brice is unhinged and dangerous. These are the rantings of a disturbed mind and deserve further scrutiny. Indeed, these are a series of death threats that cannot be ignored. With your permission, I'd like to discuss them with Derek Wynn with a view to taking action against Brice."

"You don't think it will make matters worse?" Cyrus was ashen.

"I think Brice is a bully. He wants you to be so terrified that you will give him the map and keep your mouth shut. Whether he is prepared to carry out his threats or not we will never know, because this ends now."

"Oh, Harriet, thank you with all my heart. I wish I'd come to you sooner."

Harriet gave him a hug. Although she was bursting to talk to him about the text from Ben, it could wait until he'd regained his equilibrium.

Chapter 24

That evening Cyrus was back to his cheerful good-humoured self as they ate dinner in the hotel but the events of the last few days had caught up with him and he happily wandered upstairs just after nine.

Harriet took the opportunity to bring Henry up to speed regarding the threats Cyrus had received.

"Poor Cyrus. I knew something was wrong, but I've known the man a very long time and he does things on his terms. So, I was expecting a conversation at some point. Well done for the intervention. What did Derek Wynn say?"

"Derek agreed this was serious enough for Brice to be spoken to. We will have to wait to see what the result is in due course. I know they were only texts, but Brice sounded extremely disturbed, so it could be an interesting interview."

"I kind of wish I could be a fly on the wall." Henry laughed.

"Me too."

"It's still early. Do you fancy a stroll into town?"

"Love to." Harriet took the arm offered to her.

They ambled slowly along the cobbled streets and took in the atmosphere. The town was busy with people eating and drinking. There was an energy to the place; happiness imbued the warm air.

"Henry, has Cyrus mentioned how he's getting on with tracking down my errant husband, Nick?"

"Only in passing. Said he needed to make some calls, but that he had located him."

"Oh, okay. Well, I'm not sure how to break it to him that I want him to stop. What was once an all-consuming need to find Nick, so that I could berate him for all he put our family, his colleagues and the wider police family through, has evaporated."

"Because?"

"Because it won't change anything, and it will just be nerve-wracking and traumatic for us both and because I really have no desire to see him ever again."

"I respect that, but wouldn't it give you closure?"

"I've thought about it long and hard and I'm not sure it would. It is what it is, the debt, the embarrassment, the hurt will still be there to deal with. And besides, if I know where he is, I'm duty bound to report this. It's complicated but he was the senior investigating officer on my last case and the powers that be are keen to get him back to account for his behaviour and decision making at an internal disciplinary enquiry."

"So is your head or your heart the motivating factor here?"

Harriet thought for a moment before replying. "It's definitely coming from my heart. For me it's time to move on. If I hold onto all the hurt and betrayal what good will that do? I'll never be free. I stumbled across a saying the other night and it just made sense: '*holding onto anger is like grasping a hot coal with the intent of throwing it at someone else. You are the one who gets burned.*'"

"I think that is very true. When Ella died, I felt such anger and rage after the initial sense of loss. Unfortunately, it grew and grew until it threatened to destroy me. If it hadn't been for Cyrus's intervention, I'm pretty sure Kate would not have a father alive today. I was completely out of control – the fury I felt was all-engulfing. It took many years to realise that I was hurting not only myself but, more importantly, Kate and, slowly and painfully, I came to terms with what had occurred and rebuilt my life."

Harriet turned to face Henry. Placing her arms around him she placed her forehead on his chest. Henry moved in closer and nuzzled her neck.

"The pain you experienced must have been unbearable. I'm so very sorry." In due course they released their grip on each other. No further words were necessary. Henry re-took Harriet's arm and she held on tight.

Next morning at breakfast, Harriet plucked up the courage to tell Cyrus that she no longer wanted him to find Nick. Cyrus took the news remarkably well.

"I appreciate all the work you've done on my behalf; I really do."

"It was my pleasure. I am just so pleased that you have come to what I think is a sensible and considered decision. I know you don't want to talk to Nick, but do you want to know where he is and with whom?"

Harriet was amazed that she didn't feel anything other than curiosity. "Go on then, have you any photos?"

"Yes, I have photos. Nick is currently in Marseille. He's crewing for a yacht company with his Danish girlfriend, Ditte. His life is migratory. They never stay long in one place, which I guess is good for him as it makes him more difficult to locate."

Cyrus handed over his phone. Harriet's gaze rested on a tanned male with his hair tied back in a man bun. He had a pierced ear and tattoos on both arms. Standing next to him, a woman, older than Harriet and with a fuller figure; she too had tattoos. Her blonde hair was plaited into two long pigtails. Harriet looked closer, scrutinising the man's image. Surely that wasn't Nick? She looked at the other two photos, searching for recognition. Nick had always been conventional, a conformist. She'd never detected anything adventurous about him and yet there he was, barely recognisable. A large smile spread across her face.

"You dark horse, Nick Lacey. Well, good luck to them, I say." Harriet took one last look before handing the phone back to Cyrus.

"For the record, Ditte is good for him. She keeps him and his drinking in check – they live a simple outdoor life." Cyrus put his phone on the table. "Good. Well, I for one feel relieved now that's out of the way." He took a large sip of coffee.

"Thank you again, Cyrus. I have some exciting news." Harriet leaned in towards her companions and lowered her voice. "Yesterday, Ben, my son, sent a text in which he suggested the symbols bordering the map might in fact be some sort of code. He'd been talking to a friend who told him that the Templars were widely known to use code to communicate. Apparently, there are apps you can use to help you to decipher these. So, I contacted Kate and, between her and Steven Leach, they've found an app which I now have. I suggest we go somewhere discreet – perhaps back to the library? – to take a look, see if we can make sense of the symbols."

"Oh, this is beyond exciting." Cyrus was already on his feet.

"But what about our unwelcome surveillance?" asked Henry.

"Ah, well, thanks to Veronica and Mike they are currently enjoying a long car journey in the French countryside."

"Inspired, but where are they heading?" asked a smiling Henry.

"To wherever takes Mike's fancy. He has all morning to lead them astray. It's a simple plan, I gave him the keys to our hire car, so they believe they are following us." Cyrus and Henry couldn't help but chuckle as they pictured the scene.

Several hours later, engrossed in analysing the map's symbols, many of which looked like triangles. Harriet's found they had started to make sense. They worked painstakingly, checking the code against the app, double checking, until they came up with a completed piece of text. In a whisper, Cyrus read it out loud.

'Friend, with my remains lies a box, the contents of which I have spent a lifetime shielding from harm. I gladly hand over custody to you. My only wish is that you continue to defend it. May God be with you. William of Hertford.'

"Cyrus," whispered Harriet, "this is absolutely incredible. Not for one minute did I actually think this might work but it has and, what's more, it makes total sense." She could feel her heart racing and her cheeks flush.

"It's not often that I'm rendered speechless," said Henry in a low voice. "But this feels like something out of a movie. It's no wonder there are those desperate to get their hands on the map."

"I know, I know! I'm so exquisitely happy." Cyrus sounded breathless. "Never did I imagine when I found the map that it would lead here. Never did I imagine that it might put us in danger. I wonder what could possibly be in the box? It's so intriguing."

"It's more than that, Cyrus. I feel like we are on the verge of something considered so important by William that it has been hidden from the world for hundreds of years." Henry ran his hands through his hair.

"It's a real life mystery that we just might be able to solve." Harriet kept her voice low. "I've been thinking, as William's map is the mirror image of Odysseus's maybe, just maybe, William headed to Ithaca too. What if he made the island his home? Maybe that's where we'll find his remains. At the very least I really think it's worth a look."

"Couldn't agree more." Cyrus was still beaming.

"That sounds like a good plan but, before we go, it might be sensible to do some research so we have some idea of where to look." Henry reached for his mobile.

"Good idea," said Harriet. "Why don't you two do that while I go into town to book the flights and accommodation?"

"Okay, see if you can arrange flights for tomorrow or the day after," said Cyrus. "We will all meet up for dinner at the restaurant in the main square. You know the one with the red and white checked tablecloths?"

"Yes, that sounds good. See you about seven?" said Harriet.

Cyrus nodded. Henry was looking at his mobile but stopped to give her a wide smile.

It didn't take as long as she'd anticipated to make the travel arrangements. Harriet, Cyrus and Henry would fly to Kefalonia the following day and after a short drive take a ferry across to Ithaca. Harriet found she had time to go back to the hotel to shower and change into a pretty multi-coloured maxi dress. She also made contact with Mike. His drive in the country had gone off without a hitch but there had been no sign of Cleo. Veronica, had, however, received a phone call from her around lunchtime. She sounded worse for wear, was slurring her words and ranting about Harriet being impossible to get to.

Dinner that evening was a lively and happy occasion. Cyrus was full of beans, at his most exuberant. About ten, they left the restaurant together, Cyrus in fine voice serenaded them as Henry and Harriet took an arm each and walked slowly back to the hotel. They had less than half a mile to go when Harriet's mobile sounded. It was Derek Wynn, so she waved Cyrus and Henry on and followed on behind. It was not long before the streetlights were fewer and further between and she lost sight of the two men as they turned the corner. She stopped to put her mobile back in her bag which she was wearing across her body. It was dark and she had to concentrate. Without warning an arm shot out of an adjacent doorway and hurled her backwards into the shadowy depths. Before she could get her bearings, she felt her throat being squeezed. Tighter and tighter the grip became until it was difficult to breathe, and she started to feel faint. With one last flash of consciousness she kicked out behind her as hard as she could, scraping her left heel down the shin of her attacker. The grip loosened, allowing her to take a gasp of air.

"You fucking bitch, why the fuck won't you fucking die without a bloody drama!" shouted a voice she immediately recognised. A shiver ran down the entire length of her spine.

"Cleo! What the bloody hell do you think you are doing, you absolute psychopath." Harriet's voice was hoarse. She tried to move, but she found her legs wouldn't work and she struggled to remain awake.

Then Cleo increased the pressure on her neck again. The pain was excruciating, but when her hair was also violently yanked, it did at least jolt her back to consciousness.

"Have I ever told you how much I fucking hate you? You piece of shit! You fucking left me to die."

Harriet struggled to speak.

"Is that what you think? Well, you're wrong. Why I will never know but I did come back. I tried my hardest to get you out of the car." The grip around her neck suddenly released.

"No, no, no, that can't be. No fucking way!"

"Yes, yes, yes! Despite everything you did to me, I came back to get you out."

"No, that's not true."

"Oh, I assure you it is. Now get lost, will you? I've had a belly full of your stalking and mind games. Just leave me alone. Go on, piss off."

"That's never going to happen." Cleo moved in closer. She was still behind her and Harriet could feel the warmth of her breath on the back of her neck and smell her sickly sweet perfume. Once more Cleo grasped her around the neck. Out of the corner of her eye Harriet saw something glint in the darkness and it was then that she realised Cleo had a blade in her hand.

"You are responsible for ruining my looks, for the scarring on my face, you bitch."

"No, Cleo, that was entirely your own doing, your reckless driving, your blind fury."

Cleo said nothing for a moment, but squeezed Harriet's neck a little harder.

"Go on, then, hurry up and get it over with." Harriet's voice was getting hoarser.

"You're supposed to bloody plead for your life as I cut your throat you bitch, not encourage me. This is not how I planned it!"

"Fucking get on with it. I've had enough!" Harriet felt a surge of fury. Without warning she was released from the vice-like grip. She stood rigid for a few seconds straining to hear any movement behind her. Nothing. She plucked up the courage to turn around, Cleo had gone. Harriet slid to the floor and sat with her back up against the doorway. Moments later a breathless Henry appeared. Harriet was shaking violently as Henry placed his jacket around her shoulders and helped her to her feet. Mike ran around the corner.

"I'm alright, I'm alright," Harriet rasped.

The two men exchanged looks but neither spoke. They simply helped Harriet to her feet and back to the hotel. Cyrus checked in on her briefly, then left Henry to carry out a cursory examination of her neck. He quickly concluded that she did not need hospital treatment. Mike then persuaded Harriet to talk about what had happened.

"I should be dead. What the hell was I thinking? I can't believe I actually encouraged her to finish me off! When she jumped me all I could think of was Veronica's advice, keep Cleo outside her comfort zone. She once told me that everything Cleo does is pre-planned down to the minutest detail. Force her to change the plan even slightly and she becomes disorientated and confused. Thank God!"

"Yes, you were bloody lucky," said Mike. "Thank goodness you are relatively unharmed."

"What I want to know is how you both knew where I was."

The two men exchanged looks for a second time that evening.

"Well, I suppose we were always going to have to tell you at some point. We put a sophisticated tracker in your phone," confessed Henry.

"You did what? Under whose authority? No, don't tell me. I know exactly who. Derek."

"Look, don't be too harsh on us; it was the only way we could think of to keep you bloody safe." Mike put his hand on Harriet's shoulder. "And you are always leaving your mobile on your desk, so it was relatively easy to borrow it and insert the tracker."

"I understand how a tracker works, but I didn't know it could tell if someone's in trouble."

"Look, one minute you were behind Cyrus and me," said Henry, "and the next minute you had disappeared. So, I told Cyrus to get hold of Mike and I followed the tracker for your location."

"Thank you both. Thank you for looking out for me."

"Well, thank God you are relatively unscathed, although I'm sorry to say you have quite significant bruising to your neck. Does it hurt much?" asked Henry as he put his glasses on and gently touched the base of her neck. It was as much as Harriet could do to concentrate; his touch was the gentlest she'd ever encountered.

"No, it's uncomfortable but not too painful. It's my voice I'm more concerned about. Any idea how long I'm going to sound like a lifetime smoker?" Harriet managed a smile.

"A couple of days, I expect. I think you could probably do with some paracetamol and ibuprofen. I'll go and get some."

"How handy to have my own personal medical practitioner." Harriet grinned. Henry smiled and they locked gazes until he had to turn to make his exit.

"Harriet, I'm so fucking relieved you aren't too worse for wear. Please take care and let the lovely Dr Squires look after you." Mike was smirking.

"What? What are you trying to insinuate, Mike Taylor?" Harriet had her hands on her hips, but she was grinning.

"Nothing, nothing at all, but would it be so bad?"

"Er, goodnight, Mike! See you tomorrow." Harriet held the door open.

"See you tomorrow. Now get some sleep!" said Mike, chuckling to himself as he closed the door. A minute or two later Henry reappeared.

"Henry, can I ask you a massive favour? I still feel a bit shaky; would you mind staying while I take a shower?"

"Of course."

Half an hour later, Harriet emerged from the bathroom in a fluffy dressing gown.

Henry got to his feet and walked across to her. "Now, have you taken the paracetamol and ibuprofen?"

Harriet nodded.

"And are you going to be alright on your own? I'm happy to sleep on the sofa," said Henry gently.

The thought of having Henry close was exhilarating, to the point that Harriet felt herself colouring, but she was totally drained, shattered and she didn't trust herself. The last thing she wanted to do was ruin their blossoming friendship.

"You are such a kind and thoughtful man, thank you, but I think I'll be fine. I just want to sleep now."

"Good idea. How about I stay with you until you drift off?"

"That would be perfect."

"Right then, into bed you go."

"Okay, but I'm naked under here," said Harriet grinning.

"Best I turn my back then!" Henry was laughing.

Once she was safely ensconced in bed, Henry kicked off his shoes and jumped up beside her. For a moment or so they just looked at each other.

"Harriet Lacey, you are one of the bravest women I have ever met. Beautiful, educated, intelligent, graceful and funny and I really quite like you!"

Harriet beamed back, but she was barely able to keep her eyes open. Never before had she felt such joy. Never.

Chapter 25

It was late morning before Harriet emerged. She found Henry and Cyrus sitting in the sunshine together reading in the hotel's walled garden.

"Oh, my dear, how are you?" Cyrus got to his feet and hugged her warmly.

"I'm feeling remarkably good, considering," said Harriet, her voice still hoarse. She turned to smile at Henry who had also stood up. "Thank you for looking after me so well last night."

"It was my pleasure." Henry greeted her with a kiss on the cheek. "The bruising doesn't look too bad this morning," he said as he peered at Harriet's neck.

"No, I was very lucky. Last time Cleo laid hands on me, it was a completely different story. Any contact from Mike at all this morning?"

"Not yet, but I'm sure he'll be along shortly. Are you up for travelling, though?" asked Cyrus.

"Yes, I feel okay. It will be fine."

It was early afternoon when they set off for the airport. Harriet opted to travel with Mike and Veronica and, although it was against the rules set down by CPS, Mike figured that after what had happened in the last twenty-four hours, it was permissible. So Mike drove one hire car, a Renault Megane, with Harriet in the back and Veronica in the front passenger seat and Henry drove the other, accompanied by Cyrus. It wasn't long before Henry noticed they were being followed. After several miles, he flashed Mike who was in front and both cars pulled into a lay-by. The offending vehicle drove past and stopped further up the road.

"Mike, see that red Citroën about a hundred yards ahead?" Mike nodded. "Well, I'm pretty sure it contains our unwelcome surveillance guys. The car has been aggressively driving close to my bumper for the last ten kilometres."

"Fuck."

"Are you sure?" asked Harriet who'd joined them.

"Yes. Look, the way I figure it, they are only interested in Cyrus and Harriet and, as luck would have it, you are in separate cars. So how about we make it tricky for them and take different routes? The road forks about two kilometres from here. If I take the faster or more direct route, the A26, and you take the left fork, the secondary road, the D677, they will have to make a decision about which car to follow. In the meantime, the other car can contact the local police for assistance."

"It could bloody work, you know," said Mike. "Yes, let's go with it."

"I agree." said Harriet over her shoulder as she ran back to the car and got in. She had barely closed the door when the Renault Megane's tyres screeched on the tarmac and the car flew up the road minus Mike. The red Citroën immediately fell in behind and it too shot off at speed.

"Cleo, you need to stop this now. Stop the car and let Harriet out," said Veronica keeping her voice calm.

"Why the fuck would I do that, Mother?"

"Please just listen to me for once in your life. Stop the car and let Harriet out."

"What's the matter, Harriet, cat got your tongue?"

"Cleo, please…Oh my God!" Without warning the red Citroën car had rammed the Megane from behind, jolting the women forward with some force.

Cleo started to laugh loudly, perhaps even hysterically.

"Cleo, this isn't going to end well. Please just stop the car," pleaded Veronica.

"But this is such fun, Mother."

Another shove from the car behind and then another.

"They're trying to force us off the road," said Harriet to no one in particular.

Cleo's response was to speed up. Veronica turned and exchanged fearful looks with Harriet. A strong smell of alcohol pervaded the car.

"Please, Cleo, please don't do this." Veronica was less calm now.

The next shunt made the Megane leave the road. How Cleo missed the road sign, Harriet would never know. The car bumped across the grass verge at speed before returning to the carriageway.

Harriet could feel her mobile vibrating in her pocket but, such was the speed and erratic way Cleo was driving, it was impossible to access. It was as much as she could do to hang on.

A few minutes later, the red Citroën pulled up alongside. The driver scowled as he jabbed his finger violently indicating that they should pull into the side of the road. But Cleo merely put her foot down and sped off again.

Harriet could hear her heart thumping in her ears and was aware of sweat beads on her top lip. Despite this she felt strangely detached from the drama around her. It felt surreal. She just didn't know how she should be feeling, how to react. She had survived last night by the skin of her teeth, only to be thrown into a new nightmare, except this time Veronica was in the mix. Part of her wanted to shout, to scream, to berate Cleo, but deep down she knew Cleo didn't tick right and shouting at her would be pointless. Part of her wanted to weep. There was just no way of knowing how this would end.

The impact when it came was far more severe than any previously, but it was the shattering of the rear nearside window that freaked them out the most. Luckily Harriet was not injured. Now, however, she could see the fear in Cleo's eyes in the rear view mirror.

The occupants of the car were silent for a moment or so, each lost in their own terror.

"Cleo, you bloody owe me. I've spent the last ten, twelve years in turmoil covering up for you, living a lie, hurting. My life has been on hold. Enough, you are going to fucking listen to me for once." Veronica grabbed the handbrake.

"What the hell are you doing?" shouted Cleo, as the car veered to the left. "Okay, okay, let go of the hand brake. As much as I loathe you, Harriet, I don't particularly want to die. I'm pretty sure that they are after you, not me, so here's what we're going to do. I'll speed up, try to get sufficient distance to be out of sight long enough to allow you to exit the car. Mother and I will then drive on, before slowing and pulling over. When they see you are no longer in the vehicle, they should lose interest in us. Got it?"

Harriet nodded.

"Thank you, Cleo, I knew deep down in your dark soul there was a speck of humanity left," said Veronica.

"I'm not doing this for you, Mother, nor for Harriet. I'm doing this for me."

Harriet decided it was best not to comment. And so it was that when they reached the village of Voue, a hamlet on a straight flat road, Cleo put her foot down, overtook a small black car and without warning veered to the left, into a church car park, before slamming on the brakes and bringing the car to a crawl.

"Now would be a good time. Jump, Harriet, jump. Go! Now!" Harriet did as she was told and landed with a thud on her knees. Without looking back, she scrambled to her feet and ran to the churchyard throwing herself over a wall, she landed with a thud on the other side. Lying on the damp ground beneath, she attempted to catch her breath, but then she heard a vehicle enter the car park at speed. She could hear the sound of gravel spraying in all directions as it came to an abrupt halt but then it sped off again. She stayed where she was, her heart thumping like fury. She struggled to regulate her breathing. She again heard a vehicle enter the car park. It too came to a halt before at least two doors were opened and closed. There were approaching footsteps on the gravel. Harriet's heart was in her mouth. She closed her eyes and held her breath.

"Fuck me, the tracker says she's in the car park, please don't let it be wrong." It was Mike's voice.

Cyrus walked towards the entrance to the churchyard just as a little head appeared to his right. "Thank God, my dear, are you unharmed?" he asked.

"Oh, you lot are a sight for sore eyes. I'm not sure what it is about me, but I seem to attract trouble." said Harriet both laughing and welling up at the same time.

Cyrus gave Harriet an enthusiastic hug, followed by Mike. It was then Henry's turn. Gently wiping a tear from her cheek, he leaned in and kissed her long and hard. For Harriet, nothing else mattered, nothing at all, in that moment. The world around her didn't exist. She was lost.

As they walked back to the car, Harriet explained how she'd ended up behind the wall. As she was describing how she'd leapt from the moving car she was interrupted by an almighty blast, so loud the ground shook. Startled, they looked around to see a rising plume of dark smoke in the distance.

"Bloody hell!" shouted Cyrus putting his hand to his head. "What the hell was that?"

"Oh my God, Veronica," shouted Harriet.

They ran back to the car and drove towards the smoke; it wasn't long before they came across a scene of carnage. Cyrus grabbed his mobile and called emergency services. The others ran towards the mass of twisted and burning wreckage. Both sides of the road were blocked. Harriet counted at least seven cars, a lorry and a tanker, but it was impossible to be accurate. The tanker was clearly the source of the explosion. Some of the vehicles were engulfed in flames, and there was no getting near them. They did, however, manage to free an elderly couple at the back of the pile-up, and help them to a safe area of verge. A young woman in another car was carried by Henry to join them. Henry's medical expertise was in demand. Mike went to the aid of the driver of a lorry and helped to get him out of his twisted cab. As he glanced back over his shoulder he noticed the index plate of his hire car poking out from under the burning overturned tanker. He ran back to Harriet and Cyrus who were busy finding blankets and coats to keep the injured warm.

"Any luck in finding Veronica and Cleo?" asked Harriet.

Mike put his hand on her shoulder. "It doesn't look good. Of course, we don't know the circumstances yet, they may have escaped. The road's completely blocked, they may have made it out and be at the far end of the crash."

Harriet leant her head on Mike's chest. There were no words. A cloak of sadness engulfed her.

The emergency services arrived about forty minutes after the explosion and slowly but surely they worked their way through it. Several hours later, tired and smelling strongly of smoke, Harriet, Cyrus, Mike and Henry were driven by taxi to a Paris hotel for the night. Much to Cyrus's delight, the Hotel Louvre Marsollier had once been the residence of Oscar Wilde, in 1899. It was located five minutes' walk from the Louvre in the Opera area of Paris. They had missed their flights to Kefalonia, but no one seemed to mind. Exhausted by the events of the last couple of days everyone seemed happy to take a moment to reflect. Having showered, they met in the hotel lobby and walked around the corner to a restaurant where they ordered steaks and frites. They all ate hungrily, only slowing a little for the cheese course.

"Am I the only one who feels a bit disjointed, dazed?" said Henry. "Actually, I'm not sure how to feel."

"Bewildered?" suggested Cyrus.

"Disconnected?" suggested Harriet.

"Emotional?" was Mike's contribution.

"All of the above, I think," said Henry with a rueful smile.

"It has been a surreal day," said Cyrus. "And we are left in limbo. Did Veronica and Cleo make it? Are they still alive, or did they perish?"

"I know," said Harriet. "I feel worried, concerned and emotional about Veronica and, as for Cleo, I don't know how to feel. Part of me wants to feel relieved that she may be gone and I don't have to deal with her shit any more but, if she is gone, then it's highly likely that Veronica is also and that makes me very sad."

Henry took her hand.

"It was such a fucking awful scene that I think it's going to take the gendarmerie a couple of days to gather forensics and work out exactly what did happen," said Mike. "And, of course, there's the fate of our two stalkers to discover yet."

"Yes, indeed," said Cyrus. "Well, tomorrow morning we might get a little more clarity. We have an appointment with a Captain Bernard of the Gendarmerie Nationale. He wishes to speak to us all individually and also as a group. He has kindly offered to come to the hotel at ten."

"Thank God you speak fluent French, Cyrus," said Harriet. "Otherwise it could be very awkward to explain how we all came to be at the scene."

"Hear, hear," said Mike.

"Yes, well, I'm happy to be useful," said Cyrus. "However, whilst I'm optimistic, I still think it's going to be tricky." Cyrus cut a huge slice of cheese.

"What do you mean, old friend?" said Henry. "All you have to do is tell it how it is. 'Well, Captain, it's like this. Some of us travelled to France in search of a Templar Knight from the twelfth century, some of us were here in search of a psychotic killer, who by the way also just happens to have a pathological hatred for one of our party, and who attempted to strangle her the night before the crash. I think I should also mention that the mother of the psychopath was also present to assist British police to detain her daughter. Oh, and before I forget, there were also two individuals who were aggressively stalking us whilst this was all going on, who by the way instigated the car chase which appears to have been a major factor in the tragic pile-up.' Piece of cake."

Everyone around the table broke into spontaneous laughter.

"My dear boy," said Cyrus, chuckling. "When you put it like that, I can see it's going to be a walk in the park."

Captain Bernard was not what Harriet had expected, not at all. Standing at least six foot four, he was lean, almost willowy, with immensely large feet, short dark brown hair, a full beard and a hooked nose. Aged perhaps forty, forty-five? He was wearing a fully pressed dress uniform. His command of English was reasonable, but by no means fluent. Cyrus, she thought, would have his work cut out. Harriet couldn't decide if he was shy, emotionally inhibited, or just arrogant.

"Silence, s'il vous plaît!" was the signal that things were not going too well. Captain Bernard had his hands on his hips and was frowning. "One at a time, if you would be so kind." He did not look happy.
Two and a half hours later, Bernard was still grilling them and Harriet had had enough. She walked across to Cyrus and took him to one side.

"I think we might need to get Derek Wynn on the phone to talk to Bernard. I'm not a fluent French speaker but I know enough to recognise that this debrief is not going to plan and that's in no way a criticism of the sterling effort you're making. I just get the distinct feeling that Monsieur Bernard is someone who is impressed by rank which currently we are unable to provide him with. Also, I'm worried if this goes on much longer Mike may thump him." Harriet gave Cyrus a cheeky grin.

"I totally agree. Would you mind calling him this instant? I'm not sure how much more of this pompous twit I can take. And besides, I'm really anxious to get to Ithaca as soon as we can. By the way, have you noticed how laid back Henry is? Look at him, he's leaning against the wall over there, taking it all in, and smiling with amusement." Cyrus rolled his eyes in jest. Harriet laughed, but the sight of Henry made her pulse race.

An hour later, Derek Wynn had expertly dealt with Captain Bernard and they were in the process of making statements to the various officers the captain had marched into the room.

At three that afternoon they were done. Immediately Bernard had left, Harriet rang Derek Wynn.

"Derek, I can't thank you enough for your intervention."

"It was my pleasure. Captain Bernard is probably the most pompous and superior police officer I have ever had the misfortune to come across. How did you manage to stop Mike thumping him?"

Harriet laughed. "Funny you should say that, I really thought he was about to, that's why I contacted you. It seems, however, that along with his new dress sense he's also found new depths of self-control!"

"Pray tell."

"Well, today he's wearing a really classy blue and white flowery shirt. Last night, he wore a purple and blue one."

"What, Mike did?"

"Yes, well, to be fair, his suitcase was lost in the crash. I was lucky, mine was in the other car with Cyrus and Henry."

"I see. Can I have a word with Mike, please?" Harriet could hear the amusement in Derek's voice.

For the next twenty minutes Mike and Derek were clearly engaged in good-natured banter, but towards the end of their chat Mike's expression changed. Harriet could see the look of concentration on his face. "Okay, yes, sir. I've got it. Don't worry, I'll pass it on. And thank you again."

Mike indicated that they should all gather around. "Okay, I suggest we decamp to a bar somewhere for a chat. Derek has asked me to pass on what he's managed to glean from Captain Bernard. But first we should organise our travel arrangements. I'd say it's probably too late to get to our preferred destinations today, unless we travel overnight. And I for one would rather not do that." No one contradicted him; indeed, they all nodded in agreement.

By five o'clock, taxis, hire cars, flights and ferries had all been booked and everyone set off for a light and airy bar a short walk from the hotel. They found a table at the rear of a large glass conservatory area and ordered a round of drinks.

"Mike, I'm dying to know what Derek found out from Bernard." Cyrus was smiling widely.

"Well, I'm not going to repeat everything he said, it was too rude." Mike laughed.

"No, surely not!" said Harriet. "Not Derek Wynn, he doesn't swear."

"Rarely swears," corrected Mike. "And today was one of those occasions."

Harriet nodded, smiling as she recalled the first time he swore in her presence. It had come as a surprise.

"Derek Wynn sounds like a man much like myself, for I never bleeding swear, never." Henry grinned.

"You are always bloody swearing," said Cyrus, his shoulders shaking with laughter.

"I can bloody vouch for that." Mike was laughing as well.

With the tension of the day released, Mike was now able to tell them what Derek had imparted to him. He lowered his voice. "Okay, I have several bits of information I need to tell you. Firstly, it appears our stalkers are deceased. The gendarmerie are trying to identify them. It seems that they may be hired ex special forces."

"I wonder if they were employed by Colonel Tim Brice?" interrupted Harriet.

"Derek's one step ahead of you. He has passed on his details to Bernard. Did Derek also tell you that Tim Brice has been detained under the Mental Health Act?"

"Oh God, yes, with all that's happened it completely slipped my mind," said Harriet. "That's the call I received in Troyes just prior to my encounter with Cleo."

"Can you give us a bit more detail?" asked Cyrus who was now sitting on the edge of his chair.

"Yes, no problem," replied Mike. "When he was brought in for questioning about his threats to you, Cyrus, his behaviour was bizarre and he seemed completely unhinged. He made no sense, talked codswallop, took his clothes off without warning and then began to sing Abba songs at the top of his voice. A mental health assessment was conducted, and he was detained for further assessment at hospital."

"Blimey," said Cyrus, wide-eyed.

"The second bit of information concerns how the collision occurred. Again, it's early days, and Derek stresses that Bernard was showing off, but initial thoughts are that the red car, containing our stalkers, made contact with Cleo's car at speed. Cleo lost control and veered into the path of an oncoming tanker. The driver of the tanker tried to take evasive action but his brakes locked and he hit the curb, which put the tanker on its side, it then continued to slide across both carriageways. The driver of the red car ploughed into a stationary car immediately in front of it and, at such speed, both cars careered into the tanker, which was still sliding. Current thinking is that the driver of the red car was too busy looking at the carnage it had caused to notice the car in front had stopped. And a lorry behind the tanker swerved to avoid the scene immediately in front of it only to hit a car on the other side of the carriageway, which in turn hit another vehicle."

"Good God!" said Cyrus. The rest of them stayed silent. Harriet felt a wave of sadness flood across her and stared at the floor as she tried to process Mike's words.

"The third bit of information pertains to Veronica and Cleo." Harriet looked up, sat upright and took a deep breath. "Veronica and Cleo are missing presumed dead," Mike went on. "However, due to the ferocity of the fire, much of the potential forensic evidence has been destroyed. Some fragments of human remains have been recovered from the car but DNA analysis will be challenging. In short, it is likely to be quite some time before we have a result. Hopefully when it does come it will be definitive."

"There are advances in forensics all the time," said Henry. "I'm confident the results will be conclusive. Harriet must know whether she still has to contend with Cleo. I have a friend at Kings College London who is an expert in the field. I'll give him a call."

"Thank you, Henry." Harriet managed a smile but deep down she felt sick. Would Cleo's hold on her life never end? Was it possible she had escaped? Or perhaps Veronica had survived? Harriet just couldn't shake the sense of guilt she felt for having pressed so hard for Veronica's involvement.

Chapter 26

Present day: Ithaca, Greece

As soon as they took their seats on the plane Harriet felt less tense. As the flight progressed, she contemplated her excitement. Well aware that they may not find what they were looking for, she decided as she gazed out across the French Alps that, for her, the search was as important, no, more important than the result. And she couldn't think of two more charming companions in the hunt than Cyrus and Henry.

The flight from Charles de Gaulle airport to Kefalonia took over four hours, so it was three in the afternoon when they landed. Once they'd cleared customs and retrieved their baggage they went in search of their pre-booked taxi, which was to take them to the port of Sami. As they left the shade of the airport buildings to locate the cab, a wall of hot air slammed into them. It took Harriet's breath away. The taxi journey took about fifty minutes. At times it was terrifying, as they were driven at speed insanely close to the edge of the road. To describe it as a road was generous, it twisted and turned and often fell steeply away with nothing but sea at the base of sheer cliffs. From Sami the plan was to take the ferry to the tiny port of Pisaetos on Ithaca, a journey time of forty minutes.

It was a magical boat trip. Opting for the top deck of the ferry, they sat on wooden benches in the shade of a tarpaulin. Harriet was struck by the clarity of the deep blue, almost aquamarine, water. To begin with the ferry chugged along hugging the coastline, rocky, with scant vegetation, wild herbs, the odd scraggy tree and a mountain goat or two. The breeze was deliciously warm with a hint of saltiness to it. Harriet beamed from ear to ear. Every so often she looked across at Henry, who was sitting opposite, to exchange grins. He was such a self-assured, handsome and kind man. She couldn't stop staring at him – but only when she thought he wasn't looking.

At the harbourside, they located their hire car and a short time later Henry drove up the steep hill out of the harbour on a single-track concrete road. Cyrus positioned himself in the front passenger seat to map read. Their hotel was approximately twenty minutes by car and located in the capital, Vathy. They arrived some time after six. A former nineteenth-century neoclassical mansion, it was located on the quayside of the picturesque port. Travel weary, Henry suggested they dump their bags in their rooms and head to the harbourside for food.

They found a little taverna on the waterfront and chose a table that allowed them to look out across the harbour dotted with colourful local fishing boats. They ordered fried squid, juicy tomatoes with garlic and Greek basil, Greek salad and the catch of the day. Henry opted for a lager, Cyrus red wine and Harriet retsina.

"This is absolutely perfect. The warm air, the smell of the sea, mouth-watering food. It's heavenly." Harriet sipped her wine.

"I can't believe we actually made it," said Cyrus. "I'm so grateful to both of you for juggling your commitments to stay on for a little longer." He raised his glass to them.

"I for one wouldn't have missed this for the world," said Henry. "It is years since I've felt so alive, so happy."

"Nor me," said Harriet. "Do we have a plan for tomorrow?"

"Well, back in Troyes Cyrus and I did some research and have some ideas, let's put it that way." Henry winked at Harriet.

"Yes, indeed. I was thinking that we should rise early tomorrow morning to avoid the crowds of tourists who will descend on what is believed to be the site of Odysseus's palace. It's located just outside the village of Stavros, I think about eighteen kilometres from here. Of course, this site is controversial: some experts argue that the physical description of the island in Homer's epic poem does not correlate with the island itself. I'm open minded about this; there have been numerous landslides and earthquakes over the years which will undoubtedly have impacted the landscape. Anyway, I digress. We know William was familiar with the tale of Odysseus, hence his map. Therefore, it's entirely possible he came to see the ruins and I believe it's also feasible he could have settled nearby." Cyrus took out a map and laid it on the table for them to look at.

"That makes absolute sense," said Harriet. "When you say early, exactly what time were you thinking?"

"I'd like to be on the road by six, if that's okay?"

"Yes, I can manage that."

It was nearly seven when they left the car in the centre of Stavros and began their walk out of the village on a narrow single-track country road. After a mile the incline became steeper until they found themselves winding their way uphill. Gradually they left behind small fields of crops and livestock and their surroundings became rockier and increasingly forested. It took forty minutes to reach their destination. For a major archaeological site, it had a remarkably low-key entrance. They followed a rocky path to an opening in the pine trees. Harriet took her time to look around. There was an aura to the place as the early morning sun began to warm the air and create a golden glow. It seemed they were the only ones there save for the awakening cicadas.

"Now, I don't believe we will necessarily be able to interpret much of the site," said Cyrus. "It's my understanding that excavations have been piecemeal, and a lack of funds has severely hampered progress. But I think this visit is more about the atmosphere for us than anything else."

"Well, I for one think this is one of the most truly impressive locations I've ever seen." Henry exchanged a smile with Harriet.

As they climbed up a set of huge uneven stone steps, they reached another level of the site with a view of the sea through the trees.

"I tell you what, this is a fantastic location for a palace whether it was Odysseus's or not," said Henry.

"Totally agree, old man." Cyrus was busy looking around him. "Somewhere on this site is supposed to be a well dating from the eighth century BC, roughly the period in which Odysseus is believed to have been king."

They moved on and climbed another set of irregular, shallower, stone steps until they reached a number of ruined buildings constructed using gigantic stone slabs. At the top of the site was a building that looked as if it had once been a church. Inside they came across some gravestones in the floor, almost all overgrown. Towards the back of the building, Henry began to photograph something. Harriet and Cyrus walked across to him.

"Have you found something interesting?" asked Harriet.

"I think I may have found a Templar cross etched into this stone."

Cyrus's face lit up and he moved forward and peered at the stone. "I do believe you have. Oh my. I'm going to google it if I can." He sounded excited.

"Any luck?" asked Harriet after a couple of minutes.

"Yes, that's definitely a Templar cross. I can't date it accurately but it does seem to fit within the twelfth-century timeline. I take it there's no other writing on the stone?"

"No, nothing," said Henry.

"An unexpected find, but wonderful nevertheless," said Harriet.

"It really is," replied Cyrus.

Before heading back, the three explorers sat on a low wall at the top of the site and took in the sea view while they breakfasted on sweet pastries, fruit and iced coffee. They arrived back at the hotel late morning. Harriet went for a swim, Henry a walk, and Cyrus had a snooze on the veranda. Later they met for lunch to plan the next stage of their search.

"I've been thinking about what should be our next move and I'm minded to hire a boat to take us around various parts of the coastline," said Cyrus. "I know we are probably looking for a needle in a haystack, but I had the idea that we might be able to identify possible landing sites that may have been suitable for William and his companions."

"Sounds like a good idea to me." Harriet couldn't help but notice Cyrus looked relieved by her enthusiastic response.

"I agree," said Henry in a low voice. "But I do have one question that's been bugging me. I accept that we may never find William, but just suppose we do. Do we have any idea how to access the mysterious box he mentions?"

"Bloody hell, Henry, you are absolutely right. Is it something we leave to chance? The likelihood of finding William is extremely slim."

No one spoke for some time.

"Cyrus, did you by any chance bring the bible with you, the one in which you found the map?" asked Harriet.

"I did. Why do you ask?"

"Just a thought, call it a hunch. I could be completely wrong."

With lunch over, they walked back to the hotel. Cyrus went to his room to fetch the bible before joining the others on a quiet and shady terrace overlooking the harbour. He handed the leather-bound book to Harriet, who paused to admire it. Then, taking a pair of tweezers from her handbag, she carefully inserted them into the spine. The two men watched intently. After several attempts, part of a leather cord appeared. Gently she tugged it and slowly more of the cord emerged, and a long thin iron key.

"This might be what we need." Harriet laughed as she held the key aloft.

"Absolutely amazing," said Henry, his admiring glance caused Harriet to blush.

"Beyond awesome." Cyrus got to his feet and flung his arms around the seated Harriet. "What made you think of that?"

"It was just a feeling. I tried to put myself in William's shoes. Where would I have hidden it?"

The following morning, they set out by boat captained by George, part-time fisherman, part-time tour guide. The heat of the early August sunshine amplified hour by hour, but the sense of anticipation in the boat meant it was barely noticed.

It was mid-afternoon when Cyrus spotted a bay on the west coast of the island. A deep inlet with clear turquoise blue water framed by olive clad slopes. As their boat moved closer, a second pebble beach came into sight, along with a tiny sheltered harbour at the southern end teeming with traditional blue and white fishing boats. At the back of the larger limestone beach there appeared to be an expanse of low-lying scrubland. George pointed to a small cantina at the far end of the beach nestled under eucalyptus trees.

They managed to find a mooring in the crowded harbour and disembarked. Harriet suggested they walk a little way up the hill behind the cantina to get a better feel for the place. It was incredibly steep. They were joined in their stroll by cicadas, a host of butterflies and several lizards of varying sizes. They did not need to go far before they were able to turn and survey the bay stretching out below.

"It feels to me just like the sort of place to appeal to a war weary William," said Harriet.

"Why?" asked Cyrus turning to face her.

"Because it's sheltered and tucked away in a quiet part of the island and there is land at the rear of the bay. If you look closely you can just see the outline of ridges and furrows. These are the result of prolonged ploughing. The soil builds up in ridges. In the Middle Ages in Europe it was *the* method of farming. It is really only possible to see it on land ploughed in the middle ages but not since."

"My dear, you have such hidden depths," said a wide-eyed Cyrus. Henry interrupted. "Guys, on the north side of the bay there appears to be a series of walls in various states of disrepair. I'm not sure, but I think they are the outlines of buildings." He pointed into the distance.

"Do you think it could have been a farming settlement?" asked

Cyrus.

"I think that's a distinct possibility. Do you both fancy exploring a bit?" asked Harriet. Her companions nodded enthusiastically.

They had almost reached the cantina when Harriet just happened to glance to her right. Out of the corner of her eye something caught her interest and she turned to explore it further. Nestled into the hillside was an unexpected find. Her cry of surprise sent Henry and Cyrus scurrying to join her.

"Oh, my goodness," she exclaimed. "I didn't expect to find this. None of the tourist books mention it."

Before them was a tiny stone chapel. Only parts of the walls remained and a corrugated iron roof had been erected on wooden stilts to protect it. Most surprisingly, inside there was still a pew or two, religious paintings, including a small altar and a lamp hanging from a central piece of wall. It had clearly been the victim of one of the island's many earthquakes. As they explored they came across yet another surprise, a second stone Templar cross leaning up against an outside side wall.

"I don't want to get our hopes up but is anyone else feeling that we might just be close?" Harriet placed her right hand on her chest to try to regulate her breathing.

"I've not felt this nervous for many, many years." Henry traced the lines of the cross with his hand.

"I think I'm going to faint."

Harriet and Henry rushed to Cyrus's side.

They rested at the cantina until Cyrus had regained his strength and his blood sugar levels had been restored. He was insistent that they didn't leave before exploring the ruins spotted by Henry on the north side of the bay. So they sauntered along the beach until they reached its end, clambered into the first of several ancient olive groves, then followed old goat tracks until they turned a corner into an open area that may once have been a large courtyard. Although in ruins, it had clearly been an impressively large farm, maybe a commune, thought Harriet. There were stone pens, the remains of houses, barns and a larger manor house all contained inside what had once been a mighty wall. As they explored, they found the remains of two old wells, and five granary stores, not to mention numerous fragments of stone olive presses.

"This was some impressive operation in its day," remarked Harriet.

"Indeed." Cyrus almost seemed overwhelmed by the scale of the place.

"Guys, I think I might have found something." Henry shouted across from the far corner of an inner courtyard. He had almost disappeared beneath the undergrowth.

Harriet took Cyrus's hand and they made their way as fast as they could. Under the briars they could see the outline of a stone doorway. "Stand back," said Cyrus as he used his walking stick to hack away the thorny branches. Henry used his mobile to light the way down a narrow passageway of approximately twenty metres. At the far end, they came across a door, or rather the remains of a solid wooden door the like of which none of them had ever seen. Above it, an inscription was just visible in the stone frame: *'Familia nostra'*.

"Our family," said Henry out loud but to no one in particular.

"Do you think we can get in?" asked Harriet, her brow wet with anticipation.

"Well, we can try," replied Henry. "If I can manage to dislodge one or two panels we may be able to squeeze through."

"We've come this far," said Cyrus. "I'm not turning back now. I need to see this through."

It took Henry several attempts to prise open a couple of rotten panels. "Cyrus, do you think you can crawl through this space? I'm not sure I can make it any bigger."

"Don't worry about me, old boy, I will make it. I must." And he did.

They found themselves in an enormous stone room. Using their mobiles as torches, they began to explore. Cyrus and Henry moved to a far wall to look at a huge glass panel containing a series of scenes. In the central section, a Templar Knight held his sword aloft. Harriet remained in the centre of the room with her back to her two companions and tried to stifle sobs as she realised what she was looking at. As Cyrus and Henry turned back to join her their lights illuminated the tears crafting patterns on her cheeks.

"Oh, Cyrus, I can't believe it," she said, transfixed. "I can't believe it. We've found him. And, after everything they found each other! Who'd have thought, their love was stronger than all the obstacles of culture, of faith, they found a way to be together. Oh my God, look!" she sobbed.

As the two men moved forward, their lights came to rest on a stone Templar Knight, one hand placed on his heart, the other holding the hand of a woman lying next to him. An inscription at the foot of his tomb simply said, '*William beloved husband of Rabia*'. At the foot of the woman's tomb '*Rabia beloved wife of William*'.

Henry moved forward and put his arm around Harriet who buried her head in his chest.

"Well, I never. I never thought we would find them, let alone together. This is a true love story." Cyrus stood, head bowed and motionless, by the tombs for some time. Then he seemed to shake himself and continued to explore the rest of the room. There were many further graves in the floor of the room. Having recovered herself, Harriet joined him, with Henry.

"This truly was a community, a family, *'Familia nostra'* and, whilst we will probably never know what happened to William to bring him here, one thing's for sure, there were many Knights who chose to follow him and who made a new life alongside him. They are all here, along with their families. I've found some familiar names. Salma, she's over here. Notice how she's been laid to rest facing towards Mecca. I've also found William's manservant, Zafir, who, it seems, married a woman named Lubna. And Thierry of Tyre, who is mentioned in several of William's letters." Cyrus was smiling widely.

"Unbelievable," said Harriet, once more feeling awash with emotion.

"Before we go, we need to decide whether we search for and take custody of William's box," said Cyrus.

"Are you having second thoughts?" asked Henry.

"If it helps, I think William would be grateful if you took custody of it," said Harriet. "It clearly meant a great deal to him."

"I believe you're right," said Cyrus, looking at the floor. "It's a duty, it's not something I have a choice over."

"Come on, my friend, we're all in this together. We will be by your side." Henry handed Cyrus the key.

"Any ideas?" asked Cyrus, waving the key in the air.

The three of them peered at the tombs.

"Has anyone else noticed their faces?" asked Harriet.

"Oh, goodness me, are they are smiling?" Cyrus bent down to take a closer look.

"Yes," said Harriet, once more welling up. Harriet noticed that Henry was closely studying the carved image of William, resplendent in his chainmail complete with trademark Templar tabard.

"Have you spotted something?" she asked.

"A keyhole in the centre of the Templar cross over William's heart."

With shaking hand Cyrus inserted and turned the key. For a moment nothing happened but then a drawer low down in the side of the tomb creaked open. Cyrus and Henry peered into the dark recess. Using his torch, Henry shone the light into the depths. At the back of the space he spotted a shape. He leaned in closer and saw an old box which appeared to be made of wood and metal. He carefully placed it on the stone floor.

"Hang on a minute, there's something else." Henry's torso had all but disappeared inside the space. He reappeared moments later clutching something wrapped in the remnants of an embroidered cloth. It turned out to be an elaborately carved sword.

"Good God, it's heavy. It must have taken two hands to wield it. It's a thing of beauty. Look at the craftsmanship." Henry placed it on top of the tomb.

Cyrus moved in closer. "It has a chilling beauty to it, don't you think? It must be a metre long, double edged, tapering to a point. Look, the pommel, the circular disc at the top of the grip, has been carved with a depiction of the Templar Seal, a war horse carrying two Knights, typical William I'd say. An incredible find."

"What's it made of?" asked Harriet.

"Undoubtedly steel." Cyrus replied, running his hand along the blade. "This blade has seen some action – look at the dints running along its full length." Cyrus ran his hand along the blade several times.

"Do you think the key opens both the tomb and the box? Why don't you try the key in the box?" Henry picked it up and placed it on top of William's tomb.

"Let's give it a go." Cyrus's hand was shaking in the torchlight. As the key turned, he tentatively raised the lid, only to let out an enormous gasp. Harriet and Henry immediately leaned in.

"Surely that can't be?" said a wide-eyed Harriet.

"I think it is," said Cyrus

"What, *the* crown of thorns?" whispered Harriet.

"Yes, the bible tells us that when Jesus was crucified, Roman soldiers put a plaited crown of thorns on his head before mocking him *'Hail, King of the Jews!'*" said Cyrus.

"We need more light; did I see you put a torch in your rucksack, Cyrus?" asked Henry. Cyrus nodded, and took it from his bag.

"No wonder William guarded it so closely. It's astonishing," said Harriet.

"It's so very fragile." Henry pored over the box. "It seems to have been fashioned from a series of thorny twigs, the thorns are large and almost barbed on the ends, it's been twisted, maybe plaited, into a rudimentary crown."

"How did it survive for so long?" asked Harriet.

"Well, I suppose, the conditions here are ideal. Dry and temperate but how and why it came into William's possession, we are unlikely to ever know. Clearly though, he was convinced of its authenticity." Cyrus's voice was hoarse. "I need to think very carefully about what to do with it."

"I remember reading somewhere how it was believed to have been plundered in a crusade and sold to French royalty," said Harriet. "King Louis IX I think, apparently used to break off thorns as gifts to those who married into his family."

"Ah yes, now I come to think of it, wasn't one of those thorns supposed to have ended up in a public school somewhere in the UK?" said Cyrus.

"I don't know about that," said Henry, "but I do recall being told as a child that it was in Notre Dame Cathedral, and that the thorns were tied together with gold thread."

"Whatever the truth," said Cyrus, "one thing's for sure, it's incredibly important to Christians as a symbol of Christ's suffering. I don't think we can underestimate what a crucial decision we are about to make and of course at the centre of it is its provenance. A large part of me wants to leave it with William."

"You're not seriously thinking of leaving it here?" Henry's eyebrows were raised.

"I just don't know." Cyrus sighed. "I suddenly feel the overwhelming weight of responsibility."

"You are not alone my friend, we are all in this together. Maybe we should look at it differently, view it as a revered relic that should be accessible to all? My friend, this is the stuff of dreams. You should be immensely proud." Henry patted his friend on the back.

"Oh, I am, beyond words. But I now need to make sure I do the right thing by William."

Harriet put her hand on Cyrus's shoulder.

"You know, my father would often say that one should never discount the fact that *sometimes the truth is hidden for a reason.* William spent a lifetime protecting the crown from exploitation. If you think about it, other relics such as the holy grail and the arc of the covenant were ferociously fought over and lost. Indeed, today, what form they took is not even agreed upon. Some believe the holy grail was the cup used by Jesus at the last supper, others think it refers to his blood line. "

"What you say makes a good deal of sense, Harriet, but who are we to make such a momentous decision?" asked Henry.

The three of them stood for several minutes, each lost in a jumble of thoughts and emotions.

Cyrus broke the silence. "Okay, this is what we're going to do. Henry, please photograph the sword and put it back in the tomb. I think I understand why William placed it alongside the box, to symbolically guard it, but it should remain with him. We will not take the crown back with us. There is a multitude of reasons for this which include its fragility. How would we get it out of the country and back to the United Kingdom without damaging it? There is also the risk of discovery which would inevitably result in a massive diplomatic incident, and there is every likelihood it would be fought over, by the Catholic Church and the Church of England. I for one do not want to be responsible for it becoming a curiosity. It was highly valued by William; significant to his faith and to expose it to the world at large I would argue is contrary to everything he fought for. I think Harriet's father was right, sometimes the truth should remain hidden. I sincerely believe the crown will be safer left in William's care."

"Sounds like a sensible plan to me," said Henry. "But I think it's vital we secure both the door into this room and the door into the passageway to try to ensure that our visit here remains hidden. The best possible scenario would be to make it look as if no one was ever here."

"I wholeheartedly agree," said Cyrus, making his way towards the door.

Harriet was the last to leave. As she reached the doorway, she hesitated and turned one last time to shine her torch on William and Rabia. For an instant she allowed herself to wonder at how they had found each other despite everything. It was inspiring and uplifting. At that moment Harriet hoped with all her heart that one day she too might be lucky enough to find such a deep connection with someone.

Chapter 27

Present day

A couple of days later, the three companions flew back to the UK. At Gatwick, they went their separate ways, but not before Henry took Harriet to one side.

"I couldn't let you go without telling you that whatever is happening between us, it's taking quite a hold of my emotions."

"Mine too."

"I'm so happy you feel the same. Shall we see where it leads us?"

"Yes, I'd like that." Harriet took Henry's hands in hers and locked eyes with him.

"I've got to go now, but I'll be in touch." And with that he leaned in and cupped Harriet's face in his hands, gently kissing her lips. With heart pounding Harriet closed her eyes and drank in his fragrance. All too soon she found herself alone, waving the two men into the distance.

Harriet did not have long to dwell on her feelings for Henry, for the following day she drove to Sheffield to join Ben, Amelia, Mike and Annie. But Henry was as good as his word, and over the next ten days they conversed daily.

On her return, Harriet found herself feeling strangely solitary. Henry was working long hours, so there was less time to chat. Gone were the protection officers and much of the intrusive surveillance equipment in the cottage and, although Joe Wilson was still outstanding, the case against Eve was almost at the plea and trial stage. A skeleton staff remained in place in order to tie up loose ends and continue the search for Joe. But Harriet knew that she would soon be re-posted. She thought about how nothing stayed the same in her life for long. It was the nature of her work, of course. However, since meeting Henry she was aware of feeling more positive and light hearted and, despite trying to keep things between them on a steady footing, she found herself increasingly eager to get to know him better.

A week or so later, and out of the blue, Henry invited Harriet and Cyrus to supper. Harriet spent far longer than usual getting herself ready that evening.

"I need to ask if either of you has had second thoughts about our decision to leave the crown of thorns with William? And whether you are coping with the burden of the secret we carry." Cyrus searched their faces. He did not wait for an answer before continuing. "I, for one, have wrestled with the matter, but I find myself returning to the same conclusion."

"Which is?" asked Henry.

"Well, despite everything I feel we were true to William's wishes and therefore we must keep the discovery secret in order to ensure it remains protected from exploitation."

"Hear, hear," said Henry.

"I agree. It was a difficult decision that was rather forced on us by circumstance. But I'm happy it was the right thing to do." Harriet paused for a moment. "I also wanted to say that to spend so much time with you both in pursuit of your quest, Cyrus, was a joy, some of the happiest days of my life to date." A sunny Harriet raised her glass to her friends.

"Ditto." Henry smiled warmly at his guests across the table.

"I feel truly privileged that you were both able to join me. I can't tell you what an enjoyable journey it's been. I will never forget the thrill of the chase, and I will never forget William of Hertford. He's had a profound effect on me."

"On all of us," said Harriet. "You know, the other night I dreamt that, at the exact moment I turned to take one last look at William and Rabia, instead of seeing their tombs in my torch light, I saw William standing there in full armour. Our eyes met and he bowed to me. I was spellbound. I will always be a little bit in love with him. He was a remarkable man."

"He was," said Henry. "The more we learned of his life, the more I felt his charisma and a growing respect towards him. Some individuals have an aura about them. I'm not in the least bit surprised you dreamt of him. I too encountered him in a dream."

"Well, I never, he really did get under our skin. I'm so immensely proud to be related to him," said Cyrus.

"He's left behind a legacy of hope." Harriet raised her glass.

"A legacy of love too," said Henry, lifting his own glass and winking. "To William of Hertford."

"William of Hertford," they chimed together as they toasted him.

"Now, I have exciting news. In fact it's the main reason for inviting you here tonight." Henry took a sip of wine before continuing. "As you know, when Ella died I was in pieces. It took many years and much support from my good friends to get back on my feet. One night about a year ago whilst at Ella's graveside, I decided I wanted to give something back. I live a comfortable and safe life; anyway, with Kate's blessing I applied to join MSF – Médecins Sans Frontières."

At that moment, it was all Harriet could do not to shout out, not to cry. She had not seen this coming. Her hand went to her mouth. She swallowed hard and forced a smile. She shot a look at the two men, hoping that her obvious anguish had gone unnoticed. Cyrus was congratulating Henry. It appeared her distress had not been spotted. But she knew she'd be expected to offer her congratulations so again she swallowed hard.

"Good for you, Henry. To do something like that takes real strength of character. Can you tell us where you'll be going and for how long?"

"Thanks. It means a great deal to me to have your support." As he said this he looked directly at her. Harriet found her cheeks burning, for it felt as if he were searching her face for the truth of how she actually felt. "I shall be going to Yemen, where it has to be said the conditions are frankly gruesome. There's an urgent need for aid, safe water, food and sanitation – the country is on the brink of famine. There is much disease as well as injury as a result of the raging civil war. I've signed up for six months."

"I'm proud of you, Henry, and I know I speak for Harriet too when I say we couldn't be happier for you." Cyrus raised his glass. Whilst Henry went to the kitchen to fetch dessert, Cyrus took Harriet's hand in his. "My dear, don't think I haven't noticed the blossoming friendship between you two. All I can say is six months is but a mere drop in the ocean of life. If you two can survive this, you can survive anything. This is a huge step for Henry. If he thought for one moment that his plans had upset you, he'd give it up immediately. If you can find it in your heart to give him your blessing it would make all the difference. I've known Henry a very long time and I can see he has deep feelings for you. The timing may be lousy but you must decide if he's worth waiting for."

At that moment, Henry returned with a key lime pie. Once dessert was over, they continued to chat. "It seems that my notoriously fussy daughter has a boyfriend," said Henry, studying his phone; a wry smile spread across his face as he showed the photo. A widely smiling Kate had her arms around a handsome young man.

"Good for her," said Cyrus, laughing.

As Henry and Cyrus spoke about Kate and the photo, Harriet found herself troubled. There was something familiar about the man with Kate. Had she perhaps met him at work? A young officer maybe?

"Sorry to interrupt, but could I possibly take another look at Kate's photo?"

"Yeah, no problem. Is everything alright?" asked Henry.

"Yes, perfectly. I'm just trying to work out where I know Kate's friend from."

Half an hour later, open mouthed, Harriet jumped to her feet.

"Harriet, what's wrong. You've gone awfully pale, what is it?" asked Henry.

"Cyrus, Henry, do you trust me?" They nodded. "Okay, here's what I need you to do. Henry, do you have the ability to track Kate through the 'friends and family' app?

"Yes."

"Good. Find out where she is. Cyrus, call for a taxi into town, would you, please? Tell them it's urgent."

Cyrus grabbed his mobile off the table.

"She's at the Slug and Lettuce wine bar in Kings Street," said Henry.

"Okay, will she think it's weird if you text her?"

"No, not at all."

"Please text her and ask her to excuse herself and go directly to the ladies. Ask her to lock herself in a cubicle until we get there."

"Okay, but what's going on?"

"Just give me a minute, I'll explain as soon as I've made this call." Harriet picked up her phone and walked out of the room into the kitchen.

Just then, the doorbell rang. "That's the taxi," said Cyrus, popping his head around the door.

As they rushed out, Harriet turned to Henry. "Has Kate replied to your text yet?"

"Yes, just now," said Henry. "She's done as requested, but she's understandably asking why. Please Harriet, tell me what's going on."

They got into the taxi and Harriet took Henry's hands in hers. "When Kate sent you the photo with her new boyfriend, I immediately thought he looked familiar. I was sure that I'd seen him somewhere before. At first I thought he might be a young officer, but then it came to me. There's no easy way to say this, but I recognised him as Joe Wilson. Joe is wanted by the police on suspicion of the murder of a young French woman who worked in a local wine bar. Joe is also the brother of David Wilson who was charged with the murders of their brother, Philip Wilson, Philip's son Archie Wilson, and two young women. A firearms unit is on its way and as long as Kate stays put she'll be fine."

Henry looked at her in disbelief.

"I know it's a lot to process. Just hang in there." Harriet squeezed his hand.

"I'll rip his head off if Kate comes to any harm," hissed Henry.

"I'm sure it's all going to be okay. Come on, old boy, it will be fine, you'll see," said Cyrus soothingly.

As the taxi pulled up outside the Slug and Lettuce, there were blue lights everywhere.

"Please stay put until I've had a situation update."

To Harriet's relief, her colleagues had arrived within seven minutes of her call. Kate had been retrieved and was safe and well and with officers inside, but there was no sign of Joe Wilson. Kate appeared from the wine bar.

"Kate, are you alright?" said Harriet, hugging her friend. "Your Dad's over there in the taxi. He's understandably worried sick."

"I'm fine. I just feel really foolish."

"Why would you? You've done nothing to warrant that."

"I let my guard down, Harriet. Never again."

"Never say never, Kate. This was a calculated move by an accomplished manipulator and narcissist. You must have been targeted because of your job and your contacts inside the police. It had nothing to do with you as a person. I suspect it was meant to taunt us."

"Thanks, I think..."

"Listen, it's highly likely that he's a sociopath."

"Which is what exactly?"

"Traits can include superficial charm, controlling behaviour, pathological lies, a sense of self-importance, a lack of remorse, shame or guilt, hunger for power. Joe Wilson wants to be noticed. I suspect that when you didn't come back from the ladies, he realised something was up."

"Kate!"

"Dad!" Harriet left Henry and Kate in a tight embrace and entered the wine bar.

Before joining Kate and Cyrus in the waiting taxi, Henry went in search of Harriet. Taking her by the hand he led her out of sight into a narrow passageway at the side of the wine bar. He leaned in towards her, caressing her lips with his. Harriet had to steady herself against the wall to avoid losing her balance. As the intensity of their kissing reached a crescendo, Harriet could feel his muscular frame against her. For the first time in her life, she understood what burning passion was. Too soon, Henry broke off. "Thank you for saving my girl," he whispered before taking both of Harriet's hands in his and searching her face.

"I realise my timing about MSF is bloody awful but if I don't do this now I never will. I can't ask you to wait for me, I have no right, but you should know that you will be in my thoughts constantly and I will pray every day that you are here when I get back."

"Henry Squires, go, and make us all proud. I'm not saying goodbye, because that's not what this is." Henry enveloped Harriet in his arms for a moment or two before breaking away to walk slowly back to the taxi. Harriet stood motionless for a minute pondering the jumble of emotions coursing through her body.

Harriet slept poorly that night, unable to rid her head of the events of the evening. Next morning at work she struggled to concentrate on a pile of statements awaiting her attention. She wanted nothing more than to see Henry again, to touch him, to hold him. Each time he entered her head she was aware of her breathing quickening and her heart racing. Still, she knew deep down that he had to go and that she had to let him. Her daydream was rudely interrupted by the arrival of Derek Wynn.

"Ah, morning, Harriet. Thought I might find you here hard at work. Have you got a minute for a chat in my office?"

"Of course." Harriet jumped to her feet, blushing slightly as she followed, for work had been the furthest thing from her mind. She tried to focus.

"I need to talk to you. I've asked Paul Jones and Mike Taylor to join us." Derek paused and cleared his throat, which Harriet immediately recognised as his awkward tic.

"Damn it, how do I put this? Um, early this morning I received the official report into the vehicle pile-up in France. With it is the forensic report."

"Have you read it?" Harriet felt her chest tighten; she moved her hand to her neck as a queasy sensation flooded over her.

Derek was quick to take her arm. "It's okay, I haven't looked at it yet. We'll go through it together."

As Derek entered his office, Harriet followed and sat down in the nearest chair. Her energy sapped.

"I'm sorry everyone. I just feel a bit overwhelmed. I wasn't expecting this today." Harriet felt breathless. "In fact, I was completely taken by surprise. I'll be fine in a moment."

A cup of coffee later and Harriet was ready to resume.

"Right, then." Derek cleared his throat as Harriet grabbed the sides of her chair. Derek reached for a fawn folder from his desk. Mike got up and stood behind Harriet, placing his hands supportively on her shoulders.

"Paul, we are undoubtedly going to need your help to decipher this, if you would be so kind? You are by far the most qualified to interpret the data."

"Okay, let me see, I'll try to summarise it for you. Ah yes, Veronica Louise Morris and Cleopatra Morris, occupants of the blue Renault Megane." Harriet held her breath and closed her eyes.

"Interesting, the bone fragments found within the vehicle were significantly compromised, physically and chemically by the intensity of the inferno, which caused difficulties with the identification process. Most of the bone fragments showed considerable colour change, shrinkage and deformation but, having said that..."

Harriet took a deep breath and got to her feet. She found she could not sit still. As she listened intently she bit her lower lip.

Paul continued, "It does appear there were several bone fragments that were less damaged. As you probably know DNA is cellular in nature, heat damages its structure, often to the point where it is very difficult or even impossible to recover or indeed accurately assess. However, in this case it was possible to retrieve some DNA. This was compared with DNA samples provided by the family."

"Dental?" asked Harriet.

"Yes, that's right."

"And?" asked Derek, getting to his feet.

"And the forensic scientists have determined with a high degree of certainty that Cleo Morris perished."

"How high a degree?" asked Derek.

"Yes, how high a degree?" interrupted Harriet.

"All I can say is that the leading scientists are convinced that Cleo Morris died in the car," said Paul Jones.

"Fucking brilliant!" shouted Mike punching the air with his fist.

"Sorry, Paul, can I just clarify whether the report is saying that without doubt the bone fragments in the car belonged to Cleo?" asked a frowning Harriet.

"From what I've read, but I don't think they can say with a hundred percent accuracy."

"And Veronica?" asked Harriet in a whisper. "Did they find her DNA in the vehicle?"

"Now, that's less easy to answer. Such was the intensity of the fire, it's their conclusion that she also died, but remember they were closely related so there will have been strong similarities in their DNA which they may not have been able to fully isolate. Nevertheless, they have concluded that both women died. I know it's not definitive, Harriet, but I do think it's quite compelling. I will, however, look over it again tonight and get back to you if I find anything new." Paul closed the file.

"Thanks, Paul, I really appreciate that."

"Harriet, I think we can say that at last you are free of Cleo." Derek smiled as he walked across and placed a hand on her shoulder.

Harriet forced a weak smile, but whilst it seemed that everyone else in the room was happy to believe both women were dead, Harriet could not shake the feeling of unease in the pit of her stomach. What troubled her most was the DNA evidence. She wondered if it were possible it could have been mixed up or misinterpreted?

"Look, I know it's not conclusive and I understand your need to know for sure, but maybe that's not going to be possible," said Mike gently.

Needing time to think, Harriet made her excuses and left. Unable to take her mind off the report's findings, she decided to tackle the pile of mail that had accumulated on her desk. She didn't have the stomach for anything more taxing. Amongst a stack of manila envelopes, she came across a postcard. Recognising the drawing on the front as St Albans Abbey, she frowned as she turned it over. On the back written in black ink was simply; *Psalm 145:20.* Intrigued, she scrabbled around in her desk drawers in the vain hope of finding a bible and when she drew a blank turned instead to her computer. *'The Lord watches over all who love him, but all the wicked he will destroy.'*

A smile slowly spread across Harriet's face as she realised that the postcard was from Veronica Morris. She was alive! And it then dawned on her that in lieu of an actual body, Veronica was the only person who could put her mind at rest and confirm Cleo's fate. Although Harriet knew she should report this, she couldn't bring herself to do so, at least not until she'd looked into it further. But where to start?

Two weeks later a second postcard arrived. This one had a photograph of the Nave of the Abbey on the front. With her heart thumping in her ears, Harriet turned it over: written in black ink were a date and time.

Harriet arrived early, not wanting to miss the appointment. She chose to sit in the same seat at the back of the nave as on her first visit. She was deep in thought when she became aware of someone approaching from her left. She got to her feet and turned. Veronica looked different; she had changed her hair to a short layered cut. It suited her face, thought Harriet. The two women embraced.

"I can't tell you how happy I am to see you. I felt so guilty for involving you. But you took a risk in making contact." Harriet's eyes filled up.

"I decided to take the chance. You remind me of your grandmother, Ann. You have kind eyes and, despite your obvious discomfort, you were good enough to hear me out the first time we met." Veronica wiped a tear from her cheek with the back of her hand.

They sat next to each other. Harriet took Veronica's hand.

"How do you feel now that Cleo's gone? Please tell me she has gone!"

Veronica squeezed Harriet's hand. "I feel relief. I feel able to breathe once more, I'm no longer looking over my shoulder. And yes, Cleo is dead and by her own hand."

"Are you sad?"

"That's such a difficult question to answer, I'm in mourning for the small, happy, cheeky little girl full of light and joy. But not the monster she turned into. I was unable to relate to the adult Cleo at all."

"I think I understand that. I cannot tell you the guilt I felt after I jumped from the car, knowing that I'd left you in that hell. How did you survive?"

"I was glad Cleo let you go. She was drunk and driving like a lunatic. There was no need for all of us to die. After you left the car it was the perfect moment to wind her up, in the hope that there'd be an opportunity for me to get away too."

"What in heavens name did you say to her?"

"I simply made fun of her. I told her she was weak for letting you leave the car. I told her she may never get another chance to finish you. I told her it was clear she was losing her grip. With that she slammed on the brakes, her face like thunder. I didn't wait to see what she'd do; I was out of the car as fast as I could possibly manage and I ran. Seconds later I heard the sound of a car speeding off. I turned to see Cleo disappearing up the road, the red car in hot pursuit, then I saw the red car make contact with the rear of Cleo's, so hard that it pushed it across the carriageway into the path of an oncoming tanker lorry. I saw the tanker swerve, hit the curb, which catapulted it onto its side. It slid at speed, taking Cleo out. Almost simultaneously, there was a massive explosion, I was thrown to the ground by the force. When I got to my feet again, I ran towards the inferno, but the heat was such that I was forced back. There is absolutely no way she could have survived. There was no time to escape, the whole thing happened in seconds. As I stood by the side of the road and called the emergency services, it occurred to me that I had an opportunity to start afresh, to leave my old life behind. So I walked across the fields to the next village and managed to get a lift to Paris."

"So, we are free of Cleo. There's no doubt?"

"None whatsoever."

"I feel terrible for Cleo's victims and their families, though. They won't get their day in court now."

"My daughter left a trail of utter destruction in her evil wake but at least she can take no more lives."

"That's very true. Tell me, what are you planning to do now?"

"Well, that depends on you. I can stay and face the CPS. Or I can leave the country and start a new life abroad."

Harriet did not answer immediately, for she was thinking.

"I'm pretty sure CPS won't want to take any further action against you. And I for one, wish you all the best. Are you sure there is nothing for you here?"

"I'm sure. My son hasn't spoken to me for years, my husband avoids me at every opportunity. Maybe, one day, I will find the strength to tell them what Cleo did, and why I behaved the way I did. But for now I just want to live a little."

"Good for you. But I will have to tell your family you survived. It's only fair – they've been in quite a state. I will tell them you made contact, that we met, but you then disappeared."

"Thank you, Harriet, you are as kind-hearted as my daughter was sinful. And, yes, you're right my family should know the truth. There's something else I'd like to share with you. No more lies, no more deceit." Veronica handed Harriet a folded piece of paper. "Please don't open it until I've gone."

"Okay. Should I be worried?"

"No. But it won't make easy reading."

A frown flitted across Harriet's face.

The two women embraced for the final time before Veronica walked off in the direction of the crossing and Harriet made her way to the west end doors at the rear of the nave. As she walked into the autumnal sunshine she spotted a solitary bench several metres away. Sitting down, she unfolded the piece of paper Veronica had given her. As she read, her left hand shot to cover her mouth but not before a strangled yelp escaped. Shaking her head repeatedly, she read on but a giddiness overcame her and she was forced to grip the edge of the bench in order to prevent herself toppling off. For quite some time after, she struggled to regulate her breathing before once more continuing.

"My dear Harriet, after everything that has happened, I need to get something off my chest. As difficult as it is I want to tell you about Cleo's father. In the spring of 1990 I was happily single, a career girl, that is until I met a dashing young police officer at a local nightclub. I fell for him almost immediately and thought he felt the same way about me. When I discovered I was pregnant, I expected him to be as thrilled as I was but that was not the case. To cut a long and painful story short, we parted a few months before Cleo's birth in June 1991. I had no further contact with him. The following year, I met my husband James Morris, who adopted Cleo as his own. I wish there was a gentler way to tell you but Cleo's birth father is in fact your estranged husband, Nick Lacey...."

Harriet felt a wave of nausea sweep over her. How could this be? She reddened. Then she remembered that last year she'd gone to the marital home to collect some personal belongings. But far from the house being empty as she'd anticipated, she'd found Nick with a young woman. Only later had it dawned on her that she might be Cleo. The smirking female had appeared at the top of the stairs wrapped only in a sheet, clearly amused at the verbal altercation going on in the hallway below between Harriet and a drunk towel-clad Nick. Harriet took a large intake of breath. Oh good God! The realisation that Nick had bedded his own daughter, albeit unwittingly, had just sunk in. Harriet began to perspire heavily. Nick was many things, but he would never have got involved with Cleo if he'd known. Harriet let out a loud sob. How could Nick have been so stupid? How could he have behaved in such a reckless and irresponsible manner? What an idiot! On regaining her composure Harriet wondered what she should do. She wondered if Cleo had known? Surely not? This was unquestionably too warped even for Cleo, wasn't it?

Feeling totally alone Harriet's head was spinning as she tried to figure out what to do for the best. No good would come from making this public now. It would wreck lives and hadn't there been enough sadness already? She did not want to be party to further heartache. As she looked around, she realised she was sitting by the old monastery gate house and her thoughts turned to William of Hertford. What would he have advised? What would the great knight have said about this? She closed her eyes and reflected for a while. The more she thought of William the more convinced she became that his counsel would centre on what her heart told her was the right thing to do and her heart told her to hide the truth. It would be her secret to keep.

She tore the letter into tiny pieces and dropped it into a nearby bin on the driveway, before pausing momentarily to take one last look at the imposing Abbey.

"Thank you, William," she whispered under her breath.

Acknowledgements

First, I'd like to thank my husband Neil for his unwavering support.

A big thank you to Gail Richards who undertook such sterling editorial work and showed such enthusiasm for this story.

And, thanks also to my daughter Harriet, for her constructive comments on early drafts and Bea Morris for reviewing the final draft for me.

Waiting to Die

The third thriller in the Harriet Lacey Series, out in 2023

When several residents at the exclusive Fairview Residential Nursing Home die in suspicious circumstances, Detective Sergeant Harriet Lacey is chosen to investigate. Her team uncover a complex web of lies and deceit and, despite their best efforts, the deaths keep happening. It dawns on Harriet there could more than one person involved. Harriet must act swiftly. But, with personal challenges and forgotten threats to the fore, life is becoming increasingly tough for her. And, then, when she unexpectedly strikes up a friendship with a resident, an extraordinary story unfolds, one she is compelled to pursue further.

Printed in Great Britain
by Amazon

55042707R00187